A
Talented
Man

Also by Henrietta McKervey

Violet Hill
The Heart of Everything
What Becomes of Us

ACKNOWLEDGEMENTS

A Talented Man is fiction, yet its origins lie partly in my interest in Florence Balcombe, whose work in fighting those who pirated *Dracula* established important principles of copyright. There is no known sequel to *Dracula* – forged or otherwise – though it was enjoyable to imagine how such a story might go. The snippets of notes and letters attributed to Bram Stoker or his wife Florence Balcombe are as fictional as Ellis himself.

Heartfelt thanks as always to my editor Ciara Considine, and to Elaine Egan, Ruth Shern, Joanna Smyth, and all the team at Hachette Ireland. Also to Margaret Halton of Pew Literary for her good-humoured, wise and willing support.

For reading, commenting, or patiently listening, thanks to Andrea Carter, Feargal Fitzpatrick, Sarah Gilmartin, Denise Judge & Ray Ruddell, Margaret Kelleher, Clare McKervey, Kathleen MacMahon and Catherine O'Mahony.

A Talented Man

Henrietta McKervey

HACHETTE
BOOKS
IRELAND

First published in 2020 by Hachette Books Ireland

A CIP catalogue record for this title is available from the British Library

ISBN 978 1 47368 271 9

Typeset in Cambria and Snell by redrattledesign.com

Printed and bound in Great Britain by Clays Ltd, Elcograf S.p.A.

Hachette Books Ireland policy is to use papers that are natural, renewable and
recyclable products and made from wood grown in sustainable forests. The logging
and manufacturing processes are expected to conform to the environmental
regulations of the country of origin.

Hachette Books Ireland
8 Castlecourt Centre
Castleknock
Dublin 15, Ireland

A division of Hachette UK Ltd.
Carmelite House
50 Victoria Embankment
London EC47 0DZ

www.hachette.ie

For Feargal

"The subject of imposture is always an interesting one, and impostors in one shape or another are likely to flourish as long as human nature remains what it is, and society shows itself ready to be gulled."

Famous Imposters by Bram Stoker (1910)

CHAPTER 1

Ellis Spender glanced over his shoulder. The man was still there. He had first noticed the heavyset figure – belted navy overcoat, hat pulled down low over his eyes – on Hampstead Lane, and thought little of it. Yet there he was again, a constant five yards behind as Ellis turned right onto the Grove. The streets were quiet and gloomy, a fine-soot mist hovering low, blurring the air around him. Would the shadow break off if he crossed the road towards Highgate Hill? Ellis turned a corner. It stuck. Yes, he was definitely being followed. Sweat stung his neck despite the near-freezing January night. He paused outside the Golden Lamb. Rainbow-coloured circles of light clung to the lamp over the door.

It took a moment to adjust to the brightness, the rush of smoke. A barmaid gave him the eye, but looked away, coy and blushing, when he met her gaze.

'Gin and French.' He rattled coins to disguise the nervous shake in his hand.

'Evening, lad.' An old sot leaning against the bar counter

half raised his glass in greeting. His slack-mouthed grin exposed greyish gums. 'Don't s'pose you got a ciggie?' he slurred. His tongue pushed the single tooth in his lower jaw forward till it leant, pitted and filthy, against his lip.

'No.' Revolted by the perversity of the gesture, Ellis moved down the counter. He looked at the mirror-backed shelves that lined the wall behind the bar. His own distorted reflection stared back through the clutter of bottles, cigarettes and stacked glasses that zigzagged halfway to the ceiling. He took off his hat and ran a hand over his hair. Blond waves flowed under his palm, like water slipping under a bridge.

There he was! Sitting alone, no more than twenty feet away. Ellis stared hard, willing the slivers of mirror to explain what was happening. The stranger was frowning, his lips folded in on themselves. Ellis was aware of the tremor in his hand again, a nervy tug up his arm into his shoulder. He couldn't possibly be from the Prudential, could he? Surely that was long since over. Virginia had refunded the money paid out on Ellis's claim (fraudulently submitted, according to the assessors, but what would those chumps know?). The only other person who knew about that ghastly business was Uncle Freddie but he was – thankfully – in America. Perhaps the man had been hired by a creditor. Was this how it happened? Arrested over a trifling sum . . . *Come with me, please, sir.* Ellis swallowed hard. How he hated the constant sensation that life was fracturing under his feet. Cracking, collapsing. Any minute the ice was going to break, and his body would plummet through the hole into a bottomless, freezing lake.

What next? If he went straight home and was followed, the man would know where he lived . . . But perhaps he already did – had trailed him from the house, in fact – and was playing this cat-and-mouse game to taunt him.

'Excuse me?' The man was beside him, one hand fumbling in his pocket. A *knife*! Ellis's fear, a vast, foaming breaker, rose again. Every pointless moment in his life, every second of greed or avarice pricked him. Regret was blood red and pin sharp. The man tugged a balled-up handkerchief from his pocket and blew his nose loudly. A *knife*? Where was he – the Odeon? Ellis flushed, embarrassed by the intensity of his private melodrama.

'You *are* Ellis Spender, aren't you?' For a moment Ellis was about to deny it. How could this stranger prove anything? But! If he was a policeman, would Ellis be in more trouble for denying it? Was denying your own self a crime?

'Ernest Winsome,' the man said, offering his hand. For the first time Ellis registered a pathetic flicker in his face, a hunger. 'I am, I mean was, an . . . acquaintance of Freddie Broughton.'

The clench in Ellis's stomach loosened. Relief rippled through his body, a pleasant feeling that dissipated as quickly as he could appreciate its cool, clean touch.

'I spotted you on the street a while back and I've been following you – gosh, doesn't that sound suspicious? I do apologise. It was only because I wasn't quite sure it *was* you at first. May I have a word?' Winsome's manner was hesitant, the words offered as though his large, fat-lipped mouth would grab them back, greedily stuffing each letter down his throat. He was younger than Ellis had thought. Ellis was twenty-nine and this man was probably quite close in age to him, mid-thirties at most, with red-rimmed, almost lashless eyes, and reddish hair too, combed fiercely back from a high, bulging forehead.

Ellis's first reaction was to refuse. Now that this stranger posed no threat to him, he realised he disliked him intensely. The idea that another person wanted something from him always made Ellis desperately uncomfortable, even when it was clear that acquiescing to the request would have been to his advantage. *Gain equals loss*, his father used to say, holding it as irrefutable as one might a law of physics. *You won't find one without the other.* If Winsome were to profit from whatever he wanted from Ellis, it would be at Ellis's cost.

'I hope you don't mind?' Winsome pushed the handkerchief around his large forehead. 'How about I order us a couple of brandies?' He gestured towards a table in a neglected corner, the sort of quiet alcove a courting couple would choose.

'All right.' Ellis's legs felt loose suddenly, coltish and giddy with freedom. Relief began to expand within him. He was rather short of funds, and another drink would be delightful. How foolish he'd been. 'Are you a pal of Freddie's?'

A flicker passed over Winsome's face, his worried expression giving way ever so slightly. He was mollified Ellis had never heard his name from Freddie, was that it? Ellis knew he must be careful or he would lose his unexpected upper hand. 'Though,' he added brightly, 'dear Uncle Freddie has so many friends that I'm sure to recall you sooner or later. I don't doubt my mother would know you at once! She's so fond of all of Freddie's chums.' *Chums* was one way of referring to Freddie's circle of shirkers and shriekers, he supposed. Ellis's mother Virginia always spoke about her adored younger brother as though the very creaks of West End stages operated on his whim. Because of the manner in which she introduced him, as a child Ellis had believed his uncle's full name was the Impresario Frederick Broughton, which sounded far more exotic than his father's set, peopled as it was by ordinary sirs and lords. Ellis's parents used to squabble regularly about Freddie, with Virginia's avowals of his greatness invariably countered by Sidney's 'Surely you mean *ingrateness*', but in the fifteen years since her husband's death, Virginia's opinions of her brother had thrived, flourishing unchecked. Spreading, Ellis thought, much as a bruise does. He sipped his brandy. It was the colour of stair-rods, and tasted it.

Winsome's throat bumped as he swallowed. 'I have been introduced to Lady Spender, yes.'

'Freddie is abroad. He took *A Fine Dalliance* to New York.'

'I heard that he didn't return with the cast, and your mother is, um, now care-taking his possessions.'

'I don't see how that's any of your concern, Mr Winsome,' Ellis replied, somewhat tetchily. Just thinking about that fiasco angered him. Not content with squandering his own substantial earnings, Freddie had greedily sucked the Broughton family fortune down to its last farthing, a situation that had come to light shortly after he'd left London for *A Fine Dalliance*'s six-week run in New York four months earlier. Having been given the distinct impression by Freddie himself that his estate included ownership of the furnished flat in Marsham Court, which he had moved into just a year earlier when it was so gloriously new as to smell of varnish, and the endless hot water still had a brackish odour, Virginia had been bewildered to receive a landlord's letter forwarded by the concierge notifying him of eviction in absentia. Six months' back rent was owed, plus interest and outstanding management fees, not to mention the sums he had run up on account with Marsham Court's private dining rooms, public restaurant and cocktail bar.

Discharging her brother's debts soaked up the majority of what remained of Virginia's funds, which Ellis had been in the silent habit of considering his inheritance rather than her money. Her horribly expensive and pointless transatlantic telephone call to leave a message at Freddie's hotel in New York – 'The poor darling, there's obviously been a horrible misunderstanding, please tell him not to worry' – received an unapologetic telegram in reply: AWFUL NEWS STOP AM INVITED TO HOLLYWOOD! UNMISSABLE OPPORTUNITY STOP BEST BEST LOVE STOP. Only a man as irresponsible and arrogant as Freddie could waste money – best bloody best! – in an exchange about his financial ruin.

Furious, Ellis had telegraphed Freddie, telling him he owed the Spenders three hundred and ten pounds twelve shillings. Weeks later, he received a breezy note by post: *Shocked at your penny-pinching attitude, old thing. So much for family. Keep the lot & let's consider what you insist on referring to as my 'debt' duly discharged. PS – Tell my darling sister I will write soonest. Best love. FB*

No letter arrived. Neither, to Ellis's delight, did Freddie: the cast of *A Fine Dalliance* returned to London without him, dispersing once more to the wearying ether of other shows, of other hopes, of nothing. Freddie's departure from his life was a desire Ellis had silently nursed for years, which made the simultaneous discovery that his uncle was as good as broke so horribly galling. Because Freddie was unmarried and appeared likely to remain so, Virginia was his next of kin. Ellis had been counting on a reasonable inheritance from

Freddie coming his way via his mother, if not directly. He deserved to get the man's money, he thought sourly. It would be the repayment of the debt to his childhood rather than a legacy.

Ellis frowned. 'I fail to see how Freddie's actions affect you.'

Winsome coloured. 'He and I had a – a friendship last year, and when it, um, concluded, I asked him to return my letters. They were of little account, quite trifling in fact, but I'd prefer to have them back. He must have forgotten, in the rush of going to New York. A mutual acquaintance mentioned he wasn't planning to return, and that your mother has his, um, belongings.'

Freddie would have kept the sweating idiot's letters out of spite, the knowledge that Winsome feared his pash becoming public making it irresistible. Ellis was beginning to enjoy himself. He sat back in his chair, legs crossed, hands loose and open. Courteous and considerate, a gentleman of leisure out for a simple evening stroll and a drink, generous with his time and attention. 'But if the letters are unimportant, why does it matter where they are or who has them?'

'Ah, well, they were a touch . . . *personal*. I am concerned they are liable to be misunderstood, you see.'

'I don't quite grasp your meaning.' He smiled through the lie. 'Misunderstood by whom?'

'My employer at the ministry, for one.'

'I see. And is there a Mrs Winsome who might also . . . *misunderstand*?' Ellis asked, draining the last of his brandy. What delicious fun this was.

Winsome halted a passing waiter. 'Two more – large ones,' he said. 'I became engaged to be married a fortnight ago.'

'Heartiest congratulations!' Time to tighten the screw on the man's discomfort a little further. 'You're correct in that my mother *is* looking after Freddie's belongings. But why put yourself to the trouble of finding *me* when you could simply telephone *her*?' He made a show of reaching into his pocket for a pen. 'Let me give you the number.'

'No! I mean, I'd hate to impose on your mother's time. I thought perhaps it was easier to arrange between ourselves. Man to man, as it were.'

'How very thoughtful! I'm not sure I can help, though. Aside from the fact you're referring to Freddie's private possessions, there are decades' worth of theatrical memorabilia and a vast correspondence' – was that going too far? Freddie was hardly Pepys – 'that would need to be painstakingly checked. A lot of work simply to locate a couple of notes.'

'They are more than *a couple of notes* to me.'

'And yet *trifling* was the word you used.'

'Well, yes, but . . .' Winsome trailed off, unable to reconcile his desire to appear unconcerned with his genuine desperation.

'Don't worry, I completely understand. As I'm sure you're aware, I'm an author myself, so I appreciate how powerful the written word is.'

'Are you? Your uncle never said. I recognised you from seeing you at the theatre with your mother.'

Typical bloody Freddie. No, he would never have spoken about his nephew's novella *The Only Boy*, or mention its excellent review in the journal *Other Writing*. To do that would have meant acknowledging another man's talent, and Freddie Broughton was incapable of that. A strange, heated thought suddenly flitted through his mind: he could pick up the filthy tin ashtray on the table and smash it into Winsome's face.

'Mr Spender, I appreciate the imposition, which is why I would be glad to recompense you for your time in locating my, um . . . material.'

Minutes later, Winsome left, having proved very understanding – almost generous, Ellis thought – about the remuneration Ellis would need to prise himself temporarily away from his own literary endeavours. It was a matter of some discretion, Winsome insisted. He blushed when Ellis replied, 'Indiscretions often are, don't you think?'

He called the waiter over and ordered another brandy. 'Shilling or one-an'-threepenny, sir?' Ellis Spender, a shilling drinker? Hardly! He picked up a discarded *Daily Mirror* from a nearby table. It was half past nine, and the news was familiar and stale. For days the biggest headline was that of the missing-torso murder: two severed arms had been discovered under a bridge in Newbury a fortnight earlier, and though the police said the search was for a body, the press insisted on referring to it as a 'missing torso'. He, Virginia and Janey had been following the story with grisly delight. The latest theory centred on a leg newly recovered from the Thames at Reading. A man and his young son fishing had found it: at first glance they thought a shop mannequin was stuck in the mud of the riverbed. *Inspector Morris*, the article noted, *is of the opinion that this case could become the first in history where a victim is identified from his leg alone. In the search for a solution to this heinous crime*, it concluded, *the*

Metropolitan Police were putting their best feet forward. Ellis laughed aloud. Janey would enjoy that. He raised the brandy to his lips. Actually, it was delicious. An attractive colour too, he now noticed: honey-toned rather than brassy.

There was little else to interest him on the front page: Herr Hitler sent New Year wishes and renewed assurances of Germany's desire for peace and co-operation; police investigating a robbery were looking for a man with exceptionally white teeth wearing a teddy-bear coat; the Army was recruiting yet again, promising good pay and well-ordered accommodation. He could think of nothing worse. He dropped the newspaper to the table and picked up his hat and cigarettes.

'No! Wait!' The drunk who'd tried to cadge a cigarette from him earlier was calling the barmaid, his voice loud in the busy room. He wobbled from side to side like a ninepin. 'Vera, I've a trick. You'll like this 'un, I swear!'

She paused, a full tray in her hands. 'What d'you mean, "trick"?'

He took unfinished drinks from her tray one by one, tossing the remains of each into his own empty pint glass. Beer, ale, gin and peppermint, the dregs of Winsome's brandy and who knew what else. Ignoring her cry of 'Here, what d'you think you're doing?' he lifted the glass to his lips, his throat pulsing as he gulped down the viscous brown mixture. He belched, long and loud, loose and wet. The landlord appeared, soundlessly taking the man by the arm and leading him to the door. The barmaid stared at his retreating back, not in horror but with a soft sadness which was somehow worse.

Ellis rose to leave. The discoloured Vitrolite roof panels were a match for the tiled floor under his feet, and he felt dizzy suddenly, and drunk, as though the room had flipped upside down and he was trapped against the ceiling with no way of righting himself.

Midnight, and the clang of the garden gate behind him pealed out clear as a ship's bell. Fitzroy Gardens was a run of ten substantial red-brick houses, which opened onto Hampstead Lane at both ends, an unexpected ox-bow bulging into the north flank of the Heath. Ellis and Virginia lived in the second to last, the terrace all but invisible from the Lane. The path from the street to his front door was long and narrow, broken in two places by single steps and bordered by tall, dense hedges. The overall effect was of having unexpectedly dropped into a trench that sloped slowly upwards until it met the front door. The eaves and roof merged into the night above, and the few stars he could pick out were pale and overworked. Save for the orange glow thrown into the hall from a single Benares brass lamp on the large mahogany table, the house was in darkness. The grey wallpaper reflected little light, and the gloom made its marbleised finish look cracked and unsteady. He imagined rooms collapsing in clouds of dust, the garden greedily gathering the house into itself.

Virginia was sure to have been asleep since ten. Ellis couldn't tell whether their paying guests, both of whom kept long hours, were at home. Janey wasn't, he decided, sniffing for a trace of Vol de Nuit ('Who do you think buys her perfume?' Virginia murmured behind Janey's back on the afternoon she moved in), while Patrick probably was. Relentlessly regular in his habits, Patrick tended to slip ghost-like into the house each evening around nine and go straight to his room. Occasionally, he had to stay over at the hospital, so they wouldn't see him for two or three days at a time. Ellis exhaled loudly and watched the hoar of his breath leave his body and disappear, absorbed into the air around him. There were days when every exhalation carried the pointless weight of a loss, as though breathing wasn't constant and necessary, but a drain, a sucking-away at his very existence.

He threw his hat and coat onto the stand, and turned, his eye caught by a faint gleam on the hall table: Virginia's pearls, spilling from her handbag. He let his hand trail over the necklace from one end of the clasp to the other, savouring the perfect shapes, his fingertips exploring the small knots that prevented each pearl from touching its neighbours. It was originally a loose string, but when he was a small boy he'd broken it, so she had had it restrung in this way. The slight detachment – each existence lived independently from the others – pleased him. The pearls warmed to his touch. He clicked the diamond clasp shut and slipped the necklace into the bag.

The long hallway led to a large room with a glass-panelled bay window that overlooked the back garden. It was cold and quiet, its wooden floor partially illuminated by moonlight slipping through the windows. The room had once been Sidney's studio, a place of unframed, unfinished lives. Of incomplete bodies, people awaiting eyes or limbs, mere charcoal outlines of themselves, or abandoned against white space, their backdrops unpainted. Real people frozen in time by paint, as insects are in amber. Freddie's crated belongings were lined up against one wall. Neither Ellis nor Virginia had opened so much as a single box. Ellis's indifference was rooted in annoyance, Virginia's because she missed her brother so much, a sadness that would only have been exacerbated by poring over his possessions. He left the room. The search for Winsome's drivel could wait until morning.

He paused at the bottom of the staircase, the polished mahogany of the newel post cold under his left hand. He reached out and touched the framed print facing the bottom step, the first of ten *Greatest Theatrical Figures*, a series of famous actors and theatre managers his father had painted between 1897 and 1908, then tried to revive as a set of prints some years later when he'd needed the money. During the war, not only had his fortunes taken a turn for the worse, but so had Sir Sidney Spender's professional reputation. By 1920, the man who, in the gold-touched year of 1902, had been elected to the Royal Academy, the Royal Society of Portrait Painters, and the Royal Institute of Oil Painters in dizzyingly quick succession, and who was so beloved by society that the King had personally asked him to do his official portrait in 1904, followed by one of the Queen a year later, couldn't have sold penny cartoons on the street. His style, which flattered and persuaded, which united manliness and keenly superior intelligence in its male subjects and created a shapely, coquettish charm in its females, was, by the end of the Great War, deemed to be old-fashioned, its flattery obsequious and embarrassing. Too late did Sidney realise that London's art world was in reality an elite private club with the power to assign or repress value at will. By the last decade of his life, nobody wanted to be *done by Spender*, as it had once been known. What used to be an honour, a sign of society's approval and affirmation, had become a display of timidity, a desperate clinging to a vanished era. Sidney had spent his last years as an enthusiastic drunk, prone to paranoia about why his former friends Tonks and Eves were spared such a cruel fate.

Virginia had insisted on Freddie's inclusion as a *Greatest Theatrical Figure*. He was the only sitter still alive. George Thompson had gone first, toppling over onstage in 1901 and landing dead as a dodo in the orchestra pit, one arm whipping a bassoon to the floor as he fell. Henry Irving – his portrait was at the top of the stairs, his black eyes focused on the wallpaper opposite as though it contained a puzzle he was trying to solve – had died four years later, collapsing on the street in Bradford a week after his portrait was completed. Sarah Bernhardt held out until March 1923, shortly before Sidney had thrown down his palette knife for the last time. For many years, the frames were regularly crooked in the morning. A creaking ship swollen with brandy, Sidney listed to bed at night, tossed from wall to banisters and back. Ellis had been in the habit of straightening them on his way to breakfast. The more askew they were, the worse his father's morning mood was sure to be.

'I see you're admiring my rogues' gallery,' Virginia would say, to any guest who made the mistake of pausing for a moment in the hallway to fuss with a hat or umbrella. 'Why, let me introduce you!' and she would drag them up the stairs, brightly peppering each description with anecdotes. 'Dear Bram! Florence Stoker and I were children together in Dublin – the larks we had! Sidney painted Bram for the National Portrait Gallery in 1906, you know, but Florence always said this little thing here remained his absolute favourite . . .

and here's Ellen Terry of course, in costume for *The Merry Wives of Windsor*. She told me once in the clearest and most unmistakable terms,' here, Virginia's voice would invariably dip, as though sharing a sacred secret, 'that she had never known a greater man in the theatre than my brother.'

Shadows flickered across each famous countenance as Ellis moved slowly up the stairs. As a child, he was convinced the ten were prone to changes of expression, that pinkish hands flickered while eyes narrowed in disapproval and lips twitched with whispers. *I can see you*, Freddie's painted mouth seemed to say. *Even here, you are not out of my sight.* He paused by Bram Stoker. Ellis wasn't quite four when Stoker died, yet because of Virginia and Florence's close friendship, he felt as if he knew the man well, although he had only a vague memory of meeting him once, in St James's Park. He was walking at his mother's side, impatient to get to the duckpond, when they happened across Florence pushing a Bath chair. 'Oh, Florrie,' Virginia whispered, looking at the slumped, dazed figure, left almost unrecognisable by a series of strokes, 'death is terribly cruel.'

The man in the picture was seated, as though he had just pushed his chair back from an unseen desk. Broad-shouldered, his jacket strained across his portly chest and stomach. Something about him fizzed with energy, as though desperate to be liberated from the oppressive stillness of Sidney's brush. Ellis leant forward until their faces were only inches apart. Stoker's intense, buttonish eyes stared into his own, the point of his short red beard almost touching Ellis's clean-shaven chin. Ellis's disappointment in his own lack of success as a writer was his constant companion, and Stoker too had known that maddening, unreachable itch, Ellis was sure of it. He had understood what it was to go disregarded, rendered impotent by the literary establishment. To watch as stories he had bled over suffocated in their unopened covers and his income dwindled. A forgotten old man in a Bath chair: was such ignominy to be his fate too?

There was the prospect of Winsome's twenty pounds at least, he reminded himself. Yes, that was a delightfully unexpected windfall. Winsome, losesome, he thought and giggled softly. Through his bedroom window, slivers of pale moonlit sky shone through rough gaps torn in the clouds. Flickers of light, they seemed to come to him from the future. Promises made manifest.

CHAPTER 2

'You got yourself a right bozo there!' Janey slicked butter across her toast with the carefree confidence of a barber wielding a cut-throat razor. Getting something over on another person was a cause for praise. And on a bozo too! Why, that was best of all. Bozos deserved it. Asked for it, in fact. Her lips, red as a butcher's block against her pale, powdered skin, parted ever so slightly to reveal slightly gappy front teeth dotted with black crumbs.

Ellis glowed in the sunlight of her approval. Janey was beautiful in the way a wild cat, a cheetah or a leopard, is beautiful, he thought. ('If one likes that rather *obvious* look,' Virginia once remarked not-quite-quietly enough, to which Freddie had added, 'But what is her sex life, do you think?' and then softly to Ellis, when Virginia had walked away, 'Is she to be had?') She had a sinewy grace, an elegance that wasn't – as Virginia would have preferred – a sign of polish and refinement, but rather a perpetual perfect readiness.

The previous June, Virginia's cousin Minette had written from Dublin to ask if the Spenders would consider taking in the twenty-five-year-old son of a dear neighbour as a guest for a year. Ellis had always thought Minette half-witted, an opinion compounded by her inability to understand his novella. Virginia had sent copies of *The Only Boy* to all her relations in Ireland, and though Minette's note of thanks remarked on how clever Ellis must be, and how wonderful for Virginia that her son was *an aspiring writer* – he gritted his teeth at the memory of such hateful words – the praise was entirely spoilt for him by her final line: *though I confess I found myself somewhat bewildered by how few events took place . . . I prefer a good detective yarn with all the trimmings of red herrings and what have you! This must be what they call 'the modern style' and perhaps this particular reader is simply too old to appreciate it!*

Her blasted letter was positively gushing on the subject of Patrick Arcourt, billing him as a particularly fine young chap about to commence a surgical speciality at the Royal London Hospital. Patrick's mother Alice wanted him to stay with a family known to them instead of taking a flat alone or go into digs, because he had never lived away before. Of course, Minette wrote – the letter was so awash with underlinings and circlings and doublings-back on itself that reading it was like watching an intemperate adult shout instructions at a stupid child – it wasn't *at all* the sort of thing Virginia would usually undertake, and she *completely understood* what an imposition having a stranger living in the house would be, that the remuneration could *never begin to* counteract the sheer inconvenience, but if she could only find herself equal to the favour then Minette, too, would be in her debt, no more so than the Arcourts, who were, Minette assured her, a well-connected family and simply a delight to know. *And for dearest Ellis*, Minette added – to Ellis's fury – in the third of four lengthily enthusiastic postscripts, *such a situation would provide an ideal opportunity for him to associate with a young and studious man of fine character!*

Although etiquette deemed an initial reluctance necessary, Virginia kept it to a minimum, and soon declared herself only too happy to assist Minette's neighbour in any way she could. Why, what would she be doing but helping a fellow countryman? A surgeon no less, a man dedicating himself to the good health of others. It was her duty, she decided. That Patrick would be paying for his bed and board and his arrival would generate a new and extremely welcome source of funds was a significant influence on her decision, and one that – to the credit of all concerned – went entirely unmentioned. The agreement was made for reasons of altruism, not income, and though a cheque arrived promptly every month, nestled inside a polite and grateful letter from Alice Arcourt, pounds, shillings and pence hadn't for a moment entered into Virginia's thinking. Maintaining reputation was the foundation of all Virginia's decisions, so while Patrick-the-guest was welcome, a frank conversation about a rental arrangement with Patrick-the-lodger would have been impossible.

In August, not long after Patrick had moved in, Freddie had asked if Virginia could, as a favour to him, also accommodate a young woman called Janey Gould, who worked at the Lyceum for his good friend George Atkinson, and had been let down on digs at short notice. As with Patrick, Janey's arrival was at a relative's behest, so Virginia was able to gloss over the commercial nature of the arrangement. No sooner had Janey unpacked than Virginia decided she was common and, unusually for her, began to regret acceding to Freddie's request. Occasionally she suggested to Ellis that they ask Janey to find somewhere else to live. So far, he had always been able to talk his mother out of it: Janey was prompt with her rent, didn't eat a large breakfast, or use much gas or hot water. She was as perfect a paying guest as one could hope to have. Virginia needed the income from Janey and Patrick to run the house. Without it, they probably couldn't afford even a daily any more, he reminded her, knowing how much she'd hate to let the girl go. Having once had a staff of eight at her command, Virginia couldn't bear being reduced to just a single servant, an anger she took out on whoever that unfortunate happened to be. Look at your magazine, he pointed out, picking up Virginia's copy of the *Lady* and flicking through it, pointing out column after column of women seeking accommodation. Just imagine the sort of undesirables lurking there in black and white, he urged. Consider the horror of having to respond to query letters . . . Showing people the room, letting them traipse around her house, and whoever she chose would be a stranger anyway. And, he added, whatever Virginia thought about Janey – Ellis was always careful when he deployed this trump card – she had come to them with Freddie's personal seal of approval. What would Freddie think if he returned from America to find his sister had cast her out?

Virginia hadn't raised the subject for a few weeks, thankfully. Anyway, Janey's working day was so long that Virginia, who preferred breakfast in bed and tended to retire early, saw little of her. Janey rarely arrived home before eleven, and often much later. It was obvious to Ellis that she had notions about becoming an actress. He imagined her as a moth attracted to the warm glow of the footlights, hanging about backstage long after her working day was over or in a public house near the Lyceum or at theatre parties, in the hope of attracting the attentions of an actor or production manager.

Janey's jaws crunched, neat and sharp, through the crusts. 'What a chump!' she added, as if there had been some ambiguity to her 'bozo' that required a footnote. Ellis grinned, thoroughly enjoying himself. Winsome *was* a perfect chump! Why, if Ellis had had him specially made to order he couldn't have got the specifications quite as good as Winsome's natural design. He could hardly believe that the man's presence on the street had ever rattled him.

When he sat down to breakfast that morning he hadn't intended to say anything about his experience in the Golden Lamb, yet when she yawned and told him she was running late and would only have a quick cup of tea and a ciggie, he heard himself launch into an edited version of the story, one containing a hidden message that begged her to stay longer. Capturing Janey's mercurial attention wasn't easy, and he had often found himself trying to lure her by setting up a question, just as a small child might. He had done so now, he realised, by casting the opening line, 'You're not going to believe what happened!', in order to land her 'What?' by way of reply – for how could he not then respond to such a direct request?

The words came out of his mouth almost despite himself, but dispassionately, as though it was another man's life he was relaying, one he was aware of shaping into a very pleasing narrative, a tale of unintended, unexpected consequences, of the gain, the power, that could be found in another's loss. Ellis was a diligent editor when it came to the details, though, explaining that Winsome was a playwright who had sent Freddie a manuscript but, because it was now being produced elsewhere, needed the correspondence concerning it returned. All to do with copyright, he added airily. His final flourish was to describe how he himself had carefully, delicately, manoeuvred the conversation into a corner whereby Winsome offered to pay for Ellis's time in locating it. Janey hadn't queried him. Why would she? Janey, Ellis believed, understood what the world was really about, so the money-for-nothing and the getting one over on the bozo were the only aspects of the encounter that interested her. He'd had a momentary panic, that she'd be suspicious because there was no playwright by the name of Winsome. And what if she were to ask where the play was to be put on? But she didn't.

'Good on you,' was all she said, and then again, 'What a chump.'

Ellis smiled. He was in the habit of waking early and listening for the sound of Janey's bedroom door creaking open so that he could time his breakfast – 'Why, here we are again, Janey' – to coincide with hers. Infuriatingly, she was unpredictable, and rose at any time between eight and nine thirty: Atkinson was either a very patient man or obliging in how she made up her hours. She had asked several times if the squeak in her door could be oiled, but despite his assurances that it had been, he'd taken care of it himself only these old hinges were so unreliable, he had no intention of doing so. He reached out his slim hands, putting one on either side of the teapot. He held it tightly, like a head between his palms.

Warmth flowed into him, a delightful pressure reaching into the very whorls of his fingertips.

He stopped talking when Patrick, unusually late for him, lumbered in, sat down across from Janey and lit a cigarette. Ellis shook open his newspaper. He began to read, taking nothing in because he was concentrating on Janey's responses to Patrick's dreary conversational sallies. Patrick began with the weather, then moved neatly into the impact of rain on his journey to the hospital and associated timings. Patrick had bought her expensive chocolates for Christmas, and Ellis knew she kept the empty box in her room, even though its contents were long gone. Concerned she was holding on to it as a sentimental souvenir or, worse still, proof of a secret promise or suspected intention, he had begun to watch them carefully. But this proved to be one of the good days, when he was easily able to convince himself there was nothing to it. Listening to them from behind the newspaper, he reassured himself that her manner was closer to that of a host who suspects they have been rude to an unwanted visitor, and now that the guest has announced their departure, tries to make it up to them in the last hour before they leave. Patrick began to describe a surgical procedure with the sugar bowl and marmalade dish deputising as body parts. When Ellis yawned loudly from behind the paper, Janey giggled. Surreptitiously, he watched Patrick's eyes follow the movement of her teacup to the red advertisement of her lips. He had the sort of stupidly implacable face one might see on a coin, a profile so removed from its original human form as to be almost featureless and unreal.

'Excuse me, Patrick,' she said, extracting the ashtray from his impromptu demonstration. 'I wasn't done with my spleen.'

Ellis grinned, hearing her words as a vote registered in his favour. Yes, breakfast-time had improved immensely since Janey had moved in.

CHAPTER 3

A large room at the back of the house, with waist-height wood panelling and port-coloured wallpaper on three walls, it had been the Music Room before becoming Sidney's studio, though the grand piano that once sat in the wide, glass-paned bay window which bulged out over the back garden was long gone. Above the picture rail, the paper was beginning to slough off here and there, thinly, as the skin of a cooked chicken might pull from the flesh. Years before, when Virginia had a reputation for hosting extravagant suppers after Freddie's first nights or Sidney's exhibition openings, she would have the Persian rugs taken up for dancing. The room would become stuffy with smoke, and loud during those evenings, with layer upon layer of babble and laughter. Ellis used to imagine the press of people pushing against the walls, forcing the glass bay further into its bulbous shape, stretching and straining it until the frame was exhausted and the glass ready to explode. When Nanny finally dozed off by the nursery hearth he would sneak downstairs and appear at his mother's side. Too early and he'd be packed off upstairs again, with the humiliating sting of a fresh slap from Sidney across the back of his legs, but if he timed it right he'd be petted and fussed over, like a lapdog, delicious morsels dropping into his mouth from the guests' very own plates. In the morning the smells – stale cigars, a sour fruitiness he later learnt was spilt champagne, the rich hint of the roast beef and horseradish sandwiches Virginia insisted were served in the hour before the party finished – would gradually dissipate, overcome by freshly lit fires, lavender and beeswax as day sluiced away night. During the war, when commissions dried up and Sidney's assistants, Max and Roderick, enlisted (Max was bayoneted on the second day at the Somme; Roderick died in a mustard gas attack a year later, his skin blistered and unrecognisable, his throat excoriated; neither had a funeral, they merely ceased to exist), Sidney gave up the studio in Mayfair he'd kept for twenty years, moving its contents into the Music Room. Until the arrival of Freddie's parcelled-up life, the room had remained pretty much as Sidney had left it.

Sidney's father George had bought number nine Fitzroy Gardens newly built in 1868. When Sidney inherited it in 1897 he changed nothing; neither did Virginia, when Sidney died a quarter of a century later. Built to be run by a silently efficient staff moving to and from the basement, as if appearing and disappearing into an automaton clock, the house had sunk into itself in the absence of such labour. Relentlessly fashionable by the standards of the previous century, to Ellis it was like living in a museum. It was a mortuary of stuffed birds trapped under glass domes, of eau-de-Nil paint and ornaments, of knee-banging tables that buckled under the weight of potted plants. The furniture was dark, the fabrics thickly woven prints of birds and ferns, the wallpapers complex trellises of leaves and flowers, threaded through with tiny creatures. He was an explorer in his own home, wandering lost through endless foliage, every movement followed by hidden eyes.

The ancient brass heater he'd switched on in the Music Room before breakfast hadn't made any noticeable impression on the temperature of the room, merely sending tears of condensation down the windows. Ellis wiped a couple of panes. It was another sunless morning, and the room was washed in the same grey light as the wrung-out clouds over Hampstead Heath. A faint odour of mice was joined by the scent of warming dust. He checked the door was shut, then made a start on Freddie's boxes. It was sure to take no time at all, though he had decided to leave Winsome to sweat it out for a few days. Not only would that make his fee appear well-earned, but he knew Winsome's worry would slowly spread inside him, a contagion building in his blood. How much consideration had Winsome given, he wondered, to the knowledge that success in retrieving his ill-considered correspondence meant that Ellis would learn the contents of the letters?

He began happily enough, confident that what he wanted would be waiting, ready to be found, trilling, *Coo-eee! Over here!* The sensation was almost enjoyable, like playing a game he had already won. But within minutes his light-heartedness was dissipating. Container after container, box after box. It was chaos! Books, programmes, letters, scribbled scraps of paper, diaries, everything thrown in together with no attempt at establishing order by date or subject. Freddie wasn't the only designer of this pandemonium, he knew, briefly regretting his decision to hire a penny-pinching firm of navvies when Virginia had begged him to organise the urgent packing and removal of his uncle's possessions.

Ellis regarded the junk stacked up around him. What a waste of three hundred and ten pounds twelve shillings: Winsome aside, nothing there was worth a jot. He'd deny it, of course, but Ellis was sure Freddie was well aware of the debts he abandoned when he left for New York, confident that Virginia would bail him out. Either that, or what he had said in his note to Ellis was truth rather than bluster: he didn't care what happened to his possessions. Though Ellis believed that the two events were as linked as if roped together, Virginia drew no connection between Freddie's near-bankruptcy and his decision to stay in America when *A Fine Dalliance* closed. Freddie had no intention of returning to London, which made the waste of money in redeeming his possessions even more galling. Virginia hadn't paid a down-payment on his return, just the laundry bill for clearing up the mess he left when he vacated their lives. Why could she never be angry with her brother? Why was she so blind to who – what – he was?

The more Ellis considered it, the less surprising Freddie's defection was: his uncle's star, such as it was, was dangerously entwined with a particular type of old-fashioned London playhouse that was slowly dying, squeezed on one side by a new breed of smaller, rougher theatres, and on the other by an army of cinemas. Even had they wanted him, Freddie wasn't the type to throw in his lot with the Workers Theatre, or the Unity. Those places were full of Reds. Freddie would be ridiculous there, a relic.

Freddie's departure had left his mother lonely and upset

in a way Ellis had never seen before, not even when his father died. By her curious logic, the prospect of becoming a widow was always a reasonable expectation for a woman who marries a man twenty years her senior. In fact, it was the preferable scenario: Virginia couldn't bear the idea of going before her husband. It was terribly sad, yes, but *knowable*. Not tragic, not shocking. Her husband was dead: there was grief, but no rage or railing against cruel Fate.

Within half an hour, he was ready to give up the whole business. It was ridiculous! He kicked a box in anger, and its paper entrails gushed out, streaming across the floor.

'I said I didn't want to be disturbed!' he shouted, as the door opened. 'Oh, it's you! Sorry. I thought it was the girl.'

Janey shut the door behind her. 'I always wanted a look in here, but anytime I try, the door's locked,' she said, clicking open her handbag to offer him a cigarette, either unaware that she had admitted to snooping, or oblivious to his opinion either way.

'We never use it.'

'It's bigger than I thought it would be.' With her foot she gestured to a scatter of pages on the floor. 'Plenty of room to make a mess.'

'Won't the boss be wondering where you are? It's close to ten.'

'Don't you worry where *I* ought to be, dear. I've come to help.' She laid her coat and hat on a chair.

'The best help would be to chuck the lot on the fire,' he said, aware of how cross he sounded but unable to stop himself. Thinking about Freddie did that. He took a breath, trying to tamp his anger back into its airless home. 'It's all rubbish.'

'No such thing. Not knowing what to do with it is what

makes rubbish.' She tugged at a cloth that covered a stack of canvases piled against the wall and peeped underneath. 'These aren't much cop, are they?'

'They're unfinished. And my father's dead, so they're not going to get any more finished, are they?'

'No offence,' Janey said airily, tugging at another drape. 'This one's better, look! I like red setters, do you? And what's that in his mouth? A duck?'

'Show me . . . No, it's some type of game. Grouse, probably.'

'Look at the way the blood's dripping down his muzzle! Isn't it fine? D'you think I could have this one for my room?'

He shook his head. 'My mother would never agree, so best not to ask.'

She bent down and collected the loose pages Ellis had scattered behind him. 'Is what you're looking for handwritten or typed? Sorting 'em that way first would be quickest.'

'Hand.'

'These all seem to be letters. How about this lot?' She waved a few.

'Let me see . . . No.'

She tossed her cigarette into the grate, then reached into the nearest box and pulled out a thin pile of letters tied together with a green ribbon, along with a sheaf of blotting paper and loose sheets headed with the Marsham Court address. Ellis remembered the morning in the flat when he'd opened Freddie's bureau and tipped the contents of each drawer into this box. She flicked through them, reading odd phrases aloud. '*Thank you for sending such sincere congratulations . . . for your felicitations, for your exceptionally kind greetings . . .* What – does he spend his entire time sending letters to people telling them how great they are?'

'That sounds about right.' Ellis grinned. 'And hoping they'll reply, saying the same about him.'

'Here's another one. *Dear Freddie. What a tonic you are! Dear Bram and I were so thrilled you came to us for the weekend . . . Holidays can be so dreadfully laborious without entertaining company, don't you agree . . .* blah-blah.' She turned the page. '*We are still laughing at your hilarious impressions of Bram – you had us simply in howls every time! He sends his love and would have written his own postscript, but his handwriting is so horrendous you would have needed me there to decipher it! With love and all best wishes. Your dear friend, Florrie.* Who's that?'

'Florence Stoker. Freddie and my mother grew up in Ireland and knew her well. Bram died more than twenty-five years ago, Florence only last summer.'

'The *Dracula* chap who used to work in the theatre? His picture's in the foyer. That Henry Irving too, a ghoul staring down at the rest of us. The doorman, Albert, he's always piddling on about them . . . *Back in the day* this, *back in the day* that. Funny when you think about it – him writing a book about a vampire, and his chief looking like one!'

'What do vampires look like?' he asked, struck by the matter-of-fact way she spoke of vampires as a recorded, identifiable species. (Though the summer after Sidney died, Virginia had insisted Ellis spend weeks away on Freddie's touring production of *Dracula*. As a result, he privately agreed with Janey: vampires were real, and preyed on pure young blood such as his own.)

'Like him, of course. All pale and creepy.'

'Have you read *Dracula*?' he asked.

'Course not,' she replied, immediately dismissive, and he

knew he could never admit to her how much he admired Stoker's creation. Oh, to write such a character! How powerful it must feel to bring to life a being so completely unencumbered by heroism, so immune to morality.

'According to Albert, the crew adored Stoker. Crazy for him. Not Irving, though. He couldn't half be mean when he felt like it, but his acting got the crowds in. If he wanted an audience to cry, by God they cried! He could make 'em believe anything. He'd tell you white was black and you'd agree, no matter what your own eyes were telling you.'

Ellis nodded. He'd heard as much from his mother. Together, Stoker and Shakespearean star Henry Irving had turned the Lyceum into one of London's foremost theatres, their partnership running for nearly thirty years. 'Bram had both a wife *and* a husband . . . according to his wife at least,' Virginia had once remarked drily – but, over time, Irving had been less and less inclined to take Stoker's advice and, following a string of failures and financial disasters, their relationship was as good as over at the time of Irving's death.

'Irving didn't leave him anything in his will,' Ellis said, recalling a conversation between Virginia and Florence a couple of years earlier in which Florence had referred to her long-standing outrage at both the personal slight and financial disappointment. Despite his charismatic, hypnotic personality on stage, Irving was difficult and reckless, inhabiting a world far removed from the drudge of keeping a theatre's doors open day upon day. It was her charming and energetic husband, Florence insisted, who had kept the business running smoothly year after year, often at the cost of his own health. 'Oh, Florrie,' Virginia had replied wearily, 'not all that again, please.'

People had often assumed Florence and Virginia were sisters because not only were they both remarkably beautiful, with pale skin and large eyes, but they sounded so alike: in conversation together, their accents would become softer and more Irish, and their voices gather speed, as if racing each other back in time, galloping towards a life Ellis would never know or understand. Virginia's looks were the type that one noticed when her face was immobile: it was a matter of pleasing symmetry, a classical perfection of arrangement and proportion. With unusually greyish eyes and a vast shining mass of soft curls loosely piled on top of her head, Florence simply *was* beautiful – it radiated from her. No frown or pinched contortion of expression could alter it. People at parties, in shops, even in the street stared at her unashamedly, as though she was a rarity, a newly discovered species to be pointed at and openly discussed. Even when she was an old lady, men would get to their feet in the theatre as she walked into her box. Fascinated and eager, they were never disappointed by what they saw. Ellis had always liked Florence. Despite her occasionally bossy manner, she was attentive and kind, and could be very amusing. Unlike so many of Freddie's set who crowed with glee over each other's misfortunes and sneered at their successes, Florence found joy in the happiness of others.

'A pot will work fine without a ladle,' Janey added, 'but a ladle with no pot to dip into ain't any good, as my pal Stella says.'

'What do you mean?'

'Sounds like Stoker was more wrapped up in Irving's life than Irving ever was in his.' She tossed the letter into the nearest box and picked up a large leather-bound book instead. 'Diary from 'thirty-three. This any use?'

'Best not.' He took it from her hand.

Janey shrugged, and lit another cigarette. They stood at the window, smoking companionably, looking into the garden. A lone robin pecked at the lawn. A couple of magpies hovered around the empty birdbath, a cracked stone cherub holding a low, marble-lined bowl. The grass ran for thirty yards until it met an overgrown kitchen garden. Most of the greenhouse's panes were missing or cracked, and those that remained intact were soiled, blurring the shapes of the overgrown plants inside. On nights when the moon was huge, its pitted surface clear, he watched low, fast shadows flit behind the broken glass. The lawn hadn't been reseeded for years, and had become a scrubby mess of weeds, a loosely tufted battleground in varying shades of green and brown. Virginia had a man come in occasionally, but he didn't do more than keep the grass low, and tame the worst of the hedges. The far wall bordered Hampstead Heath, Nature declaring its dominion where the red-brick lines finished. Sidney had had a wooden door fitted neatly into the wall to create a private entrance to the Heath, though Ellis couldn't remember when it was last used. Not for decades, probably. Unlike their neighbours', the Spenders' garden wall was cracked and crumbling, as though the Heath was trying to invade, stealthily claiming back the very ground the house was built on.

Ellis exhaled smoke and stared into the distance. Trees with winter-thin branches, like veins glimpsed through pale skin, partially blocked his view across the Heath. An easterly wind had picked up, and low clouds the colour of tin bowled across the horizon, shiftily misty, as if trying to obscure something happening far away, in the distant sky. To their right, where the grass gave way to a patch of gorse, a lone child ran without looking back, disappearing out of sight into a dense thicket of trees.

'Nasty, isn't it? The countryside,' Janey said, her lips curled in distaste. 'It'd be rotten not to have anything around, no houses or people beside you. Say what you like about the back-to-backs, I'd sooner be in one of them than in the middle of nowhere.'

'The Heath is hardly the middle of nowhere! It's not the countryside either, for that matter.'

She put on her coat, then moved to the mirror hanging above the ornate mantelpiece to adjust her hat. 'Well, I wouldn't care for it. Anyway, cheerio.' She clicked her bag open. 'Shall I leave you a ciggie or have you got some?'

'Would you? I'm all out.'

Her perfume and cigarettes filled the room and he felt the lack of her even before she had gone, despite knowing she would despise him for it. She wasn't the type to walk away from a man and wish him still by her side: to Janey, other people were just shadows that crossed with her own in a brief meaningless convergence. She was always moving forward, ever forward, her memories no more than thoughts passing through, restless, on their way to somewhere else. He found her intoxicating and humiliating all at once. Her company was like being given a passionate love letter and reading it, entranced, suffused by desire and want, only to be casually informed afterwards it was intended for another all along.

Some nights he lay awake, restless, imagining his bed a coffin and him nothing but a skeleton decaying inside it, his flesh rotten, fallen away to nothing. He wished he could go into her room and curl up on the floor at the bottom of her bed. Her company gave him the thrill of having just received good news, without the need for the news.

'Good morning,' he heard his mother say from the hall.

'Oh, hello, Lady Spender.' Janey had finally stopped calling her Virginia, thankfully. He knew the casual forthrightness of her tone irritated his mother, who expected deference from younger women as her due, and would have preferred outright obsequiousness. Patrick performed better in that department, but despite his toadying, Alice Arcourt's regular letters of thanks and Minette's equally regular notes crammed full of assurances that Alice Arcourt was deeply grateful, Virginia had decided Patrick was a dullard, whose supposed intelligence found expression in medical matters alone. His fingers were dotted with warts, and Virginia disliked these, too ('Pity his poor patients!'), suspicious of what he must be handling in the hospital to become so horribly afflicted.

The front door creaked as Janey pulled it open. He envied how smoothly she slipped from the house to the world. She hadn't shut the door to the Music Room fully behind her and it shifted in the draught. The movement was so slight it was as though a ghostly figure had slipped in by his side, its breath cold on his neck.

He heard Virginia pause in the hallway and shuffle through the post, knowing the gloom that would fall over her as she opened bills. Life for people like the Spenders had slowly eroded since the war: his class was no longer on the inside, its rights and privileges defended by those beneath it. Old money, the kind his father's family once had, that which always replenished itself, was gone, a magic well run dry. Freddie had frittered through the more modest fortune he inherited from Berners Court, the Broughton family estate in Ireland. During the war, the demand for imported produce from Ireland had boosted his income from Berners considerably but, perennially poorly managed, by the early twenties the estate had tottered back into a familiar slump. Freddie continued year after year to spend as though the war would be fought and won in perpetuity. When the house itself burnt down a couple of years later, its insurance having been allowed to lapse by the land agent because of Freddie's constant demands for money from the estate, the few remaining tenants dispersed, leaving Berners all but forgotten. Ellis had never been there – he wasn't even sure where it was. All he and Virginia had now was what Sidney had left them: the house in Fitzroy Gardens and its unfashionably unsaleable contents, plus an unbearably diminished income from dividends, out of which Virginia paid Ellis a pitiful allowance. All her life she had treated money as air: it was just there, in whatever quantity she wanted or needed, and the adjustment to being more or less broke had been humiliating and painful.

'The rotten thing about one's funds,' she had said recently to Ellis, 'is that when one has them, one never gives it a moment's thought, but as soon as one doesn't, it becomes impossible to think about anything else.'

He had understood perfectly. He thought about money and his lack of it all the time. From her mother Virginia had inherited a couple of paintings by Millais and Hayter, which Ellis was sure would sell easily when the time came, though she would have starved sooner than sell them herself. There was some good antique porcelain too, though of a rather unfashionable style unfortunately. Ellis would get everything eventually, of course, once Freddie and Virginia had shuffled off, and they both had Prudential policies, which would help, but that could be years away, and what was he supposed to do in the meantime? Money, to Ellis, had come to symbolise freedom of action with no responsibilities. His Bohemian acquaintances, the sort of people who scorned society and Metroland alike, whom he could count on meeting in the bar at first nights or at exhibition openings, delighted in squalor. How he despised their gleeful tales of freezing rooms with peeling wallpaper and furniture made from greengrocers' boxes. Romantic rot. He didn't care for chaos in the name of creativity, and he certainly didn't believe hardship to be the indispensable inspiration necessary for art. Those who cried, 'Life is for art!' between drinks were ridiculous. Art was only worthwhile if it were lasting, an influence wielded on the future. And how could it do that without allegiance to money?

Ellis stared at the mess of papers on the floor. Freddie's purple-inked scrawl scowled up at him. Perhaps Winsome was wrong, and Freddie *had* destroyed the letters, or they'd got lost in the confusion of packing up his belongings. The money was gone, snatched away from him! He felt the loss of Winsome's windfall almost as a taste in his mouth, acidic and strong. He'd had a delightful hour in bed that morning spending Winsome's twenty pounds, while he waited for the reveille of Janey's creaking door. His imagination had sucked every farthing dry! First, he was going to Wendells. He hadn't been to the club for months, not since the barman had taken to mentioning his account in the unpleasant way he had, invariably referring to the outstanding sum against Ellis's name every time he so much as ordered a drink. Well, he'd show him! He'd stroll in, offering drinks all round. 'Come on,' he'd say, the very heart and soul of geniality, to whoever was beside him at the bar, no matter how big a fool or bore they were. 'Do let me stand you a drink – it would be my pleasure.' He'd even tip the barman, to prove that Ellis Spender was a cut above the man's dreary pettiness. Ellis could imagine scenarios that painted him in a good light in achingly rich detail. Yes, there he was in the leather-and-soup-scented baronial gloom of Wendells, its ox-blood walls and tartan carpet unchanged for decades. He was on top form, witty and erudite, with a kind word for everyone. Generous, and thoughtful with it.

As usual, by the time he left off daydreaming, he had so thoroughly inhabited the scene that he no longer felt the need to make it come true. The entire picture – debts paid, social currency re-established – imagined so completely that reality could offer no embellishment to fiction. He could go to Wendells that very moment, be rude to the staff, spend nothing, and still leave believing himself benign and generous, the very soul of affability.

Virginia called his name from the hall. He didn't reply.

'Where are you?' Closer this time. 'Have you seen *The Times*? I'm simply dying to find out the latest on the torso! Oh!' She broke off. 'Why, whatever are you doing?'

'Hello . . . I was reading the paper over breakfast. It's probably on my chair.'

'What's this?' Her gesture was loose, taking in the boxes, the snow-white flurries of pages on the floor, but her tone was sharp.

'Hmm? Oh, *this*? I thought I'd best take a quick look in case there was something important we ought to have dealt with on Uncle Freddie's behalf.'

'Has he asked you to? Did he write? Oh, Ellis, why didn't you tell me?'

'No! Nothing, I've heard nothing. I was worried that . . .' He sighed, his face serious. He rose to his feet and brushed dust from his trouser legs. His expression didn't change as he scanned the sheaf of papers in his hands for Winsome's name. 'I didn't want to bother you. It's nothing. Please, go for breakfast. And there *is* news on the leg. You'll love it!'

'Ellis!' she snapped, her left hand brusquely batting aside his distractions. 'I asked you to explain what you're doing with Freddie's papers!'

'I was concerned there might be . . .' He trailed off again and looked away from her, flushing.

'Might be *what*?'

'Other debts. I should have talked to you about it, but I hate to upset you. I am sorry.' His apology landed, a grisly lump at her feet. Freddie was the one who should be sorry! He could have ruined them entirely. 'Imagine a bailiff turning up here. Wouldn't that be hateful?' He knew he ought to stop but didn't want to. 'I couldn't bear to see such a thing happen to you.'

Tears shone in her eyes, and he thought how ordinary-looking she was becoming, her beauty a guttering candle. 'Oh,' she said, and 'Ought that to have occurred to me before? Have I made a terrible mess of things?'

'No, of course not! Please don't say that. I'm sure it's all fine. It occurred to me earlier how awful it would be were anything to complicate Uncle Freddie's return. I am the one who should have thought of it before, dearest, not you. I had to pack up so quickly in Marsham Court that I didn't look through any of it, and I ought to have.'

'Yes, I see. Thank you, darling. I'd be lost without you, I really would! I've been thinking, too, about when dearest Freddie returns. I've decided he should move in here with us permanently. Patrick can stay, but Miss Gould will have to leave. Don't you agree?'

'Yes, of course. Wonderful idea.' His fingers tightened over the pages in his hands.

'Will you put everything back just so? It doesn't seem right, looking through his private belongings.'

He nodded. 'Don't worry, I'm being terribly careful. I'll put everything back exactly as he would want it.' He was glad he hadn't told her of his telegram to Freddie about his debts, or Freddie's reply. Ellis didn't want to be sole curator of Freddie's discarded rubbish. It suited better that Virginia believed herself responsible for any problems that might arise.

'Thank you, this is so thoughtful. Oh, I almost forgot.' From the sheaf of letters in her hand she gave him a fat envelope, postmarked W1.

He knew immediately what it was: the manuscript of his new novella, returned. That Gollancz was a fool! He felt a physical pain low down in his gut to hold his precious book, lumpen and disregarded, in his hand once more. He'd held out such hopes for *Varnishing Day* and its story of a man so beguiled by the illusion of perfection that he destroyed everything he believed imperfect. The painstaking detail with which he had already imagined every step on the book's path to acclaim! Such envelopes were a bitter sight. Rejection was invariably heavy: a swollen packet with a terse, disinterested letter, its unfamiliar and indecipherable *pp* halfway down the page. Acceptance was slim, swift and elegant. A single folded sheet, an intelligent observation, an expansive, elegant signature. No matter how good, how worthy, he believed his work to be during its creation, the moment it was rejected he despised his writing just as much as he hated the person whose name underpinned the accompanying letter. It might take weeks, as he knew from experience, before the pendulum would swing back from defeat, and allow him to regard his typewriter as an ally once more.

He tightened his hand around the envelope, crushing the paper. He felt desperately angry, as though his body was suddenly separate, nothing whatsoever to do with him, and its actions, while controlled by this anger, would be completely distinct from anything he would recognise. He forced himself to take a deep breath and loosen his grip while the surge passed through him. He put the packet on the desk. The envelope was crumpled and torn, his own name smudged from the sweat of his hand.

'And look at this!' Virginia was too distracted with her own letter to notice his reaction. She waved a postal order at him. 'One pound! For everything. Honestly! That fox stole was worth more by itself alone.' Virginia had recently replied to a notice in the *Lady* advertising a private second-hand dress agency in Buckingham Palace Road. 'And she has the nerve to ask me to send her the postage to return my green silk jacket. You know, the rabbit-trimmed one? Dreadful woman claims it's soiled! By *her*, I'll be bound.'

Virginia peered into the nearest packing crate, which was full of Freddie's books. She plucked *The Lady of the Shroud* from the topmost pile. 'Dear Bram. He did come up with the most frightful tosh sometimes. But he was such a dear, one could never have told him so.' Ellis stiffened, pained for his fellow author. Was that her heart's secret opinion of *his* writing, too? She returned the book to the crate, her fingertips pale against its cherry-red cover.

He heard her neat, quick-stepping tread on the short flight of steps down to the kitchen, her voice calling for the girl. The cigarette Janey had left for him lay on the mantelpiece next to a tarnished bronze sculpture: the head and shoulders of a pouting, curly-haired child – Ellis, aged four, commissioned by Sidney from Paul Montford. The tip of the cigarette rested on a neat stack of loose pages. Letters, he realised, and began to flick through them.

Dearest Freddie, Your face – that beautiful face of yours – at my door! An apparition! Yes, no more than any man— Enough! The next: *My dearest! Previous to today I never comprehended the true nature of—* He winced at the hysterical style even as he recognised what he was holding: eight letters, just as Winsome had said there would be, dated April to June 1937. He checked the signature. Winsome's plodding schoolboy hand was in delightful contrast with the sickly sweet flamboyance of the text.

Had Janey realised what they were when she placed the pages on the mantelpiece for him to find? Surely she must have . . . And left the cigarette as a clue? Or a reward! Whatever her reasoning, it suggested that she wasn't shocked by the letters' contents. Neither did she care about his fib that Winsome was a playwright. That was interesting. She rose even higher in his estimation. He smiled, his upset at the rejection of *Varnishing Day* temporarily put to one side.

He folded Winsome's letters carefully and stowed them in his jacket pocket, then began to repack the boxes. He didn't care in what order: he had no intention of wasting time on such rubbish again. He arranged the boxes against the wall, freeing a battered copy of McNeill Whistler's *The Gentle Art of Making Enemies* from between two crates. He stood back, pleased, catching his breath. Not a bad morning's work after all, thanks to Janey. He felt a quickening inside him, a shimmer of happiness, and for a moment the air changed, the light shifted. He glanced at his watch. It wasn't yet noon. The ideal time to pay her room a little visit.

Within days of her arrival, Ellis had begun to slip into Janey's bedroom while she was at work. He always left the door ajar so he could hear footsteps approaching on the stairs. The squeaky hinge would be his excuse for being there, not that he had ever needed it: Virginia never went into either Janey or Patrick's room, and she kept the girl so busy downstairs that once she'd dusted and done the beds, she wouldn't have time to wander up here either.

Ellis and Virginia slept on the first floor, she in a bay-windowed room facing towards Hampstead Lane, he at the back of the house. It was large and square and lined in mahogany panelling, with a view across the garden and over the Heath towards North Wood. Janey and Patrick were housed on the top floor, where the bedrooms were smaller. Janey's room was directly above Ellis's, a shrunken, meaner version of his, as if the air had been sucked out of it, the very walls closer, tightening around her, holding her safe and alone. It had been his room when he was a child, though the nursery furniture and toys were long gone, replaced with heavier, plain stuff, and he had few memories of the years he had inhabited the room. The lavatory was between his bedroom and Virginia's, so he could contrive no circumstances that might take him regularly to the top floor while Janey was at home.

At night, lying in bed and listening to the foxes on the Heath howling like babies, Ellis would wonder what she was doing, a dozen or so feet in the air above him. Who was she, when she was alone? She was always dressed and ready for the outside world at breakfast, shining and polished, her permanent wave set and unmoving, black handbag swinging on her arm, as though the house was merely a series of functional boxes to move through on her way to her real existence. The idea of her undone, or in transition from one state to another, was impossible to imagine, yet equally impossible to stop thinking about.

Janey had arrived with a single suitcase, and what had seemed insubstantial then had become thinner still when its contents were dispersed, and the empty case relegated to the top of the wardrobe. On the dressing-table she kept a bottle of scent, a brush and comb, and a couple of jars containing creams and cosmetics. No books, no photographs. He ran his hands through the clothes in the wardrobe, his fingers hovering over two new beaded and trimmed evening gowns: one blood red with vast chiffon sleeves, the second a Vionnet-style blue-grey with a beaded cape. He frowned. Why did she need two new evening gowns? Was she husband-hunting? He sniffed each in turn, taking handfuls of the fabric to his mouth and nose, inhaling stale sweat and perfume. Her cheap nightdress, which he often found slung on a chair, was puddled on the carpet, as if abandoned in a hurry.

He opened every jar. Touched her *papier poudré*, sniffed her cleansing cream and rouge. At what point, he wondered, did Janey become Janey? A private Janey existed – the proof of it was here, in her room – but, to his invariable frustration, he had no access to her. Whatever space she took up in the world had nothing to do with where she slept and dressed. The Janey he met at the breakfast table was not an amalgam of her possessions.

Virginia, whom Ellis considered too old-fashioned about such matters, believed make-up fast, and frowned her disapproval at Janey's carmine lips and painted nails, at her arched, thinly plucked eyebrows ('One can't help but think of a chicken'), and lashes slicked up with brilliantine. Yet Virginia was unable to see any connection, or even consider there might be a parallel, between her own annual slimming and skin rejuvenation cure at Carlsbad – which she had yet to give up, despite the cost – and Janey's painted face and trim figure.

The empty chocolate box was in its usual place on the dressing-table, satin ribbon perfectly retied and corner tassels neatly straightened. It still gave off a lingering minty sweetness. What was Patrick playing at, throwing expensive gifts at her? An assortment that size must have set him back at least thirty shillings. He opened the drawer and withdrew the *Engagements Diary 1938* that had been his own Christmas present to her. She had professed herself thrilled with its mother-of-pearl surround and tiny brass lock and key. Ellis, too, had been delighted with his choice of gift, imagining her confessing every detail of her secret life onto its pages. His hope was that the diary would give him divine powers, transforming him into an all-seeing being, a deity able to explore her soul, to peel back the skin of her sins and prayers alike. He imagined conversations in which he'd already know the punchline of every anecdote, have already explored the very hinterland of her emotions and responses. What a joyously God-like exercise in restraint that would be! He would have to police his reactions, deny himself the urge to respond! That the diary had a lock was irrelevant because he had retained the second of the tiny brass keys that came with it. As always, it was infuriatingly blank. She hadn't even written her name on the title page!

He walked to the window and, his back turned against the garden, faced into the room, aware only of the complete absence of her, of the space she *wasn't* taking up. Ellis's happiness was not compounded by her presence: there was nothing about the way he felt for her that he would identify as love, and his potential for happiness – such as it was – wasn't tied to her presence. What he desired was her approval, her attention. He wanted her to be fascinated by him, to be as obsessed by his existence as he was by hers.

He turned around. The view from her room was the same as his own, but entirely unalike too: not because it was a floor higher, but because it was hers. The slate-grey roofs that glistened with rain on the houses at either side, visible because of the curve in the terrace, were hers alone. The tall trees on the Heath, their branches crawling through the grey sleet of sky, were something only she saw. Was it possible, he wondered, that what he really enjoyed was nothing more than the constant throb of her disinterest?

Outside, clouds flittered and trembled. Stray seagulls swooped over the ponds on the Heath. Their cries called to him, telling tales of faraway horizons and distant blue water.

CHAPTER 4

Winsome's money was more delightful to the touch than any pound note he had ever held. Relieved as he was not to have any further dealings with him, Ellis had found Winsome's stupidity strangely enlivening. Toying with the unravelled edges of the man's fear excited him. It gave him a power he had never felt before, and Ellis wanted nothing more than to experience that sensation again. Janey understood what it was to feel like that, he was sure of it; she knew, too, that there was nothing indecent in it. He had been watching the furtive glances Patrick cast increasingly in her direction, the dumb, plaintive lust that flooded his eyes when she walked into the dining room for breakfast. And Patrick was so resolutely ordinary – a man who couldn't protect his face from his private thoughts must stink as a doctor – that whatever he saw in her, well, a thousand other men must see it, and be equally unable to hide it. The feeling was, he now understood, not just the *awareness* of power, but also an understanding as to how best it should be wielded. Yet alongside this, he envied Winsome's relief at having the letters back: a self-pitying jealousy that Winsome's problem was solved permanently, while Ellis's own pauper's existence had merely gained a temporary reprieve.

When he had given Winsome an envelope containing the letters and in return received one containing banknotes, he knew that the other man's fear, and his own control over it, had dissolved, rendered invalid by the transaction. It made him sad, as though he was suddenly entirely unimportant – even to someone as pointless as Winsome – and completely alone.

Obviously, there was no point in troubling Virginia with news of such unexpected funds. It was far better to view it as a fee, reasonable recompense for his labour. Virginia never expected him to contribute financially to the household – it would be ridiculous for him to return money to her from the pitiful allowance she gave him – and a delicate situation such as this was hardly an appropriate time to start.

The original plan of paying off all his creditors had been a foolish notion, he decided, as he transferred the contents of Winsome's envelope to the secret compartment at the back of his desk. Credit was essential, part of the world order. Without the immoral pleasure and profit of a couple of debts, the see-saw barter between red and black, what was there? Nothing. Instead, he settled the most pressing accounts, those businesses whose trade he relied on, or individuals who had a name for being ill-tempered, or too quick on the snatch-back.

Next, he invited Janey to dinner and cocktails. The timing had to be carefully done, so he'd suggested Thursday, when Virginia went to bridge followed by supper, and never returned until at least ten thirty – later, if a rubber took especially long to come out – and, invariably exhausted, went straight to bed. He asked Janey if she'd like to go to a nightclub too. He'd been to the Bat once, several years earlier, so had a fair idea how much an evening there would cost. She refused, sounding put out by the question: she wouldn't set foot in that place, she swore, which set him worrying that perhaps he had misjudged her interests. But, no, what he had misjudged was her information: the Silver Slipper in Regent Street was where everyone who was anyone was going. It had a real glass floor, or so she'd heard.

And what a time they had! Champagne, martinis, wine, and then more champagne, and with each fresh drink, they raised their glasses, their toast a chorus of 'To bozos!' The Silver Slipper had cost a fair bit on top of the meal and the drinks, just as he had known it would. He'd not had any change out of a five-pound note that night, not to mention the ten bob in tips on top, plus her corsage. But hadn't it been a fair price in order to become the subject of other men's envy when they saw her on his arm? To be king and queen of those secret palaces that come to life only under moonlight?

The following morning, Ellis was still dizzy from the drinks, the toasts, the touch of his arm against Janey's, of his hand resting on her slim waist. He was late to breakfast. Janey's door hadn't opened yet. Patrick had already gone to the hospital and Virginia was alone, reading. The room was gloomy after the gleaming chromium plating of the restaurant (was it only twelve hours earlier? Already the memory of their hours together was fading, a dawn dream spilt, lost to his bed). The familiar smell of kippers, the exhaustingly ordinary sight of his plate and teacup, made him almost tearful.

'Are you all right, darling? Did you enjoy your evening?' An invitation to a party for a new literary magazine had been his disguise. Virginia wouldn't have known anyone there.

'A little tired, that's all. The readings went on rather, and there were drinks afterwards. How was bridge?'

'A success for me. I came home fifteen shillings up! I shall make our fortunes yet, Ellis. I am going to treat Nancy Grade to supper this evening on the proceeds.'

'You're out again? That's unlike you.'

'Nancy had a spare ticket for a League of Health and Beauty demonstration at the Royal Albert Hall. It's quite fun, being a gadabout once more.'

Ellis sat staring out the window long after Virginia had passed him the newspaper and left. It was well after ten when Janey appeared. She greeted him in exactly the same way as always, which confused him. It wasn't as though he was expecting anything in return from her, but still . . . Why, he could have been Patrick sitting there, she was that careless in her manner.

'Enormous fun, wasn't it?' he said, pouring her a cup of tea.

'Ugh.' She threw down the lid of the kipper dish with a clang. 'What? Oh, yes, I suppose so.' She checked her wristwatch. 'Bother – twenty past already! I shall have to be off in a tick.'

'Right,' he said. 'I thought it was super. Really super,' he added, hating himself more with each heaped spoon of praise. Why did he still feel as though he was beholden to her, craving crumbs from her table? He wanted nothing more than for her to thank him for his generosity, to look at him in a new way, a private way, so that he could say, 'I don't care about the money, you know that.' She yawned and reached for the milk jug. Disliking the forced jollity of his tone, he said,

'Your dress was glorious, Janey. Everyone must have thought I had a goddess on my arm!' She smiled, acknowledging the compliment as no more than her due. Was that it? Was she prepared to let their night – *his* night – slip off into the past, her interest as exhausted as his wallet? She couldn't! He wouldn't let her. She had worn one of the two new gowns he'd come across in her wardrobe and, desperate to keep the topic alive, he heard himself add, 'Funny, but I had pictured you in the new red – I don't know why.'

Her knife stilled. '*The new red?* What do you mean? How do you know I've got a red dress?'

Fear spiked, thin and mean as heartburn, in his chest. He secretly cursed his hunger for her attention. But panic is a liar's worst enemy, so he pretended to consider while he reached into his pocket. 'You mentioned it, oh, I don't know, a week or two ago. Ciggie?'

'Did I?' She sounded unconvinced. 'Oh, yes, thanks.'

Keen to move the conversation along, he added quickly, 'What are you doing tonight, Janey? Shall we go dancing again?'

'All right,' she said. 'If you like. Won't your mother be curious.' It wasn't a question.

'It's nothing to do with her. Anyway, she'll be out herself.'

'Not the Silver Slipper again. I didn't think it was worth it, not really.'

'Oh,' he said, not entirely sure what she meant, considering every farthing they'd spent had issued from his pocket. It was the glass floor, she explained. She had found it soiled and silly.

'Choose somewhere else then, I don't mind. Anywhere you like.'

'The Nest. It's new too. The last word, so I'm told.'

He agreed gladly, ignoring the niggling voice that warned him it was sure to cost even more than the Silver Slipper. He didn't say it to her, but he wondered whether her quick acquiescence to two evenings out in a row meant he had been correct about her job: that she wasn't staying late in the theatre every evening at the behest of her boss but because she was trying to find work for herself onstage rather than backstage. She certainly had the looks for it: the admiring glances of every man and most of the women they had encountered the previous night confirmed it.

The little voice was proved right. No sooner had they sat down in the Nest than Janey excused herself to talk to a hostess, in a slim-fitting caped dress, her shining blonde waves almost a match for Janey's own. The girl reminded him of a cat in the way she repeatedly smoothed her hair by moving her head against her palm. He sat alone, drinking champagne that tasted nothing like its price tag suggested. When Janey returned, pronouncing the place terribly gay and smart, he tried to look at the décor and patrons through her eyes. What filter of glamour was she viewing through? Prices aside, the Nest seemed cheap to him. A tawdry sort of place, full of drunks accumulating hangovers and overdrafts, its shadows strewn with sadness. Did only unhappy people go to nightclubs, he wondered, as a dumpy woman who must have had a decade on Virginia waved coyly at the band leader, the diamonds on her fingers twinkling in the lights. Perhaps the happy ones stay at home. He watched a man with a thin smile and a stiff leg dance awkwardly with a woman, neither of them speaking, and wondered if a point must come at

53

which couples stop seeing the future in each other's eyes, and begin only to see the past, and feel disappointed in it, and desperately alone.

'Who were you talking to just now?'

'Who? Her? We just got chatting earlier, when you was at the cloakroom.' Janey straightened her corsage, the rosebud still alive even though it was from the evening before, its blood-coloured petals as fresh as if just picked, re-pinning it to her red dress, her slender arms visible through the chiffon sleeves. Her wrists were narrow and fragile, her ghost-pale skin drawn tight and smooth, shockingly white against her crimson lips. She was a china doll, and just as easily breakable. He drew her attention to the dumpy woman, joined now by a much younger man in evening dress, who was looking attentively at her. 'They could be from a servants' ball, couldn't they? The dowager waltzing with the footman.'

'Servants' balls? Don't make me laugh. Another way for people who have everything to torment the rest of us, who ain't got anything. One night you're dancing with the lord of the house, the next morning you're changing his sheets and he's back to being all pound-noteish with you. It's like *Cinderella*, but the prince won't marry you. He won't even remember your name. If that ain't tormenting, I don't know what is.'

The blonde hostess danced past their table, ineptly steered by a handsome young man in a well-cut dinner jacket, who pushed her around the floor with the grace of a novice jockey taught to lean too heavily on the whip. She caught Janey's eye as he manoeuvred her past their table. Ellis noticed a current pass between the two women, not sympathetic exactly, but neither was it the superficial acknowledgement – 'Hello again!' – of one new acquaintance to another. He watched the woman's back as she was cantered off towards the far reaches of the room, her companion's face set and tense. Kinship: that was what he'd seen.

'Which of them are you looking at?' Janey asked, and he blushed and busied himself with a cigarette, even though he'd just put one out. His discomfort didn't seem to bother her, for then she said airily, 'Oh! I never did tell you the news, did I? The Lyceum's being converted to a cinema! Atkinson's furious, but the owners are insisting. He has to go along with it if he wants to keep his job.'

'Is it really?' Freddie will hate that, Ellis thought, gleeful. Another theatre gone! Ellis was only too familiar with his uncle's opinion that the modern white cinemas that had sprung up all over the city not only looked like sanatoriums but were just as boring and full of germs.

'I reckon he ought to do it up proper, you know, a real picture palace. Have you ever been in the Troxy over in Stepney? It's ever so elegant. They scent it with Yardley's Lavender. Or he could do it in the Chinese style, with dragons.'

'And will he?'

'Not a chance. The owners are tightwads. He has to buy a projector and fill in the orchestra pit for extra seats, and that'll all cost a pretty penny. He says there won't be enough left for anything fancy. He's going to block up parts of backstage to save money.' She leant forward, distracted. 'Ooh, look at that chap there, Ellis – no, by the band. Isn't he the spit of Patrick, only smaller?'

The man was heavy-set and auburn-haired. His barrel chest and short, thick arms and legs reminded Ellis of a lumbering, bumbling bulldog.

She shook her head. 'You've got him all wrong,' she said. 'Patrick's a Labrador.'

Five or six bozos later, he experienced a peculiar moment, one of unfamiliar, overwhelming perfection. The swish of the band and the crooner's whispered promises, the oniony stink of sweat wafting from the dance-floor fell away to nothing. Instead, a violent happiness filled him. Calm descended on the perpetual clamour in his brain and its incessant recalibrating of every experience to assess how it fell short of what he had desired. He was a man with money in his pocket, and a beautiful girl on his arm, at the most expensive table in the room. He was the envy of every fellow in London. They were his hands on his table. His nightclub, his city, his country. The planets were perfectly harmonious and aligned, and that would never change. The world, as he knew it, was his to own. A man could go a lifetime and never be touched by that feeling.

'Fresh drinks, sir?' A waiter appeared beside their table and lightly touched his arm.

The moment was over. Gone so quickly that he knew he'd never recapture it, or be able to summon its essence again, even in dilute form. Irritation bubbled up once more. He dug his fingernails into his palm. Janey was frowning, her lips narrowed into a red slit, her impatient nod informing him he should order more champagne. As the fresh bottle appeared, sweating in its linen towel, so did the hostess, alone now. She nodded at him and angled her head towards Janey. 'Your pal's a looker,' she whispered, but he heard nonetheless.

Janey nodded, her expression the same as when she'd asked earlier, *Which of them are you looking at?* She waved her cigarette like a baton in Ellis's direction, the tip smouldering coal-black and orange. Her expression irked him, a scab he wanted to pick at. He wasn't one of *them*, if that was what she'd meant. He wasn't like that!

And then it was a week later, her scent on his evening scarf and the second rickety hangover long since faded. Winsome's cash was gone too, spent so quickly he thought he'd made a mistake, and hunted about his pockets, searching for a mislaid ten-bob note. The thrilling, hurtling excitement, the blood-letting, was over. Ellis sighed. Sitting at his desk, his back hunched, with nothing to do but consider the tedium that life consigned him to. His study had once been Sidney's library. Compared to the rest of the house, the room was warm at least. The girl set the fire first thing every morning so that the room would be ready for him after breakfast. There was a constant procession of girls in Virginia's employment. Some lasted mere days (the record was three hours), some clung grimly on for months, but none succeeded for long in the feat of endurance that was being Virginia's sole employee, and only the desperate were prepared to live in, once they realised that Virginia was no respecter of a servant's time or privacy.

He threw more coal onto the fire. To Hell with the expense, he simply couldn't write in a cold room. It wasn't conducive to the creative process. He and Virginia had agreed as much when it was decided that Ellis needed a private space in which to write – or, as she sometimes referred to it, much to his irritation, to *type*. He had taken the chaise longue from her bedroom so he would have somewhere to read and think. His typewriter was set up on a desk to one side of the small, paned window. It overlooked the garden, just as the larger Music Room next door did.

The almost-blank sheet, a gaping ugly white thing, stared sullenly back from his typewriter. He imagined the page yawning, insolent and cruel in its tedium. The only thing he'd written in a fortnight was an entry to the *Evening Standard* Topical Limerick Competition: *The police had declared themselves stumped/In the search for the missing chump/They found a torso/ Arms and legs, yes, of course-o/Then finally hit a hump.*

His entry hadn't been placed, and when he'd written to the editor to complain about the pitifully low standards of those that were, he had received a rude reply to the effect that his submission was disqualified on the grounds that it was unsavoury and likely to cause offence to the paper's readership.

Ellis leant forward and typed a couple of words. The letter *e* key was sticky, its metal post constantly getting tangled with the *r*. He tugged them apart impatiently. He wanted words to spill from him. He could picture them flowing onto the page, bright and strong and beautiful. A river where it meets the sea. But over and over, he found himself halted in mid-stream, hands raised, thoughts cold and muddy around his ankles.

It was no good. The rollers protested as he tugged the page roughly from the typewriter. He flattened it on the table in front of him and, bored, wrote his own name over and over, playing with it, his signature long and looping in one place, squat and compressed in another. He added *Lady Virginia Spender* in a perfect, practised replica of her style. He still found it hard to believe that the insurance company had queried her name on that policy: the signature had been flawless. Having inherited his father's fine hand, Ellis had run a lucrative side-line at prep school as a penman, composing essays for friends in their own hand and, for the day-boys, forging notes supposed to have come from home.

Still bored, he tried *Freddie Broughton*, the letter *e* expansive, the *B* in Broughton a treble clef of swirls and flips. It didn't take long to produce something that he was confident would fool a casual observer at least. He and Janey had both had to sign the Members' Book at the Nest so he attempted hers next. She had signed slowly, her signature both bold and immature, the squat, uncomfortable letters suggesting she was not much in the habit of writing her name, and that it was likely to vary slightly whenever she had to do so. She had added a flourish to the *d* of Gould, he recalled, an unnecessary loop at the tail, such as a child might do. He turned the sheet over and practised, *Janey Gould Janey Gould Janey Gould*, filling the page. Then he relaxed his hands and signed again quickly on a fresh sheet. Perfect. He'd defy anyone – Janey included – to tell it from her own.

It was only mid-afternoon yet a foggy darkness was descending outside. What little extra daylight the new year had brought had faltered, as though Nature had changed its mind. He considered going out, but couldn't think of anywhere interesting he could afford to visit. He felt adrift, lost in a city that seemed unwilling to make a place for him, recalling the passage in *Dracula* where the Count tells Jonathan Harker how he longs to visit London, to be '*in the midst of the whirl and rush of humanity, to share its life, its change, its death, and all that makes it what it is*'. His fire was dying down, the room a still and disquieting mess of shade and half-light. The walls facing and behind him were lined with densely packed shelves, and the room felt airless suddenly, as if the books were going to close in, an army trampling him to the ground. If only Janey was at home. Conversation! That was what he needed. Something to stir him up, to shake an idea loose! He didn't need any single person for inspiration, he believed. No, the ideas were all his, and already there, buried in his subconscious, needing only a simple prompt to be unearthed. But where was he to find it? Janey was at work, and as usual hadn't said when she'd be back.

Had he made a mistake, he wondered, in proposing a second outing immediately after the first? In his neediness to insert himself into her life, had he merely embarrassed himself by asking her again? Putting a week or more between them would have extended the experience. Stretched it thinly, yes, but perhaps having a week of anticipation would have been better. They could have compared the two more easily, with a week's hindsight: *This we did and, yes, this too – and, oh, did we? Why, how funny, it had slipped my mind.* And it would have connected them, *do you remember* lacing them together for longer, the gossamer thread of memories tying the two of them into a single perfect bow.

Yet Janey didn't seem like the type to reminisce. Everything was present with her, every action a forward-only movement. And what if he brought up something amusing that had happened in the Silver Slipper – that waiter who skidded on the wet floor and dropped his tray, or the tipsy woman who insisted the band stop and the leader ask the patrons to search for her lost diamond earring, crying because her husband would be furious it was gone, and even more furious if he were to discover where she had been when she lost it – and she didn't remember? That would be far, far worse!

No, he had played it just right: two consecutive nights was

best. It had all gone off just as it ought. What a pity, though, that he had barely seen Janey since, aside from fleeting appearances at breakfast. Atkinson was very busy, she explained, with the preparations for the cinema conversion. Without bait to tempt her otherwise, he had no choice but to smile and pick up his newspaper and say, 'Cheerio. Maybe I'll see you tomorrow morning!' She'd been chatting to Patrick more than usual, Ellis had noticed. He'd overheard them from the hall a couple of times, but the conversation had faltered when he'd opened the dining room door. Patrick's breakfast-time appearances had become more frequent. Ellis wondered if he, too, planned his mornings around Janey's erratic time-keeping? He desperately hoped there was nothing more to it. No matter how hard he listened, he couldn't hear anything unusual from upstairs, no nocturnal crossings from one room to another, no suspicious creaks or shudders, merely her door and the lavatory's catarrh-like flush. He had checked both their rooms and found no evidence to suggest that they ever visited each other. Patrick's pillow was smooth and devoid of blonde hairs; her sheets were unstained, smelling of nothing more than laundry soap. He'd said something slighting about Patrick the previous day, just to see how she'd react, and she'd replied, 'Oh, old Sawbones is all right.'

There had been a moment in the Nest, he recalled, when she'd returned from chatting to the hostess, and sat down beside him again. She said nothing for a moment, just sipped her drink, all the time watching a pretty woman dancing with a much older, awkward man, whose grip on her arm looked painful. His feet trod on hers repeatedly, but the woman's unwavering smile gave no indication that she'd noticed, and from the way his bloated paunch strained his evening coat and obscured his view of the floor, neither had he. Janey had twisted the stem of her glass in her hand, then said, 'People are weeds, I reckon.'

'Whatever do you mean?'

'People, everyone together I mean, well, we're more like weeds than anything else. To survive the war and sicknesses – all those sorts of things . . . famines and, I don't know, earthquakes. Stands to reason, doesn't it? It's the rubbish that grows no matter what, even when there's no water. It certainly ain't flowers!'

He'd laughed because it sounded so unexpected coming from her, but she was right, of course: that the human race continued to exist had nothing to do with intelligence, with belief in a common desire for protection and preservation, or even with pacifism, no matter what the papers said. No, it was down to bloody-minded resilience. The strongest, not the righteous, would always win.

He stoked the fire, the clang of the fire-irons sounding loud in the complete silence of the room. The house was empty. It was the girl's afternoon off. Patrick was at the hospital as usual. Virginia had gone to Croydon where she could get her corns removed for free in the beauty hall at Kennards. She didn't mind having to go all that way one jot, she'd assured him, because it wasn't as though any of her friends would see her, not in Croydon, and anyway, she was hoping to see the baby elephants the shop had brought in to advertise its Jumbo Sale. 'Selfridges *would* be more pleasant,' she'd added, with a sigh, 'but they only do warts. Oh, should we tell Patrick, do you think?'

Uneasily aware that he was alone and the floors above and below him were lightless and cold as tombs, he wandered into the Music Room. He had begun to do this regularly since the search for Winsome's letters, usually doing nothing more than idly flicking through some of Freddie's possessions before moving to the window to stare out at the Heath and smoke. The previous day he'd been bored enough to read through Freddie's collection of Gilbert and Sullivan librettos – Freddie's excellent character baritone had been a staple of his parents' parties – some of which were annotated and signed by Gilbert, as well as a couple of letters, the last of which had the scribbled postscript: *My wife sends her love to your dearest sister, as I would if I dared!*

He stared at Freddie's wall of boxes and packing cases. Purging them would spare Virginia the worst of Freddie's excesses. Freddie had no intention of returning, but knowing his mother, she would uncomplainingly house his possessions for the rest of her life if it kept a tether between her younger brother and herself. The problem of what to do with Freddie's junk was going to end up in Ellis's hands anyway. It was just a matter of *when*. He imagined penning a letter to Winsome at the ministry and signing it as Freddie, some overwrought tosh about missing him, in which he would beg Winsome to throw off his life in London and move to America. He grinned as he imagined Winsome's stupid face opening the envelope, terrified that his superiors, bound to be stuffy King-and-Empire types, would see it.

If only there were more Winsomes! That would generate some money. But . . . He paused. Wasn't it possible that there *were*? Wasn't it likely, he reasoned, that Winsome wouldn't have been the only man stupid enough to enter into a compromising correspondence with a charming man? Freddie was sure to know others in similar situations to Winsome, men who would pay to have the louche loose ends of their private lives neatly trimmed away. Freddie deserved to have his belongings sold from under him. Possibly there was a dent to be made in the huge sum of money Virginia had paid out. Yes: the labour would be all his own and would need to be rewarded but, when his own financial position stabilised somewhat, his mother might deserve some recompense too.

Wait till Janey hears about this, he thought, and began to pull boxes down from the stacks. A bloodthirsty pirate, he riffled eagerly through the first, a jumble of play scripts, posters advertising old, long-forgotten productions signed (*'Dearest Freddie! A thousand thanks. The show wouldn't be the same without you!'*) by old, long-forgotten cast members, and didn't stop until he had looked at every single piece of printed material that had come from Freddie's flat. Neat ordered piles began to build as he put handwritten letters to one side, arranged by author. Autographed material from the theatre, and books signed by their authors amounted to seven stacks. Quite a few were first editions, he noticed. Rubbish, ha'penny pamphlets, and a well-used copy of *For Your Convenience: A Learned Dialogue Instructive to all Londoners and London Visitors* he tossed into an empty box. They could all go on the fire. Time passed unnoticed as he worked, crouched on the rug, his body merging with the shadows creeping in from the corners, stealing up from the floor.

The letters revealed four possible Winsomes. A disappointing tally: he had hoped for more. Still, he told himself, even if one of them – the name Arnold Harris was familiar: was he in the House of Lords? He made a mental note to check his *Debrett's* later – was prepared to play along, there was surely twenty pounds or more to be made. He would contact them all, he decided, explaining that he had recently undertaken to write a biography of his famous uncle, and just needed to check a detail or two of his correspondence. 'Yes, Lord Harris,' he imagined himself saying, the very model of a studious, dry biographer, 'I hadn't realised you and my uncle were such dear, dear friends until I read the letters!' His voice would be friendly, warm. And when Harris said he'd rather not be included in any such publication— Ellis giggled, imagining Harris sweating, his voice nervous as he hastily invented a reason for preferring to keep the correspondence private. 'Well, if you're sure,' he'd say, surprised yet still perfectly pleasant, 'though I am disappointed. I've done such a lot of work already on this chapter, you see, and this is my livelihood, so I have to ensure the publication is as good, as accurate, as it can be . . .' Yes, that might be enough to scare a man into action. There was no way for anyone to contact Freddie, so he'd be safe. He pushed his hands together, feeling the movement stretch as far as his shoulders.

But was looking for letters, for other Winsomes, really the right tack? Surely the easier way to earn money was by selling off whatever things of value Freddie had. He began to search through the books more carefully, concentrating on first editions. He put aside a Forster, a couple of Somerset Maughams, two copies of H. Rider Haggard's *She*, both signed. A couple of guineas if he was lucky.

Without pausing to consider why, he began to remove the dust sheets covering his father's easels and canvases, which remained stacked around the room just as Sidney had left them. Every noise he made, every rustle and step, joined the gurgles and clangs coming from pipes that ran down the wall outside, and the wheeze of the heater. The house groaned around him, an animal abandoned by its herd to die a slow and solitary death. He threw the sheets into a corner, and began to set the pieces on the floor, leaning them one by one against the skirting. He worked his way methodically around the room, covering three walls' worth, making no attempt to curate the canvases into any other arrangement. When he'd finished, almost-complete landscapes posed side by side with charcoal sketches, and finished portraits stood to attention beside barely begun illustrations. Two corgis, squat and ghostly in outline, stared balefully at a young woman in a wide-brimmed hat. An older woman holding a bouquet stood behind her. The girl's face and long dress were almost complete – the burr of the velvet in her gown a series of minute, perfect brushstrokes – while the older woman and the drapery in the background were outlines, a loose, faded wash, and looked ghostly and unmoored.

He recognised the girl, though couldn't recall her name. Her father, the Earl of Somewhere-or-other, had commissioned a portrait of his wife and darling daughter to celebrate the girl's coming out. Yet by the time the picture was under way, he had taken up with a twenty-year-old heiress he had met on a particularly choppy voyage on the *Mauretania* and no longer wanted a commemorative portrait or, for that matter, anything more to do with its subjects. He felt full sure, he wrote from Chicago, that as a red-blooded man himself, Sidney would understand the difficult position he found himself in, and consider their arrangement dissolved instanter. A jagged tear in the canvas suggested Sidney's response.

Four Gladwell's catalogues were tucked in behind a chipped frame. The pages were scribbled on, and sale prices had been added by hand beside many of the listings. Tucked into each catalogue was a loose sheet, titled *Unsold Lots Offered at Low Reserve Prices*. In each case, Sidney's catalogue entries were repeated there.

Ellis's nonsensical exhibition grew until it snaked around the room, the way a child's picture game might. Jumbled together, the arrangement told a crazy tale of humans and animals, of rock-bound, ill-fated schooners and purplish, lonely hills, eddied by mists. It reminded him of Virginia's description of the vast new roof garden at Derry & Toms department store: a nightmarish concoction of different styles, with a Spanish garden based on the Alhambra, a replica Tudor area, and a traditional English woodland with loamy soil and thirty species of tree. 'And,' she had added, 'pink flamingos running madly everywhere!'

The oscillation from finished artwork to barely-begun and back again was dreamlike and unsettling, the completed pieces standing out like moments of clarity during a fever. The majority of the canvases were dated on the back, but none of the sketches was, so even had he tried to arrange it by chronology, it wasn't possible. What could the passing of time have told him that he didn't already know, anyway? Sidney had retained little of his work from his first three decades as a painter for the simple reason that it was so popular. The secret to portrait painting, according to Sidney, was to be devoid of emotion. He painted with a view to his sitter's purse and vanity, and his audience's tastes. Then, when the work was done, his philosophy demanded that anything that could be sold should be sold. Send it out, let it earn acclaim! Let those painted faces command respect, honour and money! Each painting was launched into society as his representative, all bonhomie and charm. It used to be said that, just as George du Maurier added two inches of height to English women by drawing only tall, graceful types in his cartoons, Spender added two inches of girth to the men, with his insistence on broad chests and strong physiques.

During the war, his work took on a more panicked quality. That, Ellis knew, had nothing to do with fear of what was happening at the Front, or the continuing enormity of the nation's losses. Instead, it had everything to do with his father's burgeoning awareness that it had been decided by the art world that Sir Sidney Spender's day in the sun was over. The Empire was imperilled, and Sidney's unchallenged and unchallenging portraits were all of a sudden found to be in bad taste.

Last in Ellis's unintended exhibition was a series of unfinished sketches. He'd never seen any of them before. Five circus freaks, each more monstrous than the last. A small, buxom woman with a full beard and dusty, sucked-out hollows where her eyes should have been. A child, dressed in a long lace-trimmed nightgown, with two heads, one male, the other female. A man holding a midget in the palm of his right hand, while using his left to stroke her cheek . . . These were not the style of preparatory sketches for a portrait Ellis was accustomed to: there was no suggestion of flattery here, no illusions being conjured. He had no way to confirm his suspicion, but from the cold, harsh light being shone on each of the subjects, from the anger in the brushstrokes, Ellis knew he was looking at his father's final drawings. In the last, a pale, elderly man in evening dress stood alone, a full-length mirror at his side. His trousers were cut off halfway to show how impossibly bent his legs were, the left folding at a ninety-degree angle from the knee. A single dress shoe dangled as if suspended from his ankle, its toe facing the floor. Each hand was split almost up to the wrist, creating two fingers shaped like lobster claws. One hand extended outward, as if about to grab hold of the artist and bury the long, curved fingers on either side of his neck. The mirror showed only a hint of a figure, as though his form was too appalling to bear true reflection, a sombre shape that somehow resolved itself into an overweight man dressed all in black, his features unclear yet desperately sad, the suggestion of a slim implement in his hand. Unrecognisably yet unmistakably, Sidney Spender.

They were stunning, each bolder and more illuminating than the last. Ellis shivered. These grotesques would have been – should have been! – his father's finest work. How infuriatingly typical that they were incomplete.

He stood in his customary place at the window and smoked a cigarette before looking around the room all over again, from the very first oil painting to the freaks. Was this ridiculous, incoherent collection all that was left of his father? This motley ship of the unknown, the unwanted or unloved? Perhaps, he thought, that was all he and Virginia were – two of a thousand souls caught in Sidney's art, except their fate was to be trapped by poverty rather than a frame.

During the heady years of kings and queens, of commissions pouring through the door faster than Sidney could execute them, Sidney hadn't needed to source models, but for a year or so, when Ellis was four he had become his father's favourite subject. He sat for him regularly, sometimes decked out in costumes, occasionally standing beside Virginia or perched uncomfortably on her knees and aware of the staccato rhythm of her breath on his neck and hair, but more usually alone, as himself. *Artist's Child at Play* and *Ellis Dreaming* – the latter unintentionally posed as, despite Nanny's mutters, Sidney had insisted on painting Ellis while he took his lunchtime nap – were declared highlights of the 1912 Royal Academy Exhibition, and the Tate purchased *The Tinker Boy* for its permanent collection. The last time he had posed for his father had been in 1919. He hadn't really wanted to, but Virginia had insisted, and refusal could not be countenanced. It was embarrassing to lie on a chaise longue in the middle of the Music Room floor, naked apart from short trousers, his father's cool gaze on him, frowning, working him over as though he was an inanimate object to be sized up; a body whose frustrating faults had to be enumerated, then expunged by paint. Sidney never showed a sitter a work-in-progress, and it was a relief to be told after only a week that his father had finished with him. The portrait was accepted by the Royal Academy for the Summer Exhibition, Sidney's first acceptance in three years.

The day before the official opening, Sidney took Ellis with him to the Varnishing Day, the final opportunity for artists to make last-minute adjustments to the hung work. As they walked under the stone arch and entered the galleries, Sidney read aloud from the catalogue, denouncing those names whose work he disliked or whose reputation now outshone his own. Clouds passed over his face, heavy and thunderous, until he reached his own entry: 'Gallery III. Number 15. *Repose.* Sir Sidney Spender RA, RP, ROI.'

The relief in his voice pained Ellis, who was aware of how much his father's star had dulled. Aside from Uncle Freddie and Virginia's theatre friends, guests no longer visited as much, or as gaily, as they used to. His parents' social life had shrunk considerably, and he couldn't remember the last time a commission had brought a sitter to the studio. Although the room was crowded with artists feverishly adding finishing touches to their work while surreptitiously assessing each other's for quality and potential popularity, no heads had turned when his father appeared at the entrance to the room. He stood in the doorway, waiting for the room, which was full of peers, friends and colleagues, to right the wrongs meted out to him. Nothing. Observing his father's distress was agonising, yes, but embarrassing and bewildering too. In that moment Ellis would have done anything for someone – anyone! – to spot them and push through the hubbub, delighted and honoured to have none other than Sir Sidney Spender in their midst once again.

Yet . . . wasn't there something *he* could do? Perhaps he could be the one to praise his father. He hurried across the gallery to find his portrait. Yes, he could thank him for painting it and perhaps – yes, why not? – ask him for the portrait as a gift, or even offer to save and pay for it himself. Then if it didn't sell at the exhibition, it wouldn't matter: it would already have found a home in a private collection, that of Master Ellis Spender!

He skidded to a halt in front of number 15, *Repose*. It was a painting of a small terrier, lying on a densely patterned olive and brown carpet in front of a log fire, asleep, its whiskery muzzle peppered with white. From the intricate design on its tiled surround, he recognised the mantelpiece in the Music Room, its colours muted to resonate with the dog's coat. Sidney had submitted this dog – whose pet was it? Ellis had never seen the horrid animal before – instead of him.

'It didn't work with you, was the long and short of it,' Sidney said, from behind him. And then, 'House-dogs sell these days, I'm told, especially small mutts.' He picked a brush from his box to make a minute adjustment to the dog's lolling pink tongue. 'Budge out of the light, there's a fellow.' Ellis couldn't move. 'Hurry,' his father snapped. 'You're in my way!' The dog snoozed happily, warm and cared for by the glowing, painted fireside, as Sidney tweaked its muzzle.

Nineteen years had passed since that day at the Royal Academy but Sidney's *It didn't work with you* remained perfectly clear. Ellis lit another cigarette and continued leafing through his father's discarded work. On the back of a rough charcoal drawing of a man in uniform, Sidney had scribbled a quote from Milton: *Peace hath her victories/No less renowned than War*. In an otherwise-empty sketchbook he saw a small face he recognised, without realising at first why it was familiar. He held it to the light to make out every mark on the page where his father's pencil had tried to bring the face back to life.

Bad things left untouched find their own course, Ellis knew. It was how the world worked, after all. But was that sufficient justification for leaving such things alone? Yes, he decided. Yes, it probably was. He smoked and watched the light drain from the Heath outside, noticing how dusk crept up the garden, rolling towards him.

A latchkey twisted in the front door.

'Ellis?' Then, as always, a second 'Ellis!' louder, over the sound of shoes scraping across the mat. In the pause, she would have been taking off her hat and coat, patting her hair back into shape at the mirror. Next, her heels on the tiled floor. He counted silently. One, two, three, and . . . right on cue: 'Where are you?'

'Coming!' He ripped the sketch from the book, rolled it tightly and tucked it up the sleeve of his jumper. 'I'm here,' he said, shutting the door to the Music Room firmly behind him. 'Tell me, how are the corns?'

'They are no more! Why, Ellis, I could go dancing, my toes feel glorious. A floor walker – that pushy type, you know, all patter and compliments – tried her best to get me to buy new shoes afterwards, and it was terribly difficult not to, but I resisted. I think it must be a plot concocted between them, for she as good as pounced on me the moment I left the cosmetics hall.'

'And the elephants?'

'Not a success this year, sadly. Terribly sweet, of course, but apparently the mess was appalling.'

Virginia went to make tea. Ellis returned to his study and switched on the desk lamp. He slipped the rolled sheet gently from his sleeve and flattened it on the blotter. The baby stared up at him, her fine-featured face serious and watchful. He knew who it was, of course he did: Lucy Genevieve Spender, his younger sister. She was three months old when she died, not long after Ellis's fourth birthday. He couldn't recall exactly what she'd looked like, and would never have been able to describe her, except in tangential ways, such as how the very sight of her swaddled form turned Nanny, usually stern, into an unfamiliar cooing and giggling figure – yet he knew with complete certainty that this drawing was of her. His few memories were dreamlike, wispy, and always slightly troubling, the way an old ghost story can continue to upset in low, rolling waves, even years after reading it, when the characters' names are long forgotten. Lucy was a series of fixed moments: small fingers, pink and soft and topped with neat slivers of nails, wrapping around his own; a mewling, hollow sort of cry; his mother, sitting beside an empty bassinet weeping, her arm outstretched to push him away from her as he tried to grasp her, calling, 'Mummy, Mummy!' 'No,' she shouted. 'No!' He ran around her to wrap his arms around her neck, but his fingers caught in her necklace. It snapped, pearls scrambling down their slim rope at speed, falling on his face, like beautiful soft hailstones, then dropping away to the floor. A long, thin white worm with a diamond head landed in the folds of her skirt. She pushed him away and began to cry, her face in her hands. He walked away, crying too, hating the hard roll of pearls under his slippers.

Lucy was nowhere to be found in the Spender house now. Not in pictures or photographs. Not in memories or conversations. He wondered if he would ever be able to recall her as she really was or was it inevitable that she would fade further away as the space between his life and her death continued to widen with the turn of every new day. Perhaps what little of her he held inside him was already lost, cast into the blurred bottomless abyss that separates memory and history. And had he never found the sketch, wouldn't it have faded even more?

Lucy. He couldn't remember the last time he'd heard her name said aloud, or witnessed her existence being clutched back from the dead air.

CHAPTER 5

He would avoid bookshops in London. Someone he knew might spot him or – Ellis knew it was unlikely, but best to be safe – Virginia might chance upon a window display and recognise something as Freddie's. He was spending the day in the British Library reading room, he told her, but instead took a train to Oxford, to a bookshop he remembered passing regularly but never entering while he was at university. The parcel on the seat beside him rattled and shook with the motion of the train, as if desperate to draw attention to itself, a kidnap victim signalling for help.

The carriage was empty apart from a man of about his own age wearing Army uniform. He had a broad, heavy face, his features clustered closely together, as if relying on each other for company, while the extra flesh just loitered about, waiting to be put to use. A loose constellation of shaving spots on the side of his chin looked as if they could simply slide down the fat to the ground. He'd stood close enough for Ellis to inhale the scent of Gold Flake and, underneath it, the sullen smell of rain-damp fabric. He chose a seat diagonally across from Ellis, and smoked in silence, lighting each new cigarette from its predecessor. His feet moved constantly, up on his heels then down on his toes, over and over as though he was warming up, trying to summon enough energy into his heavy boots to spring forward. What life did a soldier have on the inside? Ellis wondered. Was it a rough terrain, stony and utilitarian, or was it something entirely different, a secret place of beauty, of wildness and meadows?

'Are you going far?' Ellis asked. The man met his gaze and, eyebrows raised, exhaled a smoke-ring, slowly, without looking away. Ellis blushed, and turned his head. How dare that fat fool look at him as if he thought he was a pansy on the pick-up? It was a relief when the soldier got off at Radley.

Chatterton & Chatterton Antiquarian Books on The Turl, its faded and double-fronted shopfront a series of mahogany wood-framed glass panels, was exactly as his memory had conjured it. He was surprised at how well he recalled every detail of the facade. Books in the window were propped up on stands, each accompanied by a handwritten card. They were all either first editions or listed as rare privately printed volumes, he noted, recognising *Observations on the Greek and Roman Classics* from his undergraduate reading list and *Moralités légendaires*, designed by Lucien Pissarro, whom Sidney had been quite taken with during a mercifully brief flirtation with the New English Art Club. The gold-edged card adjacent to an illustrated edition of Sheridan Le Fanu's *Carmilla* proclaimed *Specialists in Gothic literature and the super-natural.*

Next door had changed entirely. Once a dingy bar popular among undergraduates for its cheap meals and laissez-faire attitude towards bar tabs, the Quill Inn was now Quillers restaurant, a glittering temple of chrome and white tiling, its flagrant modernity a taunt to the ancient stone of the street.

He stood for ten minutes in a doorway across the road and watched. No one entered or left the shop. It was pleasant, just standing there. Hovering, neither active nor passive. A thin mist hung in the air. It reminded him of his undergraduate years, a decade earlier. Of walking down the high street on foggy winter mornings, a chorus of bicycle bells trilling like birdsong. The war had been over for ten years by then: the memory of gun-smoke faded, order restored. The past, as his father used to say, was behind them. He and his university contemporaries had lived through the war in the nursery; to them it was a bruise on their collective childhood rather than a permanent disfigurement of the future.

It was mid-morning and the pavements were quiet, the life of Oxford happening indoors and in silence, weighted down by its own exhausting history. Students were cloistered in their colleges, ordinary people were at work. The commercial life of the city was an invisible stream flowing silently underground, beneath the masses of granite and limestone. From the day Ellis had left Oxford for prep school, Sidney had been unkind and parsimonious about his allowance, doling out tiny sums imperiously, in unsatisfying, uneven amounts. If Virginia hadn't upped his allowance after Sidney's death, he would have had a terrible time, impoverished and lonely. What sort of education was that?

The brassy peal of the doorbell rang long and loud into the silent room, and as the door closed behind him, it cut through the angry horn of a van outside. He imagined the books stirred to irritation by the noise. The walls were a gloomy red, lined by a series of cabinets lit by small bulbs.

'Good day, sir.'

Ellis jumped. A tall, thin man had appeared through a hole in the floor. One hand was outstretched, the other clutched a pipe. 'Ralph Chatterton, owner of this collector's haven! Welcome.' Ellis glanced behind him, noticing a narrow set of steps that led to a basement. He looked about Freddie's age. An enormous bow-tie, its pattern of red dots on jet-coloured silk oddly jaunty by comparison with a saggy tweed jacket and cardigan, rested like a propeller on his neck. His thick black hair gleamed.

'I hope so!' Ellis shook his hand, smiling broadly. He unwrapped the parcel. 'I have some books I'd like your opinion on.'

'Well, that's what I'm here for, eh?' Chatterton took the topmost volume. He had the slightly shamed stoop of a man who had been too tall as a boy and hated it. In silence, he looked them over one by one, his face betraying nothing. He put a small pile, including Freddie's Somerset Maughams, the Forster, two Dickens, one copy of *She*, and the play script of *The Three Musketeers*, signed by Clifford Grey and P.G. Wodehouse, to one side.

'Anything else, sir?'

'Oh.' Ellis's heart was thumping. 'Well, yes . . . probably nothing but I thought I'd bring them along.' He opened his satchel.

'What a darling collection. Any signed?'

'All of them.' Surely he could hear Ellis's heart thumping hard enough to knock through his chest and land on the counter between them?

'These are yours?'

'Yes. A gift from my uncle Frederick when he moved abroad

– he's referred to in a couple of the dedications as either *Fred* or simply *F*.'

Chatterton worked his way through the Gilbert and Sullivan librettos, before placing them neatly on the counter. He had made three piles of Ellis's books. 'Are you a local chap?'

'London.' Ellis took a deep breath, then, as the other man looked curiously across at him, turned it into a cough. Chatterton raised his hands. Christ, did he not want to touch the Gilbert and Sullivans? Did he just, somehow, know?

'There are plenty of dealers there you could have gone to. May I ask why you decided to come to my quaint corner of the world?'

'Oh.' Ellis glanced down with slumped shoulders, looking every inch the shy young man. 'I'm a Balliol chap and I used to pass your shop every day and look in the window, and, well . . . the wonderful collections you always had stuck with me, that's all.' He flushed. 'I'm sentimental, I suppose. I'm sorry if I've troubled you.'

'Not remotely, it's no trouble at all. I merely mentioned it because my brother Rollo runs our establishment in town. Tavistock Street, close to Covent Garden.'

'Ah, of course. Near the Lyceum theatre? I never thought to make the connection.' He must have passed it dozens of times going to or from the theatre with Virginia.

'I merely wondered whether it would have been less trouble for you to visit Rollo. Not to say, of course,' he reached up and took hold of either side of his bow-tie, and tugged it gently, 'that I'm anything other than delighted you chose my humble door!' He looked as though he were about to take off. 'So, you'd like my opinion?'

'Please.'

'Overall, the books are in very good condition. Unread, I suspect' – that could have been said of any book of Freddie's, Ellis thought – 'which is a particular irony for bibliophiles such as myself. The gilt tooling on the Dickens is particularly fine . . . The binding is tight, no cocking or leaning. A wonderful edition, in fact. The Rider Haggard has suffered, unfortunately . . . particularly on the pastedowns. Do you see the foxing, here? And it's stained on the rear board too.' He pushed it to one side. 'Having signatures on the title pages helps, as does the dating on the ownership inscriptions. People like such notation at the moment – there are bibliophilic fashions, as in most things, though that comes as a surprise to some! Few customers want single playscripts, so *The Three Musketeers* would be hard to place. This Gilbert and Sullivan collection, though . . .' He moved his hands to either side of his nose and rubbed it with his forefingers.

Breathe, Ellis, breathe, Ellis thought, and then: *Run if you need to.* It would take just a second to grab the books back, and he had the advantage of being nearer the door. Chatterton would have to come around the counter to stop him. Had he gone too far in adding the dedications and remarks? Surely not: he had been so careful to ensure the penmanship was exact and every handwritten comment precisely judged, a pitch-perfect impersonation! He had spent hours poring over Gilbert's letters with a magnifying glass to get the letterforms right – his letters to Freddie having yielded an almost-complete alphabet – and had studied the texts so thoroughly that he had felt confident enough to include a handwritten rhyming couplet on the title page of *The Pirates of Penzance.*

'Gilbert and Sullivan are out of favour with serious collectors now,' Chatterton continued. 'Popular in amateur dramatics, of course, though unfortunately for me, amateur actors aren't interested in buying original material. But Americans! Now, that's different. Rollo and I have begun to produce mail-order catalogues three times a year for American connoisseurs. The latest goes out in a fortnight, as it happens. Because you have a collection with every piece signed . . . and, unlike books, librettos often tend to be discarded rather than retained, I think one could certainly find interest in this as a single lot.'

He put his pipe into his mouth and looked across the counter. 'Rarely do people come in for my opinion and nothing else. Shall we talk terms?'

CHAPTER 6

Ellis was awake at six. The cheque was due, and he wanted to whip away the post before Virginia noticed it. Determined to act as though this were any other ordinary day, he stayed in his room until just before eight. Lying in bed, he relived the encounter with Ralph Chatterton over and over, watching it as though it were a newsreel on a loop and he alone occupied the front row. He reviewed it from every vantage point, and was delighted with his performance. That must be how a great actor feels, he thought, the delicious certainty that one holds the power and skill to make another believe something entirely fictitious. What was truth, anyway? Nothing more than whatever a man could get away with. Finding Winsome's letters had been merely a financial transaction, Ellis a messenger paid to return the man's witless drivel. But this! It couldn't be more different . . . The thrill sustained Ellis all week, from the moment he left Chatterton's with a receipt and the promise of a cheque to follow by post. Not only had Chatterton not batted an eyelid at the authenticity of the handwriting or dedications, he had appreciated the librettos for what they had *become*, which meant that Ellis had added to the very nature of the works. He hadn't so much increased their value as their essential worth. He was an alchemist, his skill and artistry transforming base metal to gold! Ellis began to regret he hadn't added more annotations to lyrics, or a couple of supposed in-jokes between 'Fred' and 'WS'. He cursed his own cowardice, his father's words – *It didn't work with you* – flaring once more.

Janey appeared in the dining room shortly after him, immediately followed by Patrick, and then, unusually, Virginia. Patrick had intercepted the arrival of the paperboy and tapped the rolled-up *Times* against his palm, as though the news was a stick to beat the others with. Damn you, Ellis thought. The only thing worse than not seeing Janey at breakfast-time was sharing her. The four looked at each other, uncomfortable as newly honeymooning couples forced to share a table in a cheap hotel.

'Aren't we the early birds!' Patrick shook out his napkin, guffawing with laughter at his own wit. 'We'll catch all the worms today.' He'd never heard anything so hilarious.

'Tell me, Patrick,' Janey said, grinning, 'were you up at dawn yesterday to collect all your Valentines?'

Was she flirting with him? Did that mean Janey had given Patrick a Valentine? Virginia, knitting bag and magazine beside her plate, looked as though she regretted her decision to leave her bedroom so early, but as the hostess she was responsible for this fools' gathering, so etiquette demanded she stay. Patrick blushed and blustered as Janey lit a cigarette.

The girl put her head around the door. 'Shall I fetch the toast, madam?'

Virginia nodded, relieved.

'I've a couple of kippers I can put on, if the gentlemen would like one?'

Ellis shook his head. Patrick rubbed his hands together, delighted. 'What harm?' he said. 'I'll take the lot off your hands.'

This proprietorial attitude towards the food she was paying for caused Virginia to rally. 'One will be plenty, I should think,' she said, seeing off any protest by adding, 'Shall we have more rain, do you think, Patrick?'

Unable to resist such a direct claim on his opinions, Patrick replied eagerly, backing up his assertion with facts about the previous day's weather, adding, 'Shall I read today's forecast aloud, Lady Spender?'

'Forecast, my eye! Do the horoscopes,' Janey said. 'Me first. Cancer.'

Virginia frowned.

'Perhaps some news,' Ellis cut in quickly, imagining himself his mother's puppeteer as her face relaxed once more.

Patrick talked the assembled group through the headlines as if international events were a series of complex surgical cases and his fellow breakfasters a medical board. Patrick's personality, Ellis decided, as the man droned on, was that of a cricket ball, his edges stitched tight and unpickable, his grey interior dense and uniform. The lone kipper joined the table just as Patrick concluded an article about an eighty-year-old widow who had lost two sons to the trenches in 1916 and was offering to pay for the screening of the anti-war film *The World in Revolt* in a thousand churches, social centres and mission halls.

'*The World in* what?' Janey asked.

'*Revolt.*' Patrick rustled the paper, his delighted smile at being the recipient of her question sitting oddly with the word. 'It says here, *The anonymous donor promised she will do anything to save the world from the repetition of such a calamity*. Ten thousand pounds, it's going to cost her.'

'Ten *thousand*?' Janey was incredulous. 'What I'd do with that!'

'War!' Virginia, who had been sorry to see Baldwin – whose wife Lucy she was fond of – retire, broke in: 'I can't bear to hear all this talk of war. Not again.' Her older brother Claude had disappeared into the mud at Passchendaele. Twenty-one years later and *missing* he remained; *in action* he most certainly was not. 'How could any rational person give so much as a second's consideration to such a terrible prospect?' It was inconceivable to her that the weight of those campaigning against hostilities, people whose memories and politics and families still reverberated with the sound of cannon-fire, would not prevail. There was simply no way history could reassert itself in a different guise: surely the human variables made it impossible.

Patrick shook his head. 'Believe me, it will happen, Lady Spender. It has to. It signifies disease.' He had been at a lecture given by an expert in Mental Philosophy and Experimental Psychology just the previous week, he explained, and had since formed the opinion that the outbreak of war was the precipitation of a symptom followed by a certain process of incubation.

Had since formed the opinion, Ellis thought. What rot. Patrick would swallow a senior doctor's opinions as easily as he'd gulp down a captain's orders on the field, no matter how obvious a lunatic his commander was. 'Would you consider yourself a Mosleyite, Patrick?' Ellis said, amused. 'You have Blackshirts in Dublin, don't you?'

Patrick frowned, his knife held in mid-air.

'Blueshirts,' Virginia cut in unexpectedly. 'They're called Blueshirts in Ireland. Nothing short of buffoons, so Freddie says, though they believe themselves patriots.'

'Better for a man to be a patriot than a rabid Bolshevik giving away everything that doesn't belong to him!'

Ellis smiled, pleased at how easy it was to nudge the see-saw of Patrick's opinions.

'Here, whatever were you going on about just now?' Janey lifted her finger to tap her cigarette into a saucer but swerved to a nearby ashtray when she realised Virginia was watching. 'What did you mean by *signifies disease*?'

'War is a disease of modern, cultured nations. The threat does not originate in savagery by any means, despite it being a manifestation of anger. And, just as one might observe in small children, anger makes human beings misbehave. By which I mean: behave without rationality.' Patrick continued, in the same ponderous tone. What a stuffed shirt he was. Ellis imagined him hectoring his fellow students, boring them to tears with his notions. He tried to catch Janey's eye, hoping for a snigger or to see her lips curl in distaste as Patrick's foolishness continued, but she was trying to read her horoscope upside down. Her lips moved slightly. 'Fighting comes naturally to man,' Patrick continued, addressing his comments to Virginia now, 'but these mass wars are not instinctive. We are driven to them by each other, egged on by man's collective defiance.'

'Weeds,' Ellis said, in an undertone, and was delighted when Janey smiled in recognition.

Virginia shook her head as if that slight movement alone would be enough to rid her table, her very house, of the word. 'But . . . a *war*? I don't really understand how we could possibly have another. I mean, what on earth would it be for?'

'As a wiser man than I,' began Patrick, his smug face beaming, 'once said, Lady Spender, *We cannot put the jigsaw puzzle of the present together, because we are sitting on the pieces.*'

Post! Ellis jumped up and left the room. When he returned Janey was directing Patrick through the headlines like a policeman organising traffic through a busy junction. 'What's that one? No, beside it . . . That's it. Ooh, a breach of promise! I love them. Stella had one last year – you wouldn't believe the palaver. Read me that one next.'

A letter for Ellis, a postcard for Virginia. 'Freddie!' cried Virginia, and, whether in surprise or delight, read the card aloud immediately. Hollywood was wonderful, he wrote. Everyone simply adored him. Henry Warner – a dear old friend from a famous London theatrical family, now a popular Hollywood scriptwriter, Virginia clarified for the table – had provided him with introductions to all the right people. So much for Freddie's dislike of the movies! The man was anyone's for a price. He signed off with the words, 'Dearest V, you would so adore it here!' Which was hardly, Ellis thought, an invitation to pack a trunk and join him.

Nor did he mention his debts. How cruel, Ellis thought. Worse than nothing. Even Virginia seemed despondent as she passed the card to Ellis. The photograph on the front showed a movie theatre on a busy, fashionable street; a stylish, two-storey building, all sharp angles and stucco, with long, expensive cars parked outside. It looked wonderful, he thought. He imagined it was painted the colours of ice-cream, sun-warmed and new, perfect for a city crammed full of dreams. It was the opposite of his life.

'What a wonderful visit he's having!' Virginia's voice was brittle.

'*Visit*? Don't sound like he's coming back, if you ask me.' Janey frowned. 'Mr Atkinson will be disappointed. Pass the tea, Patrick, there's a dear.'

Virginia pushed her chair back, hard. She plucked the card from Ellis's hand and left the room in silence. Her knitting bag fell from the table and a ball of mossy green wool bounced across the floor, a toy batted by an invisible cat.

Ellis took Chatterton's letter to his study. A cheque for fourteen pounds twelve – ten of which earned by the librettos – and a request for *more material of similar quality, should any become available*. Finally, a tiny dent in Freddie's debt to the household! The sight of Virginia's disappointment at his card meant they'd probably had enough discussion of Freddie for one day, he decided. It would be best to keep this meagre sum to himself.

He hadn't acted on the compromising letters he'd found. He wouldn't contact Harris or the other three men, he realised now. He didn't have the nerve. No matter how much he told himself that was the right decision, he hated that what was stopping him was fear rather than sense. Winsome was different: by seeking out Ellis he had instigated the transaction. Everything was above board, refutable. But there'd be no denying a charge of blackmail if Harris or one of the others decided to cut up rough. Virginia had been able to make his problem with the Prudential disappear without the police getting involved, but she would be powerless should serious trouble befall him.

His life had to change. Ellis wasn't looking to become someone else: he wanted only to be the version of himself that he was forced continually to deny. But how? The success of forging Gilbert's hand on the librettos had loosened something within him. He went back to it over and over: it had been easy to do – Chatterton believed in their veracity wholeheartedly, and Ellis had made money at Freddie Broughton's expense. So simple and so perfect. Freddie owed him that much at least.

He went into the Music Room. He'd noticed a bound copy of *The Puppet-Showman's Album* in one of the boxes, which was worth digging out again. It might be worth a guinea. He decided to search for anything that would benefit from the addition of a simple signature or dedication. Once he had handwriting to copy from, he knew he could easily do it again. He reached for a small crate of books to check through it, swearing under his breath as he kicked over the stack of papers closest to him: thirty-two letters and four postcards from Florence Stoker. Going back nearly three decades, the letters were mostly typewritten. Most dated prior to her husband's death in 1912 were signed by them both, some also with lengthy, handwritten postscripts from Bram. She was more honest about her opinions in those she signed alone, he noticed: letters lacking Bram's signature made reference to her irritation at the Stokers' diminished influence in society; she noted how exhausted she was by their efforts to remain of importance to the theatrical world. After his death she referred to him frequently, often in such a present and vital way that her correspondence read as though he was alive, commenting in harmony with her and merely unable to sign his name. In these, she appeared to have rallied from her earlier despondency and become resolute in her role as both the keeper of books and the book-keeper of her husband's legacy. She was quick to note the various successes and trials ('To Hell with these annoyances!') of *Dracula*; a postcard from April 1913 mentioned how well the sale of Bram's literary effects at Sotheby's had gone 'despite years of peevish sales and the enthusiastic lack of interest in his novels from London's *critics* (so aptly termed!)'. One from 1927 thanked Freddie for sending thirtieth birthday wishes to Count Dracula, adding that as a result of Hamilton Deane's wildly popular theatrical version in London, followed by Balderston's American smash, *Dracula* was finally ascending to the heights its author desired but hadn't lived to see. 'Three women,' she wrote, 'fainted in fear on first night – Lugosi is an utter triumph!' Ellis enjoyed picturing Freddie's chagrin on reading that remark: despite being the first to stage a British regional tour of *Dracula* a couple of years before Deane's hit, the West End show had been produced without him, to his fury. She complained that parodies of *Dracula* were disrespectful to her late husband, ticking Freddie off for remarking that to be parodied meant one had finally made it.

Topmost was the letter Janey had found weeks earlier. He read it again, pausing at *We are still laughing at your hilarious impressions of Bram – you had us simply in howls every time!* Florence was right: Freddie was a talented mimic. With his particular blend of insight and charm he could take anybody off, and he was clever enough in his teasing invariably to flatter his victim while amusing his audience. The address was the Isle of Wight, where Florence spent the summer and Bram visited when he could. Freddie had spent a lot of time with them that year: Florence referred to other weekends, to gay outings and games.

Several later letters referred to her husband's success in almost everything he attempted, yet while there was no doubting how popular his best-known novel had become in the decades after his death, his lack of literary fame and respect saddened Bram deeply. 'All those novels,' she wrote, 'living and dying so swiftly. Each one misshaping him further . . . his succession of lost children, one darling following another into limbo.' Stoker's pain at his rejection was not the result of an insatiable ache for prestige, it was the agony of a parent.

Was this to be his own future, Ellis wondered, to die with his soul, his talent, so contorted? A line in her last letter to Freddie, dated 19 December 1936, caught his attention: *How I curse fate and furies that B in despair and faithlessness burnt all his attempts at a sequel to our beloved Dracula! Tho' as his friend perhaps you realised he suffered such fits of weakness? To me, he admitted only the name,* The Un-Dead Count. *I would never have permitted such damned rash action. Oh, had he but confided in me!*

A sequel! That would have been a book worth reading. Ellis didn't doubt her bitterness at its loss, for in recent years it would surely have generated a handsome fortune. Florence had worked hard to make money from *Dracula*, beginning with *Dracula's Guest and Other Weird Stories*, which she published two years after her husband's death. Its title story was a chapter Stoker had chosen to omit from *Dracula*, and at least half the contents had already appeared elsewhere –

several pieces were decades old – but thanks to her clever insistence on using his name in the title, and the cover illustration of a man pinned to the ground by a crazed hound, it had sold quite well by comparison with *Dracula*.

An early letter mentioned a *truly ghastly* single four-hour production of *Dracula* in 1897, performed at the Lyceum at ten fifteen on a Tuesday morning just days before the book's publication. Written by Stoker himself, it was produced only so he could legally claim the theatrical copyright over his new novel. Seats were charged at a guinea each on that occasion to dissuade people from attending: *As I recall, we had a paying audience of two, both of whom gave up the ghost before the end of Act One! Henry Irving, strutting peacock of a man, strode about the house, swearing to all & sundry how dreadful it was.*

That once-off play script was sure to be worth something . . . especially if he could add valuable seasoning in the form of a personal dedication from Stoker. He studied the handwritten postscripts. Yes, Bram's signature – always in black ink no matter what colour Florence wrote in, which suggested he had a favourite pen and was consistent in its use – would be easy enough to reproduce with a little practice. Ellis rummaged through the boxes again. He found a first edition of *Dracula*, signed with the message *To my dear Freddie Broughton, without whom . . .!* The cover was distinctive: blood-red text reading out of a bright yellow background, a style that had more in common with the sort of disreputable French novel Ellis bought from second-hand bookshops. Ellis owned an illustrated version, and knew the story well, having been forced to attend rehearsals and performances in town after gloomy town that awful summer of 1923. On that tour he preferred to watch the show from far back in the wings and, unable to see the actors' faces, had listened intently, absorbing vast passages of dialogue. He made a mental note to find out what a signed first edition might be worth. With the Count's character, Stoker might have been describing Ellis, he thought: a revenant spirit, embodied and in torment. Alive, but not living, not the way he deserved to be. The very first paragraph of *Dracula* mentioned Munich, Vienna, Budapest . . . all places he had never seen.

A tap at the door, and 'Your mother reckons Freddie will be back, does she?'

'Hello, Janey. I can't see it myself, but yes. Why?'

'Where would he live? Here?' She frowned. 'Patrick and me'll be out on our ears if he shows up again! She'd hardly be bothered with our few bob if old Money-bags moved in.'

'I don't know.' Foolish of Janey to assume that Virginia would cast a single net around her and Patrick both. Better not to tell her about Freddie's penury – or their own, for that matter. Virginia would be furious with him if Janey let slip that she knew how hard-up the Spenders were, how dependent on their paying guests. She wandered over to the large table in front of the stacks of boxes. A sheet protruded from under a blotter: Freddie's name, written over and over in an idle moment, the signature gaining strength and fluidity as the page filled. He cursed himself for not burning it.

'Cigarette?' he blustered, fumbling a packet out of his pocket, desperate to lure her away from the table. She ignored him.

'What's this, then?' She held up the page, her red fingernails drops of blood against the white sheet. 'You wrote this, didn't you?'

'Yes.' His heart thumped. He hadn't told her what he'd

done with the Gilbert and Sullivan librettos. He'd wanted to, of course he had, but held back. Despite her approval for the sale of Winsome's letters back to their author, forgery was a different matter entirely.

She studied the page. 'Is it a good likeness? I've not seen his writing.'

'The last few, there in the right column, they're indistinguishable from anything he'd produce himself.'

'What about me? I bet you can't do mine!'

He should have refused, of course he should, but her appeal to his vanity was irresistible. 'Probably.' He would never have let on he had tried her signature many times. She took a blank piece of paper and wrote her name. 'Go on, then, copy this.'

'It's not copying, not really.'

'Rubbish, of course it is. Same as if you was a teacher at the blackboard, with me at a little desk learning my ABCs.'

'That's not how I think of it. Mine's a copy only in the same way that whenever *you* sign your name you're copying yourself.' *Miss Janey Gould*, he wrote, deliberately imprecise.

'Not very good after all, are you?'

Stung, he crumpled the sheet and took a fresh one. He wrote her signature again, knowing it was as perfect as anything she'd have written herself, right down to the small loop on the *d*.

'Ooh, that is something,' she said. 'Even I'd take that as my own!'

Her reaction delighted him as much as his own ability. How wonderful of Janey to be entirely lacking in qualms about morality or legality; her concern was only for its success as a likeness. Emboldened, and wanting to test her reaction, he picked up the pen again and added *Mrs Patrick Arcourt.*

'Cheeky sod!' She giggled. 'You reckon you could do anyone's writing if you put your mind to it, don't you?'

'Yes.' Her praise gladdened him too much to feign modesty.

'All right, then . . .' She glanced around, then plucked the topmost letter off the nearest pile. 'What about this one? Who's it from?'

'Florence Stoker.' He studied it. 'There's not a lot to go on because only the postscript is done by hand, and she's used only a small proportion of the alphabet, but it's very even, which makes it easier. Regular letter shapes and a light stroke . . . I'd have to practise but, yes, I think I could.'

'Have you ever done it for real?'

'You just saw me!'

'You know what I mean.' Her eyes challenged him to understand. 'For money.'

He hesitated. It was a risk. A secret shared was a secret spread.

'You have, haven't you? I can see it on your face! Aren't you the dark horse!' She whistled, her red lips full and pursed. 'I'm impressed, Ellis Spender. Go on, spill the beans.'

While the prospect of her approval dimmed his fear, nothing would have made him admit to his failed attempt to cash in Virginia's insurance policy secretly. Instead he told her about Ralph Chatterton and the librettos. She smiled her approval. 'Is there anything else you can dickie up and sell?'

'I prefer the word *embellish*, if you don't mind. I've been searching, but I'm damned if I can come up with much – a couple of guineas' worth, maybe. There are some decent first editions, but I haven't got the authors' signatures to copy from.'

She nodded. 'So, for this to work, I mean work proper-like, not just piddling about adding autographs to old books, you need two things: a person's real handwriting to copy, and a story or whatever to add the name to. Is that it?'

'Exactly.'

'Wouldn't it be easier to make your own?'

'What do you mean?'

'You're a writer, ain't you? So write! I dunno . . . Try a play or something. Can't be that hard, if the shows Atkinson puts on are anything to go by. All you've got to do is say that it's by some famous person who's been dead for years, and sign their name on the front. Bound to be worth more.' She shrugged. 'That's how it seems to me, anyway.'

Before he could reply, the door opened.

'Can't you knock?' He slid the page with Janey's signature under a pile of papers.

'Apologies, I was looking for Lady Spender.'

'She's not here, obviously. Any message?'

'I forgot to mention I'm overnighting at the hospital.'

'I'll tell her.'

'Right.' Patrick looked at them curiously 'Well, I must get on.'

'Me too,' Janey said. 'Cheerio, Ellis.' She followed Patrick into the hall, then popped her head around the door, grinning. 'Keep up the good work!'

As he listened to their footsteps fading down the hall, he took out Florence's final letter to Freddie once more. Unusually for her, this one was short and entirely handwritten. He read a single paragraph about her husband, again, and then a third time, slowly, lingering over every word, understanding its meaning as surely as if Bram Stoker was next to him, whispering urgently in his ear, entreating his help.

Ellis grabbed the nearest of Sidney's old sketchbooks, the one that had contained the sketch of Lucy. He was aware of a lightness building in him, the moment when a valve that has been resolutely stuck unexpectedly releases. Holding the sheet up to the light, he fancied he could just make out an impression on the blank page underneath. Faint indentions suggesting a small head, a pointing chin, a scanty twist of curls. The slimmest deboss, his sister's life fainter and fainter each time he encountered it. He ran his fingertip over the paper, trying to trace her face, but his fingers merely slid across the blankness.

He opened a new page. The paper was heavy, creamy and rich, the pen light in his hand. He experienced the same pure, swelling sensation he had felt when Chatterton had accepted the Gilbert signatures as true, when Janey had whooped with admiration at his perfect execution of her name. He was powerful suddenly, and completely clear-headed. It was as if he had been wandering, lost and panicked, through strange foreign lands, and had just stumbled upon a glittering city.

How I curse fate and furies that B in despair and faithlessness burnt all his attempts at a sequel to our beloved Dracula!

Stoker would know. He would understand what this was and why it mattered. He pictured Stoker's face on the stairs, his intense restless eyes willing Ellis to take up his pen. He opened *Dracula* at the final page and began by transcribing its last line, as written by its protagonist Jonathan Harker: *Already he knows her sweetness and loving care; later on he will understand how some men so loved her, that they did dare much for her sake.*

CHAPTER 7

Janey was late. Waiting outside Covent Garden station, Ellis felt unaccountably nervous. He shifted the envelope from one hand to the other. The pavements were busy in an ordinary sort of way, no more than the usual criss-cross of people, yet they felt alien to him, as though life was taking place on the other side of a plate-glass window, a silent movie without titles, muted and unfathomable. Men and women wove an invisible tapestry, strangers permitting each other's free movement even as they ignored one another. How curious it would be, Ellis thought, to crack open the secret hearts of these unknowns, to be privy to their private monologues, the endlessly spinning tales of desire and fear, disturbance and disruption. Those passing him must be joyous, or miserably sad, or frightened, yet their faces looked the same, all flat and preoccupied, the happy no different from the desperate. Virginia had once, in a rare reference to Claude's death, said how wretched it had been to walk down the street during the war and pass strangers with tears on their faces, and know why, but feel unable to do anything to comfort them because you, too, were equally sickened and lost. 'I found myself hating anyone who *didn't* look miserable,' she said. 'Why did they deserve happiness when I had none?'

Ellis had been standing outside the station for just under half an hour, loosely timing the wait by the waves of people disgorged onto the street. Every three minutes brought a fresh surge, as though an unseen underground enemy was hunting Londoners to the surface.

The newspaper seller competed with a shrill, red-faced woman hawking apples and oranges by the entrance, while a girl holding a three-legged terrier by a piece of string stood close by, staring at the fruit. A street cleaner whistled as he pushed his cart slowly down the road. He paused when the woman greeted him, letting the handles of his cart fall to the ground. The girl dropped the string and, darting forward, grabbed an orange.

'Oi! Come back, thievin' bitch,' the woman shouted.

The street cleaner reached out to grab her, but the child was gone. The dog, pissing on the cart's back wheel, wasn't so quick, and the cleaner slammed his broom hard on its back. The dog fell, splayed, against the cart, then toppled into the gutter. 'Away an' fuck off,' he said. It limped off down a laneway beside the station, as if dragging its phantom limb behind it, slowly tracing the route the girl had taken.

'Plague o' rats, those kids,' the fruit seller said, to no one in particular. 'I'd have 'em taken out an' whipped.' The cleaner nodded and took up the handles of his cart. He walked away, whistling again.

'There you are, Ellis!' He kept his smile even, inwardly bristling at the suggestion in Janey's tone that it was *she* who had been kept waiting. She nodded in the direction of the fruit seller. 'Patrick told me about a chap who slipped on a banana skin and landed on his head. Dead as a doornail before he even got to the hospital.'

'When?'

'How should I know?'

'Not when did it happen, when did Patrick tell you about it?'

'Oh,' she said. 'What a funny question . . . Haven't a clue. Could have been anytime, really. Here, take this, will you?' She passed him a cardboard box. It was light but big, too awkward to fit under his arm. He had to hold it in front of him, his envelope balanced on top. He walked carefully behind her, a nervous supplicant, worried he would trip over a crack in the pavement. He followed her until she paused at a recess around the corner from the Lyceum's main entrance. Ellis had never noticed the stage door before.

'The finest theatre in London, or so Atkinson always said. He claims it'll be the best picture palace, too, by the time he's finished with it. The conversion is costing twelve thousand quid, did I tell you?' Janey added, pushing the door open.

'Hello, miss.' A man sitting in a wood-panelled cubbyhole just inside the door leant forward and smiled.

'Albert,' she replied. He beamed, as though there was no finer and more benevolent greeting than his own name, thrown to him with barely a glance. Mounted on the wall outside his cubbyhole, a large board's surface was divided into thirty rows. Each row had space for a name, and next to it, an In/Out slider. She moved the slider next to the scribbled letters J. G. to *In*. What a clever device, Ellis thought. If only he had one of those at home to keep tabs on her.

Albert tilted his head in Ellis's direction. 'Do you need the Visitors' Book, miss?'

'No. This chap was at the door with drawings from the engineer.' She gestured at the box. 'I'll bring him through, then let him out the front.'

She led the way through a labyrinthine series of stone and brick passageways. Each was painted brick-red to waist height, a dull chalky white above, and lined with framed photographs and posters. He recognised a few titles of plays he'd seen with Virginia, and noticed Freddie in a couple of the photos, but Janey walked quickly, so he didn't get a chance to examine anything properly. The corridors were windowless, and each door was illuminated by an old-fashioned, wall-mounted bulb. Over and over he watched Janey's figure turn to shadow only to be illuminated once more as she passed through irregular pools of light. Each door had a small nameplate beside it, with a handwritten card tucked into its brass frame. Wardrobe and costume stores took up the first corridor, dressing rooms the second – male on one side, female on the other. Doors were open and rooms abandoned. Empty hangers dangled from scored metal rails. A dressing-table running the length of an entire wall was bare, grubby with spilt make-up and powder, its line of mirrors smudged. Aside from the faint monotone of a wireless in a distant room, and the echoing tap-tap of their own steps, the place was quiet. He realised he had pictured the building as invariably busy – even during the day a theatre has a bustling, feverish life, as concentrated and animated as whatever happens onstage. It was unnerving, this faded silence created when the myriad cords and chains, the traps and flies, were forced to lie idle. Eventually, she stopped and, taking the box from him, opened a door into a junk room. She tossed the box onto the floor. The lid opened as it fell. It was empty.

'Albert's not the sharpest knife in the drawer, but I didn't want to take a chance. Tuppence says he wouldn't know you again – you're just another messenger as far as he's concerned.'

She took off again, rounding a corner that led to a short flight of steps before she finally came to a halt. He could see lights ahead of him, and a wide expanse of dense red velvet. Faint traces of sweat and paint hung in the air. They were alone, yet he had the sense of pushing through a crowd, as though generations of invisible dead hovered around him, all of them trapped on the stage together, their ancient breath the air touching his skin.

She nudged him forward. 'Might as well, while you can. It'll be gone for ever soon.'

He walked slowly from the wings onto the stage. The boards were scuffed and scored, a palimpsest of faint scratches, old taped lines and chalk marks. The main house lights were off, and he felt as though he was on a raft, with rippling red velvet waters lapping on three sides and a charcoal horizon behind him. He was lost, alone and adrift in a foreign sea that rose as high as the gods above.

'Why, it's huge,' Ellis said, suddenly disconcerted by the sound of his feet, by how weak he sounded in this vast auditorium.

'What're you whispering for?' Janey sauntered downstage. She raised her arms. 'Thank you,' she called across the crepuscular void of the empty orchestra pit to the blank, staring seats. Her voice was different. Louder, yes, but also warmer, fuller. 'You are too kind! Too, too kind. I thank you all.' Her slim arms were raised, palms turned towards her invisible audience. The ends of her blunt bob formed a shining blade across the nape of her long neck. Everything about her was fragile, he thought. Breakable. She dipped into a deep curtsy, then turned to him, laughing. 'Go on,' she said, 'it's easy. Take a bow!'

He imagined commanding the centre of the stage, every pair of eyes in the house staring at him, enraptured. Thousands of people impatient to be made happier, sadder, wiser, and trusting him as the harbinger of that change. What must it be like to exert such power, even if only for an hour and a half at a time? And to know that everyone in the audience is experiencing you in their own way, thus multiplying you into three thousand different people . . . He glanced up at Virginia's usual seat in Box G, her favourite because it commanded excellent views of the stage and the Royal Box, half expecting to see her waving down at him. He saw suddenly the horrible gap between the man he was and the one he had always wanted to be. No, more than that: the person he'd once assumed he would become. He'd thought it would just happen, an evolution in the same way he'd gone from being a child to an adult, but it hadn't. His life was that of a grown-up child. For years he had been like a fool at a bus stop, waiting hours for the wrong bus, refusing to accept that he wasn't in the right place to begin with. He stared at Virginia's seat. Well, that was all about to change. The envelope held tight in his hand would make sure of it.

A door slammed somewhere in the building and he jumped. 'What if someone catches us here?'

'Atkinson's at the architect's in Maida Vale. The cheapskate's let pretty much all the staff go to save money, saying he'll hire new when the cinema opens. The builders aren't in until next week cos the rest of backstage has to be cleared out first. I'd say you could put circus animals out here today and no one would notice. Won't be a better opportunity, said I to myself.'

'Clever Janey.' The place was as good as deserted! It was perfect.

'Come on.' She walked towards a narrow opening in the wings, which in turn became another dimly lit corridor. After about fifty feet, she turned again, eventually stopping at a doorway about halfway down. This passageway was shabbier than the others, colder too. A thin layer of dust coated the dado rails and doors. Mould bloomed on the ceiling above their heads. It was cold, the air damp and unmoving. Were they underground? He wasn't sure.

'This was Stoker's office. Next one along was Irving's.'

'Really? I'd have expected them to have something grander.'

'This used to be the fancy part, according to Albert. There was a spiral staircase leading directly from this corridor to the green room and the side door to the street. It was taken out years ago, when the theatre became a music hall for a while. Irving and his cronies were long gone by then. I don't know if anyone's used these rooms since, cos they're full of junk. Atkinson told me to organise getting them cleared out before the builders start. He's going to wall off all the backstage areas that won't be needed any more. He said it's all rubbish and I can take anything I want, as long as the rooms are emptied in time. The offices upstairs are bigger, and Atkinson likes to stay close to front of house, so nobody ever has reason to be wandering around down here. It's haunted, the actors say.'

He laughed. What self-respecting theatre wouldn't have a ghoulish story of its own? 'Some fogey actor, I suppose?' he said. 'Let me guess: he stalks the circle at midnight, dressed in doublet and hose, talking in sonnets, and searching for Yorick's skull.'

'Wrong, clever-clogs. A young lad, killed when a stage tower collapsed. Landed exactly where you were standing not five minutes ago.' She looked straight at Ellis. Her face was so close to his that he could see the powder on the bridge of her nose and a dusty smudge on her forehead. Her cheeks, her neck . . . Her bones were so close to her skin that if he reached out a hand he was sure he could touch one, that his hand would break through the skin of her throat and disappear inside her, or grab her, shattering her fine, porcelain beauty to shards. 'Come to think of it . . .' she added, holding his gaze, her eyes clear and wide, shiny and as hard as marbles. Could she read his thoughts? '. . . he was called Ellis too. I wonder if he'll stay to haunt the cinema. Poor little Ellis.'

His name hung there between them for a moment, sibilant and cruel. She turned away. He said nothing. The corridor was completely quiet, cold and still. A light behind them guttered briefly. He could hear his own breath, then hers, discordant at first until they folded into each other. She tried the handle of the first door. It refused to budge. She twisted it forward and back crossly. 'Bloody thing.'

'Is it locked?'

She shook her head. 'Swollen. Put your shoulder to it.'

He passed her the envelope and leant his full weight against the door. The room was larger than he had expected, square, windowless and damp-smelling. Two mismatched chairs sat in front of an old-fashioned mahogany desk. One grey wall was lined with empty shelves. Dirty rectangular marks on the others created ghostly frames where pictures had once hung, and the paint around the gas jets was streaked and sooty. In front of the shelves, two armchairs were set at an angle from the wall, as though a hearth and fireplace had once fitted between them. Dirty stuffing spilt from ripped armrests. He peered around behind the door. A face! A black face staring at him through the gloom! Vast glittering eyes, a wide nose.

'Good God!' He jumped backwards, bumping into Janey behind him, feeling as though his brain had split into two to accommodate the terror that was exploding inside him and the touch of the long line of her body, of her chest against his back.

'Get out, Janey! Go!'

She ducked away, laughing, and opened the door to the corridor further. In the dim light, the features slowly solidified into a horse head. 'It's a prop, you bozo!' Janey grabbed it. 'Look!' Hanging on a coatstand, the head was attached to a leather cape that would have draped around the wearer's shoulders. Ellis's cheeks flamed. He hated when she turned her disregard on him. She grabbed the horse by the ears, dropping it onto his head before he could stop her. The very air surrounding him disappeared as the hard leather interior scraped over his head and down his cheeks. It smelt mouldy. The cape part landed heavy and damp on his shoulders. Vomit hit the back of his throat. He heaved and swallowed all at once. God, was he going to be sick into it? He'd choke!

He reached up, fumbling and disoriented, his hands catching in the thick fabric. It was so heavy! As he tried to shove it up and off, the thin slits cut into the leather for the wearer to see where he was going briefly lined up with his eyes. She was laughing, a horrid, sneering laugh. He tugged again, hard, his ears burning, and pulled it off. She took the head and, holding it by a leather handle he hadn't found when he was struggling, threw it to the floor. It thudded against the side of the dresser, causing the single glass-fronted door to crash against the wall. He turned away, flattening his hair with his hands, the sting of tears in his eyes.

'Oh, for Heaven's sake, don't take on so, Ellis.'

She took the thin stack of pages from his envelope, and flicked through them. They were all typed, some also carefully annotated in black ink. From the desk drawer she withdrew the remains of a ream of blank paper, a perfect match for the sheets in her hand. '*The Un-Dead Count*,' she read aloud. 'Chapter twenty-two. *Twenty-two?* Where's the rest of it?'

'I'm beginning at the end. It's better this way,' he said, swallowing again, quickly. A rancid stink of dirty leather and Macassar oil hung around him.

'What do you mean? How will the dealer chap know what the story's about if I'm just giving him the last bit?'

Her senseless remark calmed him. He shook his head, forcing a smile. 'The story doesn't matter, Janey. Story's got nothing to do with it.' He had no intention of telling her in case she sneered again – he couldn't have borne that – but he already knew how good *The Un-Dead Count* and its tale of Dracula arisen to spearhead an invasion of hooded vampires from the backward, disordered east was going to be. A plague of Székely creatures, possessed of the power to spread a ferocious disease without either succumbing to it or being weakened by the deadly germ. He still had a long way to go, yet *The Un-Dead Count* was flowing in a way his own writing never could. There was no struggle: it seemed to come from a place beyond him, pouring steadily out as though his job was to harness the might of the stream rather than – as was his experience with his novellas – gently coax its thin, gruel-like trickle.

There were moments, alone in his study late at night, his eyes straining in the low light, when he looked down and didn't recognise his own hands. He became Stoker in those precious seconds, convinced that Stoker's imagination, trapped on earth and seeking a home, was merging with his own. So clearly had he begun to visualise Stoker writing this book that what he was creating wasn't a heartless materialistic attempt to steal from a dead man but a glorious relic, a lost artefact essential to Stoker's legacy. Ellis was bringing Stoker back to life.

Dracula was the tale of the making of a tale, and incorporated many different elements: newspaper reports, journal notes, diary entries, a ship's log, telegrams. Ellis was reusing this style because such broad source material meant that adapting and maintaining different characters and their individual voices was simpler. He had cherry-picked pieces of *Dracula* that served his purposes, and was reusing some of the language and elements of the plot. It was as though he was doing an exotic puzzle in which he'd been handed a strange object from a foreign land, told to feel it all over, examine every crease and crack, then identify its purpose, and be the first to give it a name. Stoker, who had enjoyed secret scripts and codes, would have appreciated this approach, he was sure of it.

During the previous weeks, in the few moments when he wasn't working, he considered the plan carefully, attacking the strategy from every angle to ensure it was foolproof. 'Don't overtire yourself, darling,' Virginia had commented, surprised at how much time he was spending locked in his study, the only sound the gunfire crack of typewriter keys.

A single chapter was to be found here in the Lyceum, supposedly discarded in a long-forgotten box of junk in Stoker's former office, with the remainder of the manuscript to come from the chaos of Freddie's possessions. Stoker, Ellis decided, had begun to work intermittently on a sequel to *Dracula* while still employed by Irving at the Lyceum, but didn't complete the book until September 1905, at which point he had given it to Freddie to read. He spent seven years writing *Dracula*, hence it was reasonable to assume a sequel could have taken a similar amount of time. An untidy man, when the fifteen pages that comprised chapter twenty-two became jumbled up in the mess on Stoker's desk, they had accidentally ended up in a box of unused typing paper. Irving had died suddenly in October 1905, and barely a year later, Stoker published a hefty two-volume *Personal Reminiscences of Henry Irving*. Ellis recalled his mother and Florence discussing how Irving's estranged wife had upset Bram terribly by trying to freeze him out of the funeral arrangements. Her aggressively anti-Irish sentiments had always irritated Virginia to such an extent that even had Virginia agreed with her on anything she would never have admitted it. It was reasonable, Ellis decided, that between his shock at the loss of his formerly dear friend and colleague and the well-judged decision to cash in quickly on their relationship, Stoker had put aside the sequel, intending to return to it at a later date, and simply forgotten he had ever given it to Freddie. Stoker was in the habit of making under-copies of all his fiction and related correspondence, and retained a complete manuscript for himself, which he had later burnt.

The vampire-adoring public would disagree with Stoker's private assessment that *The Un-Dead Count* was imperfect,

Ellis was sure of it. And if they didn't, who was to care? He'd get a tidy sum for the manuscript either way, now that Florence was dead and couldn't be asked to authenticate it. She had treated the Society of Authors as her personal enforcement agency and, as Virginia had once remarked, championed her husband's legacy 'to frankly quite exhausting lengths'. Nothing to do with *Dracula* escaped her notice: she'd insisted that all the prints of a German film version she hadn't sanctioned were destroyed. Their son Noel – whom Ellis had met once or twice years earlier and remembered as such a shy chap that even the prospect of the dullest social conversation could upset him – didn't pose any threat. The likelihood of Noel being aware of the detail of his father's work was remote, he knew: even as an adult, he was rarely in his parents' company, Florence particularly appearing to regard him with a benign casualness. But, being cautious, Ellis off-handedly mentioned his name to Virginia, wondering aloud what had become of Noel since his mother's passing. Virginia didn't know, recalling Noel's wife saying something about how busy his accountancy practice had become, and the long trip on the Continent they were planning because he needed a rest. It was perfect.

'No, Janey.' He shook his head. 'If you show up with just the start of the book, who's to know that Stoker wrote more? It could have been a one-off that he disliked and discarded after the first chapter. But having the last chapter suggests the rest of the book exists too. And if my plan fails, you're not to blame because you did nothing other than find some old pages in the theatre. Doing it this way will get the Chattertons salivating. We'll leave it a couple of months so by the time I turn up with the rest of it, they won't be able to resist. Wait and see!'

'And the rest!' She laughed, and read aloud: '*For I shake still at the memory of watching that castle begin to quake. How it suddenly began to crack and split as the very ground it was built on began to part, opening up like a secret dark fissure in the very depths of the earth, and drawing the castle to itself, inside itself, inside its red, fiery heart! That place of evil was once alien to me – and oh, that I had stayed away from those eastern lands, and remained in ignorance of the devastation wrought by the hands of that creature and his desperate plague of cruelty and damnation—*'

She broke off and turned the page closer to the light. 'Wait – devastation is crossed out. What's that scribbled next to it? *Desolation*, is it?'

'Yes. Stoker types up a draft at home, then brings the typescript with him to work to reread, which is when he marks by hand the changes he wants to make. That *desolation* is a pentimento.'

'A pentiwhato?' She looked at him suspiciously, as though sure he was laughing at her; inventing words to show her up.

'Pentimento. In painting it means a repentance, a second thought. After all, why would a forger have a second thought? An artist might change their original work, but someone copying it wouldn't.' He was planning to make a number of handwritten changes in the manuscript, and was pleased with such erasures, enjoying the weave and curl of Stoker's language between his fingers. 'And what is a forged painting, anyway? Nothing but a portrait of an imaginary art work.'

'Clever, ain't you?' Her tone suggesting that to be described as clever couldn't possibly be a compliment. She read another line or two aloud then broke off, abruptly.

'What is it? Is something wrong?'

'Seen enough, that's all.' She put blank sheets of paper on either side of the manuscript and tucked the lot into the desk drawer. 'Let's get you out in case Albert decides to take a wander, though it's not very likely. He only leaves his cubbyhole to go to the pub. I still don't see why you're insisting on all this palaver of planting it in Stoker's old office. All I need to do is to say I found it here – it's not as though anyone could ever prove different. I never took you for the superstitious sort, Ellis!'

'I'm not.' He walked ahead of her down the corridor. Superstition? That was for fools. No, if anything, it was purity. Bram Stoker had written vast swathes of *Dracula* in the Lyceum during breaks between shows, so where else would he have begun this unknown remarkable sequel? Ellis wanted to know Stoker's world, no matter that what he was looking at was a faded, disregarded echo of it. If only he could lower himself into the chair Stoker had risen from! Write at the desk he had rested his head on, run his fingers over the drawers the man had opened and closed every day, as though Stoker had just popped out on an errand, leaving Ellis alone, waiting patiently in his office.

For Ellis to make this fiction plausible, he had to believe it in its entirety. Although he already knew the story so well as to recall entire sections word for word, he had reread *Dracula* four more times, going from the last page back to the first without pause and making notes as he went. He had heard the line, *in all the mass of material of which the record is composed, there is hardly one authentic document! nothing but a mass of typewriting, except in the later note-books of*

Mina and Seward and myself on the last page as a warning. A stage direction, it was instructing him to be scrupulously honest in his dishonesty.

The majority of *The Un-Dead Count* was to come from the hands and mouth of Quincey Harker, Jonathan and Mina Harker's adult son, who first appears in the last paragraph of *Dracula* as a small child, sitting on Professor Van Helsing's knee and listening to their tale. In Ellis's story, vampires have risen once more, massing uneasily like birds at sunset as they prepare to invade England by sea and air, seeking revenge against the children of those who tried to destroy them. Dracula can tame the elements to his will, calling up storms, fogs and thunder, directing wild and tame creatures alike. The dead remain his to command.

Janey was to come across what she assumed was an unused ream of paper when clearing out the desk in the room and take it home for her own use, where she would discover the typewritten chapter tucked between the blank pages. Atkinson had told her she could have whatever she wanted as long as she had the basement corridor emptied in time for the builders to start the following Monday. Ellis suggested she take a few other things too, playbills, a couple of photographs, maybe a small prop or two, to ensure she left the theatre with a box full of worthless bits and pieces.

'A forgery only becomes a forgery when it is found,' he told her. 'Why, every single word we'll ever say to each other is salvage, already used in a thousand other conversations.' The world was full of forgeries; it could not survive without them. Every fable and folktale, every myth and belief that society was constructed upon arose in imitation of what had gone before. Forgery was a chain, not an isolated act. He knew it made no sense to her, and he didn't care whether she understood or not. But before the act of discovery, what *were* those pages she had just planted in Stoker's former office? Authentically forged or not, they had no value other than homage at best, and pointless scribblings at worst. The act of finding the manuscript, that single beautiful chapter, was irrelevant in one way – what really mattered was the recognition of it as a discovery. That moment! Even though he could not be present, he found himself fizzing with joy at the thought of it! The point at which value would be transferred, and his painstakingly typed and entirely worthless pages would rise from the flames, becoming a lost work, a glorious found object of desire. He was using Stoker's ideas, Stoker's language, even Stoker's paper! *The Un-Dead Count* might as well have been written by Stoker: Ellis was a chemist, creating a new compound by distilling the same proprietary ingredients in an original and different way. His creation may have been a fake, it was a genuine one. If art was life, and life was continuance, then what was he doing but perpetuating life?

She laughed. 'Don't fool yourself, Ellis Spender! Fake is fake. This was a phoney the moment you took the cover off your typewriter.'

CHAPTER 8

From the way Janey described it afterwards, she delivered her lines perfectly. She took a box containing the newly found pages to Chatterton's in Tavistock Street, 'what with the Lyceum being just around the corner'. She had been given unwanted office supplies and discarded theatre memorabilia, she explained to Rollo Chatterton, and found the pages tucked in the middle of an old ream of paper she had taken to write employment letters ('I'm looking for a new position, you see, but . . .' with a coy giggle '. . . promise you won't go telling my boss!'). The chapter was mixed up in a nest of faded stage photos, programmes and Lyceum headed paper. Rollo Chatterton swallowed it hook, line and sinker and, to her emphatically professed amazement, offered her seventy pounds. He suggested thirty up-front as a deposit while he satisfied himself as to its provenance, and now, just over three weeks later, its authenticity attested to by both an expert at the British Museum and a retired editor by the name of William Jaffe, who had once worked for Archibald Constable, Stoker's original publisher, Chatterton professed himself delighted. The forty-pound balance was ready to be collected.

A glorious, invigorating sensation coursed through Ellis's veins, warm and vital as blood. His plan had worked perfectly. The only snag to the scheme as far as Ellis was concerned was that, because Janey had to profess herself entirely ignorant of the value of her find in order to keep herself at arm's length from the manuscript, she was in no position to negotiate. That Chatterton was prepared to offer seventy so quickly suggested the chapter was worth far more, Ellis was sure. In fact, when she described the encounter, he wondered if she had overegged her ignorance by saying, 'No offence intended, sir, but that can't be right. Are you sure it's not just scrap paper?'

Having to wait didn't trouble Ellis: he had anticipated such a delay while Chatterton satisfied himself it was genuine. If anything, it took less time than he had expected. Ellis had done enough of the other kind of waiting, that which holds only anxiety or sour, repetitive drudgery, so he had quietly savoured the days and their attendant anticipation of riches. The delay was merely that of a rising wave. All he had to do was to hold his nerve while it crested around him, high and foaming and pure, dropping treasure at his feet as it receded.

Anyway, he was so busy completing *The Un-Dead Count* that he barely had time to think about anything else. As he travelled further and further into the secret chambers of the book's heart, he began to enjoy emulating *Dracula*'s Victorian fears and flourishes, and sympathised with Stoker's fascination with change and the speed of progress. The excess zeal and sentiment reminded him of his father's portraiture. Sidney had believed he was capturing the essence of a sitter, yet in reality painted as though he was determined to impose a particular shape and view on the world; in claiming to reflect reality, he was actually trying to create it. Did that make his father a forger? Perhaps, though an unwitting one, stumbling blindly on, in thrall to a fleeting, unreliable power.

Even if the worst did happen, he was completely in the clear: should Chatterton query the chapter's provenance, there was nothing to trace it back to Ellis. Neither did Janey have anything to worry about. Because of Ellis's insistence on planting the chapter in Stoker's disused room for her to find, she had done nothing more than come across a sheaf of pages that had been sitting in a drawer for decades.

He was glad he had settled on a two-part plan in preference to a single discovery of the complete manuscript. Selling one chapter by itself was a perfect test of the work's success and value, as well as a safe way of ensuring it remained distant from him. The seed had been planted, and now Rollo, as well as his business partner and brother Ralph had a vested interest in reaping the harvest.

Within a fortnight of beginning *The Un-Dead Count*, he was so confident of success that he began to consider forging some other works by Stoker, perhaps in a year's time. No, not *forging*, he reminded himself. That was a nasty legal term, not remotely harmonious with his momentous undertaking. *Discovering*. Short stories preferably: Stoker had published plenty. Perhaps something set in Ireland would work, because he could base it around the folklore Virginia was so fond of. The long-standing friendship between Virginia and Florence might come in useful: the books Florence must have known in childhood would have been the same as those Virginia had read, some of which she still had. There were references in Stoker's fiction that would make such a book believable, and an Irish setting would serve to distance the text from Ellis and assist in establishing its provenance. An unknown stash of unpublished stories from half a century earlier maybe, a collection begun when Stoker was a bored civil servant in Dublin, long before he had become enthralled by Henry Irving and moved to London and the job at the Lyceum. Stoker's writing wasn't a constant dip-dip into a well till it dried up. No, his prolific output – and the variations in quality – suggested that he had died with his head still crammed full of stories.

Though Ellis woke very early, keen to run through the plan for collecting the balance of the money that afternoon, he waited in his bedroom, listening for the creak of Janey's door from above. Somehow, she eluded him on the stairs – how did she do that? – and was sitting at the breakfast table, Patrick's head bent and close to hers, when he eventually caught up with her. They broke off their conversation and looked up at him. Patrick, Ellis noticed, leant back in his seat but Janey didn't move. She nodded at Ellis, one hand just brushing Patrick's arm, her smile suddenly striking him as scornful, as if she was laughing quietly at a joke he wouldn't have understood. Another new blouse, Ellis noticed, an expensive, milky-coloured silk, trimmed with lace and mother-of-pearl buttons.

What was she playing at, on such an important day for them both? She had begun to act as though it was all just a bit of a lark; that all his work on *The Un-Dead Count* didn't add up to much, which was unfair, given that he was the one creating the book and all she'd had to do was convincingly sell a single chapter! She'd been happy enough to take her share of Chatterton's thirty pounds, hadn't she? 'Don't take on so, Ellis,' she'd said when, briefly alone in the hallway the previous day, he'd asked her to run through the plan for collecting the balance of the money. 'It's dull, when you take on.' He apologised, wanting to make it up, to make her like him again, laughing off his preoccupation as tiredness, a nervous exhaustion caused by his hard work on the manuscript, but it had stung him to do so. He had felt alone in her company then, and suddenly sure that she would always have the power to make him feel so. The certainty sent a tingle down his spine, a premonitory fear.

Virginia was at the table as well, and Ellis inwardly cursed her and Patrick. He really wanted to get Janey alone. It was the fault of the new servant: just as Ellis had known she would, the previous girl had left after a fortnight, throwing curses in Virginia's direction as she slammed the door behind her. Her replacement's breakfasts were a vast improvement, which encouraged prompt and regular attendance at the table.

'I have an announcement,' Patrick said, as Ellis sat down and took out a cigarette. He was going home for a holiday, he told them, in mid-May. He had worked all through Christmas, and was due to work through Easter, too. It would be his first opportunity to leave London since his arrival in Fitzroy Gardens the previous summer, he explained, and when that generated no response, added, 'The six-five express from Euston, then the night boat from Liverpool at ten fifteen.'

Virginia was first to rally. 'Patrick, how lovely,' she said, and then, 'A week at home . . . how pleased your dear mother will be.'

'Actually, I've been given two weeks off. And, lest I forget to mention, I have to stay at the hospital tonight. Oh, may I?'

Virginia nodded so he reached out and slid the last egg onto his plate.

'Really? A full fortnight? Surely your poor patients can't possibly spare you for so long.' Virginia's fingertips tapped the edge of the table, as if playing a gentle tune only she could hear, the diamonds and emeralds on her slim fingers sparkling their private chorus. His mother had lost weight, Ellis noticed, watching her rings slide up towards her knuckles as her hands moved.

Patrick smiled awkwardly, unsure whether she was teasing him to amuse herself, or genuinely believed he was such a wonderful doctor that the fortunes of the Royal London rested on his rounded shoulders. Following months of winter gloom, the dining room was bright again, full and fresh and eager with new-minted April light. Virginia had put a vase of daffodils on the sideboard the previous day. 'Did you pick 'em on the Heath?' Janey had enquired, to Virginia's horror.

Ellis alone understood that Virginia's remark meant she was concerned about the implications Patrick's holiday would have on the household income. Would the Arcourts' May cheque take account of his absence or not? Virginia had grown to love the sight of Alice Arcourt's handwriting on the mat during the first week of every month, and Ellis knew that she would fret in silence about the possibility of a temporary halving of Patrick's board, yet refuse to do the only thing that would put her mind at ease, and enquire.

'Dublin won't have changed a jot, I'll wager,' said Patrick, completely unaware of his hostess's worries. His cheery tone marked him as a man who delighted in such certainties. 'It never does.'

'I met a chap from Ireland once,' Janey said thoughtfully, taking the cigarette Ellis offered her.

'Yes?' Patrick said. And then, puzzled, 'You mean me, don't you?'

'What? No, not you, silly. I can't remember the chap's name now . . . O-something-something. Foreignish, you know? Talked about fox-hunting all the time. Complete bozo – begging your pardon, Lady Spender – if I'm being straight. Maybe they're all like that.'

'They? I'm Irish!' Patrick protested.

She shrugged. Smoke streamed from her nostrils. 'You're a doctor. That's different.'

Ellis grinned and reached for the marmalade spoon. There was no point in arguing with Janey's logic, though he hoped Patrick would persist because it irritated Janey to have her point of view, no matter how ridiculous, challenged.

'When do you leave us, Patrick?' Virginia asked, pointedly pushing the ashtray closer to Janey's elbow. 'We shall miss you, of course.'

'Thank you, Lady Spender. I've booked passage' – (Passage! Ellis thought. What a chump. It's the mail boat, not the bloody Queen Mary) – 'for May the eleventh. My professor has been very generous. I'll spend four nights in Dublin, followed by a couple of days in Donegal, with a final visit back home before I leave. I do hope the weather is fine. I'm keen to get some rock-climbing and hill-walking done.'

'That sounds like an admirably sensible holiday, Patrick. I assumed you were going home on a spree. Turning the slate, it was referred to in my young days.'

'Far from it. There is but a single mountain range in Ireland I have yet to master!'

'Like hell there is,' Ellis muttered into his cup.

'I beg your pardon, dear?' Virginia said. 'What was that?'

'Bell. I said, bell. Do you want to ring for more tea?'

Patrick continued as though Ellis hadn't spoken. 'Climbing the rugged coastline . . . stiff scrambles in the highlands . . . There is no finer way to spend a day than in the heart of nature and under God's own blue sky, take my word for it, Lady Spender.'

'I shall have to.'

Ellis was desperate to catch Janey's eye, but she was looking down, rummaging for something in her handbag. 'Buggering thing,' she muttered, so completely distracted that she didn't hear Virginia tut-tutting. 'Bloody lining's snagged.' He needed to regain her attention, to make her laugh, privately, together. The balance was all off, and the unspoken pact that anointed Patrick their secret buffoon was in danger of falling apart. A show of unity, of strength, was required. Couldn't she see that? When Ellis had first met Janey she had seemed as simple as sunlight to him, but recently he had begun to realise the extent to which he had misunderstood her. In fact, she had the ability to create a disquieting uncertainty. The light she shone in this perpetual twilight could be the glow of a lamp or the cold lure of sirens, it was impossible to know which. Janey's scrabbling in her bag finally produced a Woolworth's compact no bigger than a shilling, and a lipstick. Virginia stiffened as Janey clicked open the tiny mirror and puckered up.

'My brothers and I have our sights set on finally climbing the Blue Stack Mountains,' Patrick droned. 'There are more than ten summits, the highest of which is Croaghgorm. I'm no geologist, but even to an enthusiastic amateur such as myself, the quality and variety of the rock formations are magnificent.'

'How interesting,' Virginia said. 'What an enjoyable pastime.' (Pastime! Well done, you, Ellis thought, relishing her subtle admonishment.) 'Ellis, doesn't it sound wonderful?'

'Yes.' He heard the sullen tone in his voice and didn't care. As Patrick went on and on about ranges and ravines and knife-edges, Ellis shook open *The Times*, using it to obscure his face. He knew Virginia would consider him rude, but that didn't bother him either. The news was full of comments from Von Ribbentrop on his recent return to Germany from London, and a particularly violent robbery in Manchester. The torso murder sputtered on, though no longer commanding the biggest headlines. The story was of little interest to him now that the victim had been identified as a sixty-year-old retired Army man from Kettering. Police continued to hunt his erstwhile servant, Alastair Harper, who had become the main suspect, primarily because, as a former butcher, he was believed to have both the skills and equipment required to efficiently dismember a body.

Ellis was happy for anything to distract him from the rubbish Patrick was spouting about his prowess as a climber. He pictured a stupid lumbering giant, leaping up mountains in a single bound, naked but for the stethoscope around his neck, his warty hands plucking rocks from crevices and hurling them into the crashing seas far below. He turned the page. A man had died after a gas-mask test in a church hall.

'That would be marvellous! Don't you agree, Ellis?'

'I beg your pardon?' What had he missed? Three faces were trained on his own. Virginia smiled expectantly, Janey's lips twitched, as if she was trying not to laugh, while Patrick's expression was one of wide-eyed dismay incompetently overlaid by an artificial smile.

'I said, I've had the most marvellous idea: you should take a holiday in Dublin with Cousin Minette, and join Patrick on his trip to Donegal!'

'It's more than a trip, Lady Spender. Closer to an expedition really.' Patrick sounded as panicked as Ellis felt. 'Experience is required—'

'Experience? For walking up a hill?' Virginia interrupted. 'Nonsense.'

'Equipment, I meant to say.' Patrick's cheeks pinked.

'Nothing more than stout boots and a strong stick, I imagine. Ellis, I shall treat you!'

Patrick's mouth opened and shut. He was trapped.

'Ooh, Ellis,' Janey was almost cooing as she glanced from one man to the other, 'just imagine! What an adventure.'

'I don't think so,' Ellis said quickly. What was she playing at? He looked at Patrick's ugly face, the smattering of reddish freckles that dotted his forehead and nose, like a pox. He would sooner die. 'I'm far too busy with my writing . . . and climbing hills isn't something I've ever been interested in.'

'All the more reason to try! You've been working so hard recently, you look exhausted. Getting out of London for a while would do you the world of good. Oh, the fresh Donegal air! Why, you'll be inspired by it, I simply know you will!' Virginia rose and Patrick half jumped up, too, the toady. 'I shall write to Minette immediately.'

'Perhaps enquire about the equipment,' Janey said. 'Your cousin might have a pal Ellis could borrow it from or whatever.'

'How clever of you, Janey.' Virginia looked surprised to

hear herself utter such words. 'Thank you.' She bundled her magazine into her knitting bag and left the room, calling for the girl to come and clear the table.

Patrick drained his teacup, swallowing loudly. He rose to leave, pausing in front of the window. Dust motes stirred in the light around him, forming an odd halo around his head and body, as though shaken into life by his movement. Backlit against the glass, his face was unreadable, his arms thick and long, hanging loosely by his sides.

A tiny bird flew past outside, reminding Ellis of a game he used to play as a child in which he would wrap small empty boxes in paper and ribbons, then use his catapult to fire them out of his bedroom window, across the garden and onto the pavement, in wait for the next passer-by. How delicious the enjoyment of a stranger's confusion and greed was to witness! He got caught when he fumbled his aim and a box fell like a stone onto the grass below. Sidney had been standing exactly where Patrick was now and saw it land. He went out and opened it, then stormed upstairs to beat Ellis for his impudence.

Ellis was desperate for Patrick to leave the room. It was an important day for him and Janey, and he needed her on her own to double-check the arrangements. It was infuriating how light-hearted she was being. He couldn't bear to think that she was behaving so on purpose, that her careless attitude was a tease.

'Right, well, of course, Ellis,' Patrick said finally. 'You'd be, um, very welcome.'

'Cheerio, Patrick,' Janey said, with a laugh, as the door shut behind him. She picked a tiny crumb from the sleeve of her blouse. 'Damn,' she muttered. 'It's stained. Bad enough at the theatre. I cover up but everything still gets plastered with dust.' As far as Ellis could tell, she was planning to spend her entire share of the money Chatterton was paying them (and the cut he'd promised her once he sold the rest of the manuscript) on clothes.

Ellis had watched Virginia silently noting each fresh outfit, desperately curious as to how she was funding them. Not interrogating Janey about a sleek new sealskin coat the previous week had almost choked her. 'She once mentioned a pal in the theatre who passes on her old things,' Ellis told Virginia afterwards, wishing Janey would be more careful. She must have opened an account with every department store in London.

Virginia regarded him pityingly. 'Take my word, Ellis, the only previous owner of that coat is Harry Selfridge.'

He'd take a look in Janey's wardrobe when she went to work, he decided, and see exactly what she'd bought. He was spending every waking hour on the manuscript of *The Un-Dead Count*, so between lack of time and opportunity, he hadn't been in her room for well over a week.

'Honestly, Janey,' Ellis snapped, when Patrick was out of earshot. 'Egging my mother on like that! I'd sooner go to Hell than Ireland with Patrick! Do you want to be rid of me for a couple of weeks? Is that it?'

'Don't be a chump. With all that money in your pocket, did it not occur to you that a trip away might be exactly the thing to do? Listen, here's what you do: go to Dublin, and tell . . . Minnie, was it?'

'Minette.'

'Tell her and Sawbones you've got an old friend, from, I don't know, university or something, who's invited you to visit him in some other bit of Ireland, then go wherever you like for a week. Treat yourself to a fancy hotel at the seaside – there must be one. How else are you going to spend your money without having to explain where it came from?'

The scales righted themselves. It was true: he deserved some fun! What a shame there was no airport in Dublin – he'd have loved to fly somewhere for a few days. He had always pictured himself holidaying on the Continent, a serious young man alone with his notebook in a pavement café, or a chic yet friendly bistro. Not Berlin, not now, but Paris? Yes, he had always loved the idea of Paris . . . maybe even Rome – or Venice! Why not? A small but fashionable hotel, nowhere too ostentatious . . . He might strike up conversations, friendships even, with fellow patrons. People similar to him: knowledgeable yet understated, interested in books and art and culture. He would be sure to pack spare copies of *The Only Boy* to give his new friends. Wasn't a taste of such a life – the authentic life he so desperately craved – the least he deserved after months of hard work? *The Un-Dead Count* had become everything to him, and it alone could serve him the life he deserved. Fuelled by money, each fresh day had the potential to be perfect.

'Oh, yes . . . I see. Sorry, Janey.' The treaty was signed: Janey and he were allies once more. 'Sometimes I—' he faltered, feeling suddenly exposed and fearful, but, buoyed by her concern, and the swing from the horror of going away with Patrick to the prospect of an extravagant holiday by himself, pressed on: 'I get confused whose side you're on.'

'Side?' She was standing in front of the fireplace, smoothing her skirt. 'You don't know me at all, do you, Ellis? And before you ask, no, I haven't forgotten: I'll be at the stage door at five thirty.'

'Perhaps I should wait for you near Chatterton's instead. I promise to keep out of sight.'

'Not again! Haven't we been over this enough? What if Ralph Chatterton is there today and sees you? Or Rollo's in Oxford when you bring the rest of the book in? First, I show up with a chapter I found in a junk room, then my pal just happens to appear with the rest of it? It'll stink. You know full well you have to stay away.' She was right, of course: according to his plan, Ellis was going to visit Ralph Chatterton in Oxford in two months or so, bringing with him the rest of the book, newly uncovered among Freddie's possessions.

'But the prospect of you carrying so much money around makes me nervous.'

She regarded him scornfully. 'Nervous for me or about me?' And then she was gone.

He stood at the window and thought of his long-ago game, remembering how the few people who had brazenly opened the parcel on the street always looked more embarrassed than annoyed when the box was revealed to be empty, and glanced around, realising they had been the subject of a petty joke.

The girl opened the door, a tray jammed under her armpit. Behind him, the draught from the hall reached the daffodils on the sideboard. The flowers' heads nodded, their movement as slight and gentle as Virginia's fingers on the tabletop, approving of the silence.

CHAPTER 9

Ellis arrived at the Lyceum more than an hour early. He waited beside a bus stop a couple of yards from the front of the theatre, which offered a good yet discreet view of the stage door. The box office was shuttered, the entrance lobby dim. Through the glass-panelled entrance to the foyer he could see where the old carpet had been ripped up, the main staircase ascending into the gloom, its newly bare boards disappearing into blackness as if it was no more than a cheap stage set. Pasted across the glass-fronted display board by the entrance was a single sign: Luxurious New Lyceum Cinema! Grand Opening "The Gang Show" starring Ralph Reader, 27 April. The two remaining front-of-house staff had also been let go, Janey had explained. Atkinson would be hiring fresh. The conversion work and projection room were nearly completed, only the box office and orchestra pit to finish off.

Just after half past four, the main entrance opened. Six labourers emerged, their clothes caked with dust and dirt, the last man slamming the door shut behind him. They were joking together, one man windmilling his arms as if pretending to fall backwards. The others guffawed, and the chap beside him clapped him on the shoulder. They looked easy together, Ellis thought. A minute later, the stage door opened slowly: Albert, a newspaper tucked under his arm. He had the self-righteous yet hesitant demeanour of a dog furtively pissing under its owner's chair. He glanced around, before ducking down the laneway that Ellis knew led into the back courtyard of the Flag & Arms. He couldn't have been more obviously skiving off had he been waving a little sign announcing it.

Ellis stood quietly, waiting, just waiting, his eyes focused on the stage door. He was about to be proved right, he knew he was, but the knowledge made him feel horribly sad. She wasn't his friend. She never had been, never would be. His life would always be like this, he was completely sure of it. Anyone he would ever love or desire – whatever that amoral artifice meant – would eventually disappoint him. His parents had. Fervent university friendships, begun in mutual enthusiasm in college clubs, had faded before his very eyes when he went down from Oxford, as though they were nothing more than a petty interregnum between child- and adulthood. He'd never understood why he was gradually excluded, friends softly cutting ties with him as they moved on to employment in the City, or left for the Continent, or lost themselves in Bohemian torpor, while he went home to Virginia and a life that now felt studied and sour. Was it him? Was he somehow corrosive? He tried so hard with people . . . He clenched his hands, feeling entirely hopeless. Why, he didn't even have the companionship that that filthy labourer had! It was ghastly, but it was true, he was sure. True, too, was his certainty that he could continue in this way, deluding himself with each new encounter, waiting for the moment when he would once again be taken unawares and blindsided by dislike. And so it would go on for ever: trapped in this existence, his life a continuous circling of Hell. He felt his breath turn harsh, knocking painfully against his ribcage. He clutched the bus stop, afraid that the weight of this realisation would send him spinning into the gutter.

There she was! Janey Gould, slipping out the stage door, sealskin collar turned up, handbag pressed to her chest.

'Ellis!' She started back, clutching the bag tighter. The look in her eyes – surprised yet cold, a sort of hardness forged in disregard – confirmed his suspicions all over again. In that moment he hated her more than he had thought possible. 'Why Ellis, what are you— I mean, you're early.'

'Yes.'

'We agreed five thirty, remember? I'm not off work yet.'

'Oh, that's a shame.' He smiled. Her shoulders dropped slightly, her face relaxed. Her first confusion was abating. He could tell she was beginning to wonder if this was no more than excitement, that in his eagerness he hadn't been able to stay away. Fine, he thought. Let's play your game. A bus pulled up nearby, and the pavement was suddenly busy with people getting on and off, plaiting invisible paths around each other. A man in Navy uniform stumbled on a loose paving stone, his kit bag bumping against Ellis's leg. He had the same distracted look that Ellis had noticed in other men in uniform recently: an awareness of a hazy, as-yet unfathomable fate.

'Just popping out for something, were you?' He raised his voice over the spluttering engine.

'Yes! I came straight back from Chatterton's with the

money and put it away safely in the office. I was gasping for a cuppa but the workmen left the staff tea-room in such a state that I goes to myself, Why not nip to Lyon's around the corner?' She tilted her head and smiled, reaching out to link his arm. 'Come with me, so's I can tell you all about it.'

'Let's pop inside and get the money first! I can't wait.' He tightened his arm to his side, trapping her hand and wrist. He squeezed, flattening her fingers against him. She winced. 'How exciting!' he continued, as he opened the stage door, pushing her forward, ahead of him.

She spoke quickly. 'The place is such a mess . . . You wait here while I go and fetch it.'

'I don't think you should be wandering around here by yourself. It's so quiet and creepy. I'll keep you company.'

'Oh, but there are heaps of people about. It's just cos of the building work it looks like this.'

He glanced at the sign-in board beside Albert's cubbyhole. 'J.G.' was the only entry with its slider at In. He reached over and slipped it to Out. 'It seems quiet to me,' he said, his voice low. And then, 'Where exactly did you say the money was?'

'The office, in the wages safe. All right, then, you go, and I'll wait here. I'll give you the code.' Her tone changed again, a thin note of worry giving way to defiance.

'So, if I looked in your bag now, it wouldn't be there?'

'No!'

He pulled the bag from her hands and popped the clasp. 'Now that's strange. Forty pounds, and a receipt: *For Chapter twenty-two of The Un-Dead Count by Mr Bram Stoker. In full and final settlement. Sincerest wishes. Rollo Chatterton Esquire, Owner, Chatterton & Chatterton Antiquarian Books, Tavistock Street, Covent Garden and The Turl, Oxford.*'

As he was reading, she snatched the money from his other hand and ducked, as if to run around him and out the stage door. He moved just as quickly and blocked her. She turned and ran down the opposite corridor instead, the same gloomy passageway she had led him along on the day he had planted the manuscript. She had the advantage of knowing her way through the dimly lit corridors, turning a corner, then another. Ellis stumbled and pitched forward, his hands stretched out to break his fall. When he righted himself, she had disappeared. He felt his way forward, his palms pressed against the cold walls. A feeble waxy yellow glow cast onto the walls from a dim bulb was the only lighting. His heart thudded. His hand touched something: a handle! The door was ajar, and he sniffed gently: Vol de Nuit. Softly, he pushed it open. Nothing. As his eyes adjusted to the gloom, he realised he had followed her into Bram Stoker's office.

'I found your suitcase, Janey.'

Oh, the ache of those words! Two hours earlier he had slipped into her bedroom to examine her new clothes only to discover her suitcase, packed and ready to go, its handle a wide, mocking smile. She hadn't bothered to take the diary he had bought her, he noticed bitterly: it lay in an abandoned sewing box, tossed on top of a stocking that needed darning. A shrivelled corsage was in the wastepaper basket, its broken petals a patchwork of red stains against a discarded white handkerchief.

He reached out, his hands flailing uselessly in the dark. 'All packed up and ready to go, weren't you? Let me guess: you were going to leave me here like a stooge at half past five while you nipped back to Fitzroy Gardens to collect your case. By the time I worked out something was wrong and went home, you'd be long gone. Where, Janey? Where were you going?'

A rustle came from a corner, but he couldn't make out what had caused it. All of a sudden, something hard slammed into him. Falling back against the wall, winded and frightened, he reached out an arm and grabbed hold of the first thing he touched. Her sleeve! She struggled, but he pushed her, hard, forcing her wrist down by her side.

'I wasn't going nowhere – you've got it all wrong! I was going to take a little holiday, that's all, same as I was telling you to do this morning. Come with me, if you like!'

'No, Janey, you weren't. You were going to run out on me.' He remembered how powerful he'd felt when Winsome had paid him for the letters, and how he had despised the man's stupidity. Had Janey felt that way about *him*? That he was easy prey? He couldn't bear it. 'But why? I promised you a cut of the rest when I got it, and that's worth far more!'

'Like you'd have paid me anything, once you got your hands on it! I know your sort, Ellis Spender! Lies and more lies, and you'd tell me to go hang if I wouldn't shut up.'

She was prepared to run out on him now because she assumed he would do so to her later on. How could she think such a thing? What had he ever done to her that she should torture him so? She half wriggled out of his grasp, one arm flailing around, trying to grab something from the floor. His eyes had adjusted to the gloom and he recognised the shape as she lifted it again: the horse! That disgusting prop she had forced onto his head! He could recall its foul weight, the decaying stink. She swung it towards him, but it was heavy and with only one free hand she couldn't get much strength behind it. He grabbed it from her and, lifting the head as high as he could, smashed it down hard into her face. She stumbled backwards, one hand raised, elbow cocked as if saluting him. Stunned, she wobbled without falling, her raised arm now in front of her face.

Alone in the deserted basement of a deserted building, who was to see? Who was to know?

'Ellis . . .'

It wasn't much more than a whisper. What little he could see of her face disappeared into shadow. Again he raised the horse's head, bringing it down with even more force. She fell now, landing heavily, and twisted on the floor. He edged forward and leant over her, one hand ready to grab her throat while the other fumbled in his pocket for his lighter. Her head was turned to one side, a pool of blood spilling from behind her. It glistened in the light, a murky halo against the paleness of her hair. A spatter of blood on her blouse grew before his eyes, soaking through the silk. Her black skirt had ripped, and was twisted up and around, exposing the straps of her suspender belt and slim, opal-white thighs. One of the straps was fastened with a safety pin. He reached out and touched the skin just above her knee. It was soft. Warm. He traced his thumb slowly around it and behind her knee, then held the flame, a quivering yellow bulb of light, closer to her face. Janey half mumbled something, he couldn't catch what. Her pupils flared in the light, the terror already fading. She blinked, and he watched the sea-blue of her eyes lose focus. With the lighter raised to guide him, he lifted the horse for a third time and brought it down hard against the side of her head closest to him. It ripped through her temple, the smell of blood overpowering her perfume.

The mumbling faltered, her words breaking up, disappearing. As he watched, all the thoughts that had ever filled her head disintegrated. Meanings and sounds faded in seconds, each one a single blossom shaken loose by a high wind and lost to the skies.

He dropped the lighter and sat on his heels, panting. His mind was blank and yet completely full, swollen as though it might burst. He ran his hand across his face and, once again, the disgusting mix of oil and dirty leather made his stomach heave. He fumbled around until he touched the lighter. His arm ached. The horse's head glared up at him from the floor, a slick of blood across its nose. He staggered to his feet and lurched out into the corridor: silence. Thank God.

He leant back against the wall, shaking, sweating. The corridor was cold, chilling his back instantly.

She was dead.

He had killed her.

He forced his breathing slower, compelling himself to calm down and think. He returned to Stoker's office. When his eyes landed on the ragged mess of her face he felt desperately nauseous. He pushed her further onto her side to release her bag from underneath her coat, and tipped its contents out onto the floor. The money and letter from Rollo Chatterton went into his coat pocket. Everything else – lipstick, glove, hankie, silver rotating pencil, splintered piece of butterscotch – he grabbed and shoved into another pocket. Coin purse too, once he'd emptied it.

He hadn't removed the gloves he'd been wearing while waiting at the bus stop – was that only minutes earlier? Anyway, even if his fingerprints were found on her possessions, what would that mean? They lived in the same house, so it would hardly be suspicious. But what was he to *do* with her? Once more he slipped into the corridor, closing the door behind him this time. No one had seen him in the theatre and he was tempted just to leave her there. Yet, no matter how little-used that corridor or Stoker's office was, she'd be found, if not immediately then soon. But he could hardly sail down the Strand like a drunken sailor on shore leave, with a woman's bloodied body draped around him, could he? Removing her from the building and taking his chances on the busy pavement outside felt like a much bigger risk than hiding her somewhere inside the theatre.

He headed in the direction of the stage, retracing the route she had led him on his first visit. It wasn't nearly as far as he had thought. What he remembered as a dizzying repetition of turnings and identical grubby walls was in fact no more than a couple of sloping corridors, the last of which ended at a narrow door, which opened into the auditorium. It slotted so neatly into the panelled wall that, unless the house lights were fully up, the audience would barely have noticed it.

The entire area around the stage was unrecognisable from his previous visit. The initial five rows of seating were taken up and piled to one side. He remembered her saying that the builders had to fill and level off the orchestra pit to accommodate equipment, but because the original foundations were only earth and rubble, Janey told him the engineer had insisted on digging down further to strengthen the new base with cement. It was fenced off by a makeshift wooden rail with a 'no entry' sign pinned to it. Most of the area looked to be complete, newly surfaced with concrete, and almost level with the wooden boards of the stage. The difference was to allow for laying new carpet over the top, he decided, noticing a large and long tube-like shape wrapped in cloth leaning against a nearby wall. A small section on the far side of the orchestra pit was still unfinished – no more than a large trench with loose bricks and blocks dumped into it, but not yet surfaced. Could he somehow pack her in and cover her up?

Back in the office, he removed his shoes first, then hers. Her stockings were badly darned at the toes, he noticed, and for a moment he felt terribly sad for her, his head pulsing with the enormity of what was happening.

He hoisted her up, her left arm draped around his neck so that the gash on the back of her head was furthest away from him. Her Marcel wave was distorted, blonde hair thickened by congealing blood. She was so slight that he found that by letting her feet drag he could move her quickly, her toes bumping along, light and pointed as a ballerina's. He half carried, half pulled her body through the corridors, moving as quietly as he could. Unless Albert had returned and decided to wander around . . . No, on a Friday evening when the theatre was closed, the workmen gone, there was very little chance anyone could hear him.

He wrapped her coat out around her so that her body didn't touch the floor, tucking the collar up over her hair. Next, he pulled out dozens of loose blocks and masonry until he'd made a large hole in the unfinished trench in the orchestra pit. He picked her up and folded her into it. He'd have put her coat in there as well, but it was too bulky. She looked so small curled up, her body that of a pretty child tucked safely into its crib. She was cooling quickly, her hands mottled. He checked the floor under the coat, but there was no blood. In a feverish haste, he laid enough of the stones on top to ensure nothing of her was showing. As if he was building a horizontal wall he raised the levels on either side too, to even it out and avoid a strange bulge in the stone course. He dumped the unused blocks in a half-full wheelbarrow by the side of the stage. He checked his watch. Almost seven! He had to leave. He knew he would never return to the Lyceum.

He had stood on this stage with her, watched her perform to a non-existent crowd. How he had adored her then, believing them to be one and the same, cut from the same cloth. But she had spoilt that moment, too, with her ghost story about the dead stage hand. Something rustled nearby. He jumped, letting out a low cry in fright. 'Ellis?' he whispered, before he could stop himself. Another rustle, and another, then a ripple of movement in the stage curtain. A rat ran across the wooden boards and disappeared.

Cursing himself, he ran back to Stoker's office and used the lining of her coat to wipe blood from the horse's head. The room was almost empty aside from a few pieces of junk lying around so he decided it was safe to leave the horse where it was, now that it was clean. He tossed it into a corner, where it hit the wall with a thud.

How was he to leave? If Albert had come back he'd never be able to sneak past him. But – those workmen! Why, they had simply walked out the front door.

He was right. The door pushed open from the lobby. He found himself on the street, standing under the portico. He knew he had walked there, that his feet had mechanically taken him from the twisted entrails of the theatre to the fake world outside, but he couldn't recall a single step from the moment he had left Stoker's office.

It was evening. A perfectly ordinary Friday in London. Another day worked and complete. Gas lamps were lit, men and women in evening clothes, their faces eager for distraction, were descending on the theatres, on suppers, on parties, on each other. The evening's news was being shouted from the corner. The falsity of that! What was peddled as 'news' was only whatever paltry information made its way as far as the newspaper offices, cut into metal slivers and remade by who knows how many different men. He must walk among these strangers who would never – could never! – know what had happened, or read any shadow of his burden on his face.

He patted his pockets, panicked suddenly that the money was gone. No, there it was! He reached in and touched the comforting, thick fold of notes. Forty pounds. Both shares, now entirely his. He had doubled his earnings without intending or wanting to.

Rain-filled clouds were gathering overhead. He was thirsty, and desperate to get home. But first he needed to carefully jettison her coat and handbag. Its contents would be easy: he'd discard her things one by one as he passed dustbins and drains. He clutched the coat to his chest, folded as tight as he could manage it. A woman passing by glanced at it curiously, then at his face, and he realised his mistake: no honest chap would ever carry his wife's coat so bunched up and creased. He draped it over his arm instead, careful to keep the bag tucked out of sight beneath it.

The alarm on top of the police box at the corner of Savoy Street began to peal, loud and shrill. Should he run? But where? A constable rushed past him, brushing against Ellis's shoulder, causing the handbag to sway from side to side, like a pendulum under the coat. Seconds later, he reappeared, hurrying away in the opposite direction to the Lyceum. Ellis breathed out. His hands were clutched tight, he realised, his fingers clawing at the coat's fine hair.

He turned towards Victoria Embankment, where he would walk along the river until it was safely night enough. He would discard what was left of Janey, and then he would go home.

The Un-Dead Count
Chapter I

Lady Godalming's Journal

London, 14 May. I have heard it observed that a mother's arms are always strong enough to carry her own child. My own arms are weaker than they once were, having been troubled by the agony of rheumatic pains the last three winters, but! This I know: – my body will summon up the force and strength of a dozen giants, should my own dear John need me to sweep him up, away from scourge or trouble. The full night I lay fretfully awake, my wits shredded with worry. And now, though faint with a tiredness from which I can find no respite, I find myself ensconced at my writing table with only a flickering lamp for company. It is breaking five yet remains dark and chill as the grave outside, with no promise of dawn. The house sleeps around me, quiet bar the rustling of creatures within these ancient walls, and the scratching of my cats as they hunt their prey. This diary has no audience but my own self, but I feel the need to record my thoughts and fears, if only so that the act of putting pen to paper may serve to make clear for myself just what is troubling me. I am no different from a servant taking a rag to a greasy window-pane. But what will the glass reveal? My own darling child, or a dreadful monster?

To begin! As these pages know only too well, it is two months since I lost my dear husband, the truest companion I could ever have wished for. Scores of blank pages attest to my sadness – but those pages are in truth secretly filled with my tears. Arthur was promised to another before he and I first met: a woman who died in the most mysterious circumstances – a blood-wasting disease, he once told me. He spoke of her but rarely, which I own was my preference. Despite all our many years together I never rid myself of the suspicion that I was a paltry replacement for her, that his love for me barely mirrored what he felt for his dead bride (for though they had no ceremony, bride was the word he employed, which saddened me greatly). His actions towards me every day showed my fear for the cunning falsehood it is, yet I found it impossible to shake off, even when on his deathbed he swore to John his love for his family. Oh, John! My darling John is travelling abroad these last weeks in the company of his oldest friend, Quincey Harker. For many years Arthur and I nursed hopes for Quincey and Veronica, our dear little mouse. Many times during the week before he left, my dear son offered to remain at home in mourning with his sister and myself, but I knew his father would have brooked no change to such long-established plans! Their voyage was long planned, with such a complicated web of connections that I barely understood the itinerary. And, though I am desperately sad without my boy's soft voice and kind arm to support me, I rally. As I vow to myself with regard to his father, if I cannot be beside him, I can live for him, can I not?

Waiting for me on my arrival home from Wiltshire (of my three sisters Maud has made herself the most miserable bed in a miserable town, yet lie in it she does, seemingly willingly . . . But, no – no digressions!), there reached me a packet, containing a Note-Book written in my son's hand. It was wrapped in a single sheet – a letter. Though I am assured he is an assiduous note-taker and recorder, and more than competent in his duties to our estate – which the land agents avow he undertakes with talent and discretion, even before he inherited the title from his dear papa – he has never been a regular or reliable correspondent with me, and, as was often the way in the past while he was away and engaged upon his studies, entire fortnights might go without more than a brief note to reassure me that all was well.

I was so taken with delight to witness his signature on a letter after an interval of several weeks, that I merely glanced at the Note-Book, curious, yes, but with no attendant sense of worry, merely wondering why my son would commit such an item to me. I opened it at random. Its text was hard to decipher initially, merely a pencilled scrawl. The letter, though! I include my son's missive here, in the hopes that rewriting his words will, like an explorer painstakingly following a treasure map, illuminate his true intention. But before I do, I pray, dear son, for the sake of your mother, please return!

> *Dearest Mama – In haste, and imploring this journal to your tender care! Dearest, I pray it does not bring my goodbye! But two hours ago I was in mortal danger – and no! Before you cry out, I have been saved in the very nick of time, but the events of the day and night were so fearful that I am shaking*

still, my senses barely lifting from the black cloud that overcame me. Were it not for my philosophy, my religion, courage, all I have been taught indeed, I might have collapsed in a paroxysm of fright. Quincey and I booked passage on a Danube river cruiser from Munich to Budapest. We believed it to be a passenger ship, but when we arrived at the quayside – laden down with luggage – in time for departure, we discovered it to be a small cargo ship. Learning that there were cabins, and four other passengers listed on the manifest, we claimed it for an adventure and took berths – ill-equipped as they were – in high spirits . . . I have not strength now to detail that strange and frightening river voyage, though I will in time, I swear it. No, I must concentrate on today and today only. I am committing this to the page in a hotel in Budapest, so I am <u>safe</u>. [I reproduce his underlining, and thicken it with my own in gratitude for the word resting above it!] *In a moment I will give this letter and my Note-Book to the concierge with instructions for the post. I commit it to your safekeeping. But! Oh, dearest mother! Quincey! I have not seen or heard tell of Quincey for six hours now, and know not what has befallen him. Please believe this for the truth it is: he disappeared from his cabin, which had no porthole or other means of egress, while it was locked <u>from the inside</u>! But I will not fail him. At first light I will resume my search. I love you, and promise to return to you and little V. Your adoring son, John*

Oh, how I wanted to cry out with fear and pain but I dared not, worried I would disturb Veronica, who since our loss insists on sleeping in the adjoining suite. The relief I felt at my son's survival was tempered with terror for his companion, whose mother has been one of my dearest friends these twenty years and more. Should I wire Mina to alert her to her son's disappearance? I cannot decide the best course of action. With trembling fingers, I put the letter to one side and took up the Journal once more. The cover was blank, but the first page was entitled Walpurgis Nacht – The Night of the Witches. Below it was a small scribble, at the sight of which my heart as good as ceased beating. I read it once, and then again – and despite myself – aloud, and trembling with a dread that fell on me with the speed and urgency of a fever. Those awful words! *The dead travel fast.*

CHAPTER 10

Week after week of alchemy, each word spilling from that which came before, each sentence birthed in the warm blood of the last. *The Un-Dead Count* was written as though he was trying to fire a new life into being. He had pulled Stoker's imaginary canvas onto a new frame and stretched it taut and even, until it became real. Since the middle of February, he had done little else, thought of little else. How he had thrilled to the fresh swell of pages each day's end brought! Two hundred and eighty-three in two months, every sheet typed, with additional notations and revisions handwritten in Stoker's customary black ink. He added amendments and errata as he went, on the basis that Stoker – a prodigious note-taker and a busy man forever short of time – would have done so too. The manuscript had hurtled along, tugging him with such force that hour after hour passed in a blur. Within weeks it would be ready to be reunited with its final chapter.

During those secret days and nights in which he worked on *The Un-Dead Count*, unleashing its volatile forces of evil and fear only to hunt them down, he felt as though he was living entirely in its world. He wasn't writing a clever assimilation of Stoker's style, he had become a dead man's confessor: his hands *were* Stoker's. The revenant's plague that had revived itself and was spreading from the east, its evil determined to destroy every native bloodline even as it boasted of its own purity, was more believable to him than any vicious murder or national scandal on the wireless. More real, too, than the newspaper, with its constant reports of rearmament, and articles full of threats and bombast. By comparison with *The Un-Dead Count*, life was empty and bloodless. He realised almost immediately that when he returned to himself and his own ill-used voice and hesitant pen, never again would he travel such a curious and satisfying path. *The Un-Dead Count* brought him a sense of contentment he never found in his own work. Imagination is only freed by happiness, he decided. Without it, the beast that is memory takes over.

On the basis that his novel picked up the threads a generation later, Ellis retained part of *Dracula*'s structure, using the children of the original cast to reanimate their parents' sympathies and attitudes. In addition to his own persona, Count Dracula has arisen as three creatures, each crueller and more vicious than the last: the first with the talons and strength of an eagle; the second the savagery of a wolf; the third, a bat spitting venom. Jonathan Harker was old and unwell and could not fight the invaders as he once did, so Quincey – heir to his father's legal practice – abetted by Arthur Holmwood's son and daughter, found himself called to arms. Arthur Holmwood died not long before the novel begins, and his son John (Lord Godalming since his father's death) and daughter Veronica forgo their mourning in their search for the un-dead. Their quest was aided by a cache of letters and medical textbooks in English, German and Dutch, which Jonathan Harker was bequeathed by Van Helsing, who, Ellis decided, died in a suspicious accident shortly after *Dracula* concluded. Gullible John Holmwood's dim-witted journal provided another voice, as did Veronica's far more sensible correspondence and notes; their mother's excitable diary; and the papers of Ernest Schleier, a dreary, language translator from Amsterdam – a character based on Winsome, whose name Ellis borrowed – who became the object of Veronica's affections, to Quincey's dismay.

Just as Stoker had, Ellis collaged a series of supposedly authentic documents. Nothing was allowed to be complete, an entirety: each piece was no more than an excerpt or a tantalising – and occasionally deliberately confusing – glimpse at another fractured piece of the story. Even the most-heard voice throughout the book, that of ambitious young solicitor Quincey Harker, was no more reliable a path than that made by fallen leaves in a forest. Ellis introduced information that claimed to be official truth despite having its origins in unknown or dubious sources. That Ellis himself was the only true apocrypha at work was a thrilling, secret irony. Never in his own fiction would he have permitted characters to weep so wildly or groan so gruesomely as Stoker's did, or delay each other's progress by stopping to declaim stirring speeches before commencing any expedition, even when their patient listeners were at pains to explain the urgency of the journey.

A story witnessed and told by so many characters became estranged from itself, yet curiously more believable than a tale told by one. The process reminded Ellis of playing Chinese Whispers at school, when they would send a message one by one down the line, knowing that what the final boy heard would be completely divorced from the first boy's whisper. Ellis had quickly understood that it made his task far easier: because of the varying styles and myriad characters in *Dracula*, he was able to adapt entire sentences from the original, delicately stitching pieces of them into his own to establish realistic parallels with Stoker's text. He was doing everything he could to make it real, to soak his story in so much authenticity that it would take on the properties of every other page published by Stoker, as testamentary to the man's existence as a private diary. Reality through absorption. It was a forgery within a forgery; individuality didn't exist, not any more. That alone, to him, made *The Un-Dead Count* a more honest novel than had he written a book in homage to Stoker's style and published it under his own name. Stoker needed him, Ellis could see that now. Through *The Un-Dead Count* he was reanimating the man's imagination: he had lit the spark that would fuse their literary intentions and channel Stoker's unwritten ideas. He had never felt so close to life, or so worthwhile.

Until Friday afternoon, when time fissured into *before Janey* and *after Janey*.

Ellis had avoided his mother all weekend and again on Monday, telling her he was on a streak with his new novella. He spent most of his time sitting in silence in his study, unable to write, rereading *The Un-Dead Count* over and over without taking any of it in, his brain stuttering through the pages, unable to grasp their meaning. Tuesday morning was no different: he seemed to see only the words blood and death, no matter what page he pulled out at random. He paused in the third chapter at the line *A vast stillness appeared to have enveloped him, for all the world a deep sleep – only broken by the low, agonised rasping of his throat*, with the words *or death* a deliberately hasty looping pencil scrawl after *sleep*.

Lunch on Tuesday was a sandwich at his desk. When the girl came to take the tray, he heard Virginia impatiently calling down to her not to dawdle on her afternoon off.

How long had Janey been planning it? From the start? Dear God, please, no, not from then. The thought haunted him and cursed him equally. Eyes closed, he saw her again and again: Janey, beautiful Janey, lying on the dirty floor in front of him, quiet and still and undone. She had given him no choice – that was the terrible thing! She had turned on him. And the awful certainty that he had always known, somehow, that she would. The world felt dissolved around him, his past failures and frustrations no more than pointless debris.

He moved to the window and smoked while staring at the Heath. In the distance a tall, slim woman holding an umbrella strolled across the grass towards Fitzroy Gardens. He watched her approach, until she was no more than twenty yards from the end of the garden wall. She peered out from under the umbrella, light dancing on her hair, before turning and walking away.

He took a breath and returned to the desk. He could not let Janey ruin everything. You are not lost, Ellis, he told himself. You have yourself. He stared at the page in his typewriter, willing Stoker to come and reclaim him, take him back to their shared world, where Janey didn't – couldn't! – exist. He touched his fingertips to the keys, picturing Stoker standing close behind his chair, broad torso leaning forward to shelter him, breath warm on Ellis's neck. Hands covering his own. Replacing his own.

Ellis closed his eyes. A warm pressure began to build in his arms, allowing his fingertips to find their flickering home and lure him away from Janey and her blood-streaked hair, the gash of her silent lips. Up, up he soared, into the air on a journey of one and a half thousand miles. Across hushed valleys and seas tessellated by thousands of long-submerged ships. Over inky lakes cocooning vanished villages, whose ghostly occupants slumbered in lost beds, and high across icy mountains, and half-lit, timbered towns, restless and nervous in the, feverish darkness.

The front door bell rang, a long, shrill peal. He jumped, disoriented and confused – it could have been a minute or an hour later, he didn't know. It sounded a second time. His body felt spent and leaden as he rose and left the room, shivering as he went from fireside warm to ankle-pinching cold. It was raining heavily and from the hallway he could just make out a blurred figure through the stained-glass panels.

'Good afternoon, sir.' A low voice spoke before he had the door fully open. The man touched his helmet, sending water trickling down the brim and into his sleeve. He was of average height but extremely thin, his uniform hanging loosely about his shoulders and waist. 'Shocking weather, isn't it?' His upper lip was invisible under a thick moustache that shifted slightly as he spoke. He lifted each foot, turning it at the ankle as though trying to dislodge water from inside his boots. Ellis realised the long pause was his to fill but his mouth was full of stones. Were his hands shaking? He bunched his right fist and shoved it into his pocket.

'Constable Smyth. Smyth with a *y*.' His left eye fixed Ellis with a pebbly stare while his right roamed restlessly, as if charged with inspecting the cobwebs strung around the uppermost reaches of the doorframe.

She'd been found.

CHAPTER 11

'Was that the door?' Virginia rushed down the stairs. 'Ellis, the rain! Bring him in.' One hand on the newel post, she looked the policeman, now fussing with his dripping helmet, up and down. 'Oh . . . I assumed they'd send me an inspector.'

Send me? What did she mean? Surely Virginia hadn't telephoned the police.

'This way,' she added, sounding put-out. 'You too, Ellis.'

The sudden booming in his head made him want to faint. What was going on? 'The, eh, the fireguard. In the study,' he said, moving away while she ushered the constable into the drawing room. Ellis hovered just behind the door, listening.

'How can I be of assistance, your ladyship?' Constable Smyth lingered delightedly over *ladyship*. Through a crack in the door jamb Ellis watched him take a notebook from his breast pocket and lick his thumb before leafing slowly through its pages. He had no idea what was happening, yet his skittering anxiety at the sight of the uniform at the door began to ease: whatever his mother wanted to complain about couldn't possibly concern him. It was a rotten coincidence of some sort. Don't panic, he told himself. If he were here to arrest you, he would have done so already.

'Ellis?' she called. 'Do hurry up.'

He took a deep breath and walked into the room.

'Close the door – you're letting the heat out. I telephoned West Hampstead police station this morning about Janey.' She turned back to Smyth. 'Miss Janey Gould, that is.'

'Janey?' Fear rose inside him once more. The previous morning when Virginia had asked if he had any idea where Janey might be, he'd answered no: he hadn't seen her since Friday, and what with the cinema opening she was bound to be extremely busy. She had dropped the subject – or so he'd thought. There had been nothing in the newspaper or on the wireless about a woman's body being found in the Lyceum – God knows he'd been checking. He'd gone back there on Saturday afternoon. He knew he shouldn't have, but couldn't prevent himself. He watched the same workmen leave through the main door at five past four, followed shortly afterwards by Albert via the stage door. Ellis had stood in the street at the same bus stop, with the most curious sensation of watching the previous day unfurl before him, a newsreel he had already sat through. Because how could it have played out differently? What other ending did such a cruel betrayer deserve?

Was he behaving strangely? Virginia would notice. To regain control, he bit down on the inside of his cheek, his own flesh soft and yielding against his teeth. The sharpness focused him enough to ask, 'Were you looking to speak to her, Constable? I don't think she's in just now, but I can check her bedroom.'

Smyth was leaning far back in a chair, legs comfortably stretched out in front of him, feet resting on his heels, giving the impression of a man lying back in bed, propped up against a pillow.

Virginia shook her head. 'She isn't. I've looked.'

'You've been in Janey's room?' It spat out before he could stop himself.

'Her room is in my house, Ellis.' She stared at him, eyebrows raised.

He swallowed. 'Of course, yes.' Ellis glanced down at the carpet, concentrating on a corner of its intricate pattern of navies and reds. He desperately wanted a cigarette but didn't trust his hand not to shake. 'Apologies, I must have misunderstood.'

She smiled, placated. 'My son is a novelist, Constable Smyth. It can take him simply ages to re-join the real world when he's disturbed from his typewriter!'

'Yes, I was entirely caught up in my work and . . .' He trailed off with a shrug, an artist unwillingly cajoled back to the dripping tap that was the real world. He stuffed his hands into his pockets again, nails scoring his palms.

Smyth nodded. 'What is the nature of your concern about Miss Gould, Lady Spender?'

Virginia hesitated. 'She hasn't been here since Friday morning, I'm sure of it. She works very long hours, but always returns at night. She never mentioned anything about going away, so I began to worry if perhaps she's met with some sort of accident.'

'Miss Gould is a relation?'

'A guest.'

'She's a friend of the family?'

'No. Well, in a way, I suppose . . . She's an acquaintance of my brother, Freddie Broughton. Are you an aficionado of the theatre, Constable?'

'Not me, ma'am. The pictures, now that's another matter! Me and Mrs Smyth don't half love a good picture.'

Virginia sighed. 'Miss Gould has been living here since last summer. We have an arrangement.'

'She pays rent, you mean?'

Virginia blinked at the word. 'You could put it that way, yes.'

'And is her rent up to date?'

'At her request, she pays in the middle of the month, so it was due on Saturday. That's only a couple of days ago I know, so of course in normal circumstances I wouldn't even have noticed a delay' – (Like hell you wouldn't, Ellis thought, as relief began to douse him like ice-water) – 'but neither the servant nor I have seen or spoken to her since Friday, and she's never gone away for a weekend before. In fact, I've always had the impression she doesn't have people to go to. It all seemed rather queer, I thought.'

Ellis breathed a slow, quiet sigh. His shoulders relaxed, hands loosened. Virginia knew nothing, the police knew nothing. Virginia was suspicious about Janey's non-appearance on rent day, but because propriety wouldn't allow her to admit it, she had to mask her worry about money as concern for her welfare.

'And . . .' She paused.

'And what, Lady Spender?'

'I rang the Lyceum theatre, where she works. There was only a doorman capable of coming to the telephone – it was very confusing because of the building work being done. I can't bear to think of the Lyceum as a cinema! It's horrid, turning such a wonderful stage over to ghastly films one can see in any old picture house.' She flapped her hands to whoosh away the flock of her own distractions. 'He told me Janey hasn't been back since she signed out on Friday. When I asked to speak to George Atkinson, the manager, a dear friend of my brother, the doorman said, Whatever do you want him for? and, thinking he had a cheek to enquire about my business, I replied, Because the manager will know where his personal secretary is, and he said Janey wasn't anyone's secretary, but more of a – well, frankly, the term he used was dogsbody! Delivering scripts, running errands, that sort of thing, he said. For the last few weeks she's been getting the theatre ready for the renovation . . . He made her sound like a glorified cleaner.'

It was a struggle to make sense of it. Just as Ellis had hoped, Albert had assumed Janey had left as usual on Friday: that was excellent. But Janey wasn't Atkinson's secretary? So what had she been doing all those times she'd claimed Atkinson had kept her working late? Suddenly upset that Janey had been feeding him lies since the day they'd met, Ellis said, 'You never told me you'd telephoned the theatre. Or the police for that matter!'

'Do I require your permission? You spend every waking hour in your study, Ellis,' she said, 'and you hate to be disturbed when you're writing.'

Smyth turned in his seat. The chair groaned under him, worn-out leather cracking like ship's timbers in a storm. His left eye looked at Ellis while his right examined the picture rail on the far wall. 'When did you last see Miss Gould, Mr Spender?'

'Hmm . . . Friday also, I should think,' he suggested politely, hoping his hesitation would come across as an artist's inability to recall such mundane matters as the habits and whereabouts of his mother's lodgers. 'Yes, I remember now: Friday morning at breakfast – just as my mother says. Janey was chatting to Patrick about his forthcoming holiday. I can't recall whether she mentioned any plans of her own.' He threw in a little shrug, then ran his hand across his hair. Well done, Ellis, he thought. That's better, finally. Friendly, helpful, yet essentially useless.

'Patrick?'

'Patrick Arcourt, our other guest,' Virginia answered. 'From Ireland. His mother is a close friend of a cousin of mine. He's a doctor, doing a surgical speciality at the Royal London. He joined us late last July, not long before Janey.'

'Do you think Mr Arcourt might have some information as to Miss Gould's whereabouts?'

'No,' Virginia replied.

'Yes.' Here was an opportunity worth grabbing.

'What? Ellis, why?' Virginia looked puzzled. 'I don't see why he would know . . . I mentioned her to him this morning and he said that as he didn't see her every day he hadn't given her absence any thought.' Addressing Smyth, she added, 'Patrick works terribly hard at the hospital. Mornings aside, I rarely see him myself.'

Not given it much thought! Like hell Patrick hadn't! Ogling Janey over the teapot like a lovestruck fool in a cheap melodrama!

'Mr Spender?'

'What?'

'You said yes, that Mr – what was the name? Arcourt? – might know her whereabouts. Why?'

'Oh! I suppose it's nothing really, but they seem to be friendly . . . They talk to each other a lot at breakfast, so I assume they do so at other times too. Their bedrooms are next to each other.'

'Ellis! Are you suggesting there is any impropriety between them?' Virginia's eyes widened.

'Of course not. I merely meant they might be in a position to be in each other's company more than we could ever be party to. And you and I are on the floor below – though in fact I'm in my study most of the time, as my mother says, and I hate to be disturbed.' He served up this comment with another bashful shrug, eyes to the floor. 'I don't take account of who comes and goes. They are both paying rather than invited guests so their movements are their own concern, not ours.' Bolder now, back in control, he slipped his cigarettes from his pocket and glanced around for the table lighter.

Smyth nodded. 'May I see Miss Gould's room, Lady Spender?'

The cigarette fell from Ellis's hand. He crouched to pick it up, the white paper bright as a stick of chalk against the carpet's dust-dulled colours. As his hand brushed the wool, the cartouche pattern seemed to expand and contract before him. An intricate navy scroll, a circle of rope with one trailing strand, lifted from the design and rose from the floor, a noose straining to drop itself around his neck. He jumped back, dizzy, his left hand reaching out to steady himself against the mantelpiece. The noose fell away, inserting itself into the ornamental border once more. His own blood sounded loud and unfamiliar in his head, its rush that of an angry river surging towards unseen and unavoidable rapids. He lit the cigarette, his elbow leaning on the mantelpiece, grateful for the cool touch of the marble under his palm. Sidney's first portrait of Virginia was reflected in the vast gold-edged mirror above it, her shoulders draped in wedding-dress lace, her changeling eyes misty. Freddie hovered in the vaguely Romanesque background, slim and young, resplendent in a fashionable morning coat, with Claude beside him, two brothers delighted to be giving away their only sister. Small diamond and opal drops swung from her ears, the brushstrokes rendering them delicate as tears. Ellis looked from the painting to his mother's face, pale and worried, her left hand nervously twisting the very same ear clip.

She gamely began to introduce the *Greatest Theatrical Figures* series as she led Smyth upstairs, but he didn't respond. Disheartened, she had fallen silent by the time Ellis, a couple of steps behind Smyth, passed under Sarah Bernhardt's haughty, disinterested face. He felt Bram Stoker's gaze on him: eyes wide open, full of curiosity for the uniformed stranger and concern for his fellow author. Ellis gave him the briefest of smiles, a swift – *Don't worry, I have it all in hand* – nod.

Virginia opened the door to Janey's room and stood aside to let Smyth pass. Once again, Ellis hovered behind, barely inside the doorway. The curtains were open. Rain pelted the window, rattling the glass in the frames.

 'As you can see,' Virginia's vague gesture took in the ordinary emptiness of the scene, 'it doesn't appear she was planning to leave. I'm not in the habit of visiting her room – nor Patrick's either, needless to say – but our girl told me there is nothing out of the ordinary.'

Ellis imagined the room as Smyth saw it, his gaze taking in the grubby clutter on the dressing-table, the creams and lotions and bottle of scent, the eiderdown open and creased on the bed, a threadbare cardigan discarded on top of it, one thin arm flung out in surrender. Smyth tugged open a couple of drawers, but barely glanced at the meagre contents. 'Suitcase up there,' he said, pointing at the wardrobe. 'Does she own more than one?'

Virginia shook her head. 'That's all she had with her when she moved in.'

When Ellis had returned home from the Lyceum the previous Friday, Janey's bag and coat carefully disposed of, the first thing he'd done was to unpack her things: he'd found the key for the case in her coin purse. He could still feel the touch of the rough leather handle, the way the thick line of stitching had rubbed against his palm. Her life, trussed up in a single case. It hadn't taken long to return her possessions to the drawers and wardrobe. She must have been planning to abandon most of her old clothes, for the majority of what she had packed was new, including a fine wool skirt still wrapped in the shop's tissue paper, and two pairs of stockings in unopened packets.

On Friday, he had spent the journey home weighing up what to do. When he arrived home shortly after ten o'clock, Virginia was already in bed. He recalled at breakfast that morning – the same day or a hundred years earlier, he was so overwhelmed and exhausted that he was no longer sure – Patrick had mentioned he would be staying overnight at the hospital. (The self-important fool reappeared late on Saturday, discoursing at great length when he bumped into Ellis outside the bathroom about some complicated operation or other that had been a great success 'from a surgical learning standpoint'. He went on to explain why it had been less successful in terms of the patient's mortality, but Ellis, tired and jittery, had barely listened.)

The house had been quiet and still when he'd slipped upstairs and into Janey's room. He knew where everything went – or knew better than anyone else at least. Earlier that evening, he'd found himself back in the Golden Lamb, where he drank three large port-and-brandies in quick succession. It was his first time there since Winsome had approached him, which felt achingly long before, an episode from a previous life he now almost envied himself for. He noticed the barmaid glancing at him a number of times, but she didn't give any sign that she recognised him. He went to the Gents and realised with a start how dishevelled he was. No wonder she was staring! He damped his hair and combed it back. There was a smear on his wrist. When he picked at it, tiny flakes rubbed off. He took a corner of the towel to it and it smudged, reddish. Blood! Her blood! On his shirt too! He scrubbed at a spot on his right cuff. The drain gurgled as the dirty water washed away, the oxtail colour fading to a reddish-pink before eventually running clear.

On the first port-and-brandy, he had decided the best course of action would be to do nothing and say nothing. The packed suitcase would stay exactly where he had come across it that morning. At some point Virginia would check the room and decide Janey had left, presumably planning to send someone to collect her things, knowing that her landlady wasn't the type to rifle through it in order to salvage some value from its contents. On the second drink, he reasoned that packing a suitcase only to abandon it was more suspicious than departing the bedroom as normal and failing to return. He would remove the case, he decided, and hide or bury it somewhere, so his mother would assume Janey had done a bunk. Only on the third port-and-brandy did he realise how muddily he had been thinking. He needed to disassociate his household from Janey's disappearance, not inextricably link the two! If he removed Janey's supposed intention, surely that broadened the possibilities for what could have happened to her. Leaving the suitcase as it was, closed and ready to go, suggested she was planning something and had been halted in her tracks. But unpacking her belongings would suggest she had left the house as usual on Friday morning for work, and whatever had happened to her after that was entirely unconnected with the Spenders. Even if anyone did begin to wonder whether some terrible or strange fate had befallen her, it would have nothing to do with her life in Fitzroy Gardens.

If only he'd known she paid her rent mid-month instead of on the first, as Patrick did! He could simply have got rid of the case, and everyone would have assumed she had packed up and done a flit. Janey was trying to fool him in death as well as in life. Why was she so desperately infuriating?

Virginia peered into the wardrobe. 'Her handbag and coat are gone. A new sealskin.' Her glance took in the cheap clothes, the spilt powder. 'Wildly expensive too. I can't imagine where the money came from.' Smyth's eyebrows lifted, his knowing expression as good as if he'd said *I can.*

'She had them with her on Friday?' Smyth asked.

'I didn't see her leave but, yes, she must have.'

'What about her behaviour? Anything strike you as unusual?'

Virginia shook her head.

'And you, Mr Spender?'

'No.'

'Do you remember what Miss Gould was wearing, sir?'

Lace-trimmed silk blouse finished with mother-of-pearl buttons, bloodied.

Black skirt, ripped.

Suspender belt, broken.

Red lipstick, smeared from mouth to ear.

'No, why should I?'

Smyth frowned but answered, mildly enough, 'No reason, sir.'

Looking at her belongings, the depth of her cruelty and deception struck him once more. Anger surged, as fresh as it had been on Friday morning when he'd discovered the suitcase. Fools like this constable could unpick her known life all they liked but would never succeed in uncovering what she really was: a liar and cheat. Why, everything she had ever said was untrue, or as good as because it was conceived in lies. The room was a pretence, a painted backdrop. It would never reveal anything true or good about her. How he longed to say it! To shout out: She's not here, she never was! She was not the person I believed her to be! That she had exaggerated her job to make both it and her sound more important, more appropriate to the Spender household, was nothing by comparison with the horrible deceit she had inflicted on him.

'Would you consider her an honest girl, Lady Spender? Given that she lied to you about her job?' Smyth asked. 'To my mind, the most likely explanation is that Miss Gould did a bunk to avoid paying her rent.'

Virginia's eyelids fluttered again at the word rent. 'But she didn't have trouble with money recently – all those new clothes!'

'Perhaps the clothes were the problem, dearest,' Ellis broke in. 'She's obviously overspent terribly. With all her theatre pals she'll have found new digs at a moment's notice. Considering how kind you've been to her, it's horrible that she chose to run away rather than admit she was up to her ears in debt.'

Smyth nodded. 'Happens all the time. Like you wouldn't believe,' he added, clearly relishing his role as expert. 'I've known people roll up again months later, assuming bags and baggage are waiting for them. Some girls have a desperate cheek, as the missus says. But if it would make you feel better, your ladyship, I can telephone the theatre and check if the boss has heard anything?'

Her nod was closer to a shrug. Smyth opened his little notebook again and, holding it and the pen close to his face, began to write slowly. Ellis watched, hypnotised by the rough scrape of pencil across paper, by the single eye fixed on the page while its companion surveyed the wallpaper. Smyth's face was a study in concentration, his expression like that of the incompetently stuffed gorilla, black eyes bulbous and confused, in the Horniman Museum. Over his shoulder Ellis watched him write *Atkinson at Lieceeum.* Ellis imagined Smyth's ugly head cracking open like a boiled egg. Hollowed out and filled with soda water, until his mouth, nose, even his eye sockets fizzed, submerged. What a bozo, Ellis thought, with a pang for Janey. She would have adored Smyth.

For the first time since the constable had arrived, Virginia looked uncertain and ready to doubt herself. Good: a second opportunity. He didn't want any awkward questions once the man had left. 'You were worried something awful might have happened, weren't you, dearest?' he said softly. 'You're so thoughtful. But she's run off and that's all there is to it. I know Constable Smyth will agree with me that you haven't wasted the police's time, in wanting to be sure.'

'Wasting the . . . Oh, I never intended that!'

Virginia leant against the wall as though she was too tired to stay upright any longer. 'You must think me ridiculous. Panicking for no reason.' She flushed. Was she embarrassed that the constable would secretly conclude her show of concern was motivated by money? Ellis hoped so. Swollen shadows the colour of bruises underscored her eyes. The faded wallpaper pattern, a narrow trellis of brown and red wrapped all over in clematis blossoms, grew behind her head and shoulders, the tiny pale flowers a misshapen halo around the thick white-gold of her hair.

'Not at all, your ladyship. Now, if you'll excuse me, I'll be getting back to the station.'

It was all Freddie's bloody fault, Ellis thought. First he'd foisted Janey on the household, then almost ruined them by sucking away what little money his mother had left. 'You're too thoughtful,' Ellis continued, his voice low and tender. 'Why don't I see the constable out? You go to your room and rest. I'll bring you up something light on a tray.'

She nodded, peeling herself away from the wall with a sigh. He half expected small cracked petals to tear away from it with her, dusting her hair like torn confetti. 'All right, thank you. What should we do with her things?'

'I'll take care of everything. Let's store her case in the cellar until someone calls for it. And if any creditors come to the door, you just put them on to me.'

'Creditors?' Her voice was faint. 'Oh, surely not!'

'I won't have you upset by her appalling behaviour, not for another second. Just wait, dearest, you'll see – she'll come crawling home some day, and I'll give her a piece of my mind, I promise.'

He ushered them out of the bedroom, then turned to switch off the light. Without the promise of her presence, the room was no more suggestive of Janey's life than a set of furniture in a shop window. As he closed the door he glanced across the room to the window. Dusk wasn't due for at least an hour, but it was winter-gloomy again outside, the rain falling in thick sheets from a sky that hovered low and heavy, tucked around the deserted Heath like a blanket.

Leaving Smyth fumbling with his helmet on the step, Ellis said goodbye. Oh, the relief of shutting the door behind him! He felt entirely worn out. He had been tensed for such a knock since Friday, he now realised: it had been inevitable that someone would call to enquire about Janey, so wasn't it good to have got it over with quickly? And so easily, too! It couldn't have gone better, he decided, as he ran over the conversation again in his mind: Smyth clearly had Janey pegged as a petty fraudster, who'd done a cheap disappearing act, and Virginia as a gullible old woman. From now on, should anyone else ever contact the police enquiring about her, Smyth would already have the answer.

Ellis was in the clear. Albert believed she had left the Lyceum on Friday and not returned. The builders had worked on Saturday and found nothing to arouse suspicion, presumably finishing the work on the orchestra pit. In the gormless form of Constable Smyth, the police were satisfied. It bothered him slightly that Virginia had telephoned the station, though. He'd have to make sure she didn't get any more ridiculous notions. Perhaps a short note from Janey . . . A dashed-off apology including a couple of pounds and a forwarding address for the suitcase? A last-minute job offer from a regional tour that left the same day, perhaps. Or something vaguer that would leave Virginia with the impression she'd gone off with a man. It would mean a day trip somewhere to post it, as well as getting rid of the case safely. Was that too risky? He filed the idea away to think about later.

The old-dog smell of Smyth's wet uniform lingered in the drawing room. He crossed to the mantelpiece and, crouching, began to examine the carpet, running his fingertips across the pile. He stared intently at the scroll, challenging it to rise again and prove by repetition what he had experienced earlier. Nothing. It remained flat and unmoving, the fibres thick and broken by wear. He moved his fingers back and forth across the surface, feeling the tips fur with dust as it yielded to his touch. But why was the pattern so painfully familiar? He realised suddenly: the carpet was the same design as the one in the painting of the terrier Sidney had submitted to the Royal Academy. He had never before noticed the resemblance. While Sidney had changed the colour palette in order to better foreground the dog's coat, he had copied the design inch for inch. Ellis shivered.

He rose to his feet and slowly walked around the room. His favourite artworks in the house were the three hanging in his study, timid watercolours (an abandoned watermill; a sea-shaken lighthouse; an empty, dusty barn) that had once belonged to a great-aunt. No such concession to any other artist was allowed in the drawing room, where Sidney's career was represented on each of the four walls: the wedding portrait of Virginia and her brothers; a minor, forgotten royal; two generals newly returned from the Boer War; and a curious grouping of long-dead family dogs. The version of Freddie in the portrait of Virginia was one he had never known: young and handsome, though the twitch of a smile playing about his lips and his knowing gaze – those of a man with secrets of many colours – were horribly familiar.

Ellis stood in the centre of the room, looking at the thickets of furniture and gloomy wallpaper, the dense maroon velvet of the curtains, uncomfortably aware of the eyes watching him from the walls.

CHAPTER 12

His original intention had been to take another six weeks – longer if necessary – to complete *The Un-Dead Count*, and at a more relaxed pace, but although he constantly reassured himself that Smyth's visit couldn't have gone better, thinking about the book unsettled him. He lay awake most of Tuesday night, wondering during the grey, panicked hour before dawn whether he should burn the manuscript and send the entire business to Hell. Could he really bring himself to kill the same beautiful, spirited words he and Stoker had brought to life on the page? To abandon the prospect of the freedom it promised? No, that couldn't happen! He had to see it through, he decided, and quickly.

Janey had given Rollo Chatterton the Lyceum as her contact address, so he wasn't concerned that Chatterton would connect her to Fitzroy Gardens or its inhabitants. Anyway, Chatterton had no reason to seek her out again: their business was done. The safest thing, he decided, would be to cut all ties with Janey, which meant getting the book out of his hands and the house.

For the next three weeks, he barely slept. Dracula's castle, genesis of the plague central to his plot, became his home. Perched high and grey and lonely on the rock, imprisoned by a river rushing below and sheer, snow-covered mountains behind, it was more real to him than his own street. When he touched the dusty nap of the flock wallpaper in the dining room, his fingers met cold, crumbling stone; his customary tired slope to bed became a shadowless tread up a flight of curving steps to a turreted billet. He was a child imagining a complete world, one spinning to its own rhythm, moving in waves of new dreads and old ghosts. As he floated between east and west, his house began to feel unfamiliar, and London a chaotic city in which increasingly he had no place. But he was never really alone: Bram was with him. In the few hours of sleep he managed each night, he was fretful and restless. A strange, unfamiliar figure came to him often in his dreams: a woman, always in shadow or, as in the strange way of dreams, with her face turned away from him, no matter how close her body pressed against his.

And then, incredibly, unbelievably, it was done.

He pushed his chair back from his desk, rising with the exhausted calm of a man whose fever has finally broken. His typewriter seemed to hum, resonating with energy and the intensity of his labour. He felt as light as the dawn breaking outside his window, and as alive. *The Un-Dead Count* existed! It was the fourth of May, he realised, and the secret harmony of the coincidence appealed to him. In Dracula that was the eve of St George's Day: at midnight on the fourth of May all of the evil things in the world would have their sway, unchecked and unstoppable, and a blue flame would burn wherever treasure was hidden.

'We've done it,' he whispered to Stoker's portrait. He reached out and stroked the man's painted hand, feeling not glass but warm, dry flesh, the ridges of veins. 'Are you proud of me?' Stoker's love for his own novels, his despair at how ill-regarded his fiction was and his faith in his work were those of a father for his children. Was it ridiculous to envy a book? What a thing it must be, he thought, to see such care reflected in another's eyes, to know they desire only your joy, your success.

For typing paper, he'd used old reams Janey had found at the Lyceum. He spent a day working on the completed manuscript – a cigar-ash stain and slight rip here, a spillage and crushed corner there, using Fuller's Earth to discolour the pages and make them ever so slightly gritty – until he was certain it was perfect. Storing each day's work in a sealed box with a slightly damp blotter had lent the pages an authentically musty smell. It wasn't necessary to work it excessively: the book had supposedly sat unread in a folder for more than thirty years, and while it would have aged, it had suffered little wear and tear.

He had created a deliciously intricate puzzle and, by offering it to Ralph Chatterton, was about to wrap it in another. Poor Janey! She had such a dull imagination, to believe she was cleverer than him, that he was no better than any of her chumps, a stooge whose job it was merely to feed her lines, then stand back while she stole the limelight and success. She had been right about one thing, though: he needed to get away from London. As soon as the manuscript was sold he would tell Virginia he had received a publisher's advance for a book of travel essays, and would be going abroad for a short while. A modest sum, he decided, fifty or sixty pounds: not so much as to generate an expectation it might be shared, yet not so small that he couldn't plausibly go away for a month or more in comfort.

Selecting a firm sure to be completely outside the reach of Virginia's social circle, he told her that an editor at Secker & Warburg had read *The Only Boy* and asked to meet him about a non-fiction commission, a hard-working lie that also prepared the ground for his soon-to-be-announced advance. Instead, he caught the twelve o'clock train to Oxford. As before, at the peal of the shop's bell the owner appeared at the top of the basement stairs.

'Ralph Chatterton, owner of this collector's haven! Welcome,' he said, as he had the first time. What sporadic subsequent contact they'd had since had been conducted by post, so not being recognised was hardly surprising.

'Ellis Spender. I had the pleasure of visiting once before?'

'Oh, my apologies. *Ellis* . . . yes, of course. The Gilbert and Sullivan libretto collection? Thoroughly delightful. Just as I predicted, it flew out the door to one of our new transatlantic collectors – I shouldn't really divulge the purchaser's name, but you're a diplomatic chap, I'm sure. None other than Yip Harburg! Imagine! Seemed perfectly fitting for one such renowned lyricist to collect the work of another. Should you ever come across similar material, do please let me know.'

'Of course,' Ellis replied. 'I'd be happy to. Though that's not why I'm here, Mr Chatterton.' He smiled shyly, having decided that presenting himself somewhere between politely reserved and slightly guileless was the best approach, as though he had only the simplest understanding of the potential value of the folder in his possession. 'I was visiting my college chum again so thought I'd pop by before my train.

I do so hope I'm not wasting your time, but it's the most curious thing . . . As you may recall, my uncle gave me his old papers and books when he moved to America because he wasn't in a position to transport them. Most of it is personal correspondence, of no interest to anyone, not even' – with a self-deprecating smile – 'to him. A couple of days ago I came across a folder I hadn't noticed before. I was about to discard it when something made me take a closer look, and, well . . .' He pushed the folder across the counter with a slight shrug, as though he lacked the vocabulary or ability to explain further.

Chatterton extracted the manuscript. His hands moved slowly for the first ten or fifteen seconds, then began to speed up until his fingers were gobbling the pages. For a minute, more, there was silence, apart from a continuous faint rustle. He extracted a single sheet – Ellis couldn't make out which page exactly, but guessed it was from the sixth or seventh chapter – carried it to the window and held it up to the light. Ellis couldn't breathe. What was he looking at? Or, worse, looking *for*? Was there a mistake in Stoker's handwriting style? Dear God, had he left in the folder one of the working or discarded pages – all of which were either written in Ellis's own hand or typed and badly annotated in Stoker's style, and any one of which would give up the entire thing as a fraud? He'd checked and double-checked! He began to perspire, suddenly remembering how he had felt months earlier, standing at the very same counter, wondering if he should grab the Gilbert forgeries and run.

'Twenty-one,' Chatterton muttered. 'Twenty-one. My word!' He addressed Ellis at last, his voice cracking, 'I can't believe my eyes!' He clutched his hands as if thanking the gods. 'Rollo! I must telephone Rollo!'

'What is it?'

'You understand what this *is*, don't you? You, dear boy, have the sequel to *Dracula*! *The Un-Dead Count* – what a wonderful title. *Dracula* wasn't Stoker's original choice. He changed it from *The Un-Dead* just days before the book went to print. I'd heard the rumours, of course. We all had – stories have circulated in the trade for years that Stoker had written a sequel only to destroy it.'

'Incredible!' Ellis stuttered. 'I can't – I can't believe it!'

Chatterton nodded, his face pink and excited. 'Please, tell me everything.'

'Gosh. I'm not sure there's much else to tell. The folder was in my uncle's possession for many years, and is now mine.'

'Do you have something confirming your ownership?'

'Yes. A letter.' He paused. 'It's, ah, a touch embarrassing for my mother and I, Mr Chatterton—'

'Ralph, please.'

'Thank you. My uncle found himself in a somewhat compromised situation as regards funds, so he sold rather than gave me theatrical memorabilia and papers he no longer wanted.' That careless, dashed-off note would come back to haunt Freddie yet! Ellis could have hugged himself with glee. 'The folder containing the manuscript also included this.' From his bag, he withdrew a brown-spotted letter, dated 5 October 1905: *My dearest young friend Freddie B! You know I desire this second tale of the un-dead to be greater in power, magnificence . . . yet I fear my pen struggles in vain. So, my rapscallion, I would be most grateful for your honest – & only your honest – thoughts!* Ellis had signed it, *from Bram, devoted scribbler!* He recalled how his hand had hovered before committing the word *honest* to the page, but only for a moment.

Last, he took out an envelope, the only page in his bag that was no more than it purported to be. 'Stoker's widow, Florence, died last year. My uncle received this letter from her in December 'thirty-six.'

Chatterton read Florence's letter aloud, his voice gaining speed and tripping over the words – *fate and furies; sequel; admitted only to its name* – in his excitement. 'This is the most remarkable provenance,' he declared, his face pink. He stopped suddenly. Frowned. 'But why didn't your uncle inform Mrs Stoker he had a copy of the manuscript she believed destroyed?'

He'd been expecting this. 'How astute you are, Ralph! I wondered that too. Judging by his note, it seems Stoker was hoping my uncle would critique the book, but Freddie doesn't appear to have done so – he certainly didn't annotate the manuscript and I found nothing in the form of comments anywhere else, nothing at all, in fact, to suggest he had even *read* it. Freddie has toured extensively over the last four decades, and with more than thirty years separating Bram Stoker's note and his wife's letter, it's highly likely my uncle had completely forgotten that Stoker gave him the manuscript. Henry Irving, Stoker's former employer, didn't rate *Dracula* at all and, unfortunately, I suspect my uncle may have had similar feelings about his friend's novel-writing.'

Chatterton nodded. 'Little of Stoker's work stayed in print for long during his life. I remember him as very sensitive about how the literary world viewed him.'

'Is that so? How sad for him.' Ellis paused, as though parsing the meaning of this new information. 'My uncle is a conscientious and honourable man. The prospect of upsetting a dear pal – Stoker was something of an early mentor to Freddie and they were very fond of each other – would trouble him desperately. Freddie would think it wiser to "forget" to read it rather than risk a valued friendship with an unfavourable, even if well-intentioned, judgement.'

Every word complete rot, and Chatterton couldn't swallow it quickly enough.

'To think it was just languishing in your family's possession all this time! Why, it's just too thrilling! You've read the entire manuscript, I take it?'

Silently apologising to Stoker, Ellis replied, 'It's not my sort of thing, Ralph, to be honest. I'm a modernist.'

Chatterton had begun to work through the pages once more. Running his index finger gently over a handwritten note added to the margin, he read aloud: '*Mem. Original practice in churches when newly built, of walling a person up. Now wall up only shadow. Should V lose her shadow?*' He spoke so excitedly that spittle gathered at the corners of his mouth. A barely visible globule fell from his lip and landed on the page, but he didn't notice.

Ellis winced. He couldn't bear the idea of his precious manuscript sullied in any way. He resisted the urge to lean over and wipe the tiny spot in case the ink would smudge, calling attention to its own freshness.

'You are familiar, Ellis, with the practice of immurement? The reference is to the necessity of a human sacrifice to ensure strength and divine protection for a church. It sounds barbaric, doesn't it, to trap a person in a small space and leave them to die? However, I believe it was traditional practice in many European cultures, not just among natives, as one might expect . . . vestal virgins, errant nuns and suchlike. I wonder if his reference is suggestive of that. Perhaps this V character referred to has shades of Mina Harker. I've always thought her a touch forward. In *Dracula*, Van Helsing describes her as having a man's brain, you know.'

'How interesting. There's no such reference to Veronica here.'

'Oh?' He looked puzzled. 'So, you *have* read it?'

'Yes. I mean no.' He felt light-headed. 'I skimmed through it when I found it first because I was curious as to what it actually was, but I didn't pay much attention to the story. I'm obviously not able to approach a manuscript with anything like the authority and close attention of a professional and connoisseur such as your good self.'

'What a tedious place the world would be if we were all experts!' Chatterton beamed.

Because he had understood the significance of Ralph's earlier *twenty-one*, Ellis was keen to nudge him onto the subject of the book's final chapter. Once again offering silent apologies to Stoker, he said, 'His fiction isn't to my taste, as I said, yet I did wonder if this is in fact a very early draft because the ending struck me as inconclusive. Flat, even.'

Ralph extracted chapter twenty-one again, turning to its last page. 'Quite the contrary. Your manuscript concludes, yes, but the novel doesn't! What you have doesn't include the final chapter.'

'It doesn't? That is disappointing. Perhaps it's somewhere else in Freddie's papers—'

'No, no,' Chatterton interrupted. 'Let me explain. By the most incredible good fortune, chapter twenty-two was discovered in the Lyceum theatre earlier this year. The character of Dracula was always reputed to have been based on Sir Henry Irving, you know. My brother Rollo – our London establishment is practically at the Lyceum's doorstep – purchased it. Isn't it the most perfect provenance? Stoker's own writing, discovered decades later in Stoker's own office, which apparently had been disused, a store room of sorts, for years. It is a wonderful piece of fiction.'

'Remarkable!' Ellis said, thrilling to the praise. 'Fateful, one might say.'

'Completely unheralded, a volcanic cataclysm destroys the castle. A convulsion of nature no less, flames quenching blood! And while it appears as though Dracula has finally been killed – again! – when the castle is broken into fragments and sinks into the void, there is just enough left unstated to leave the suspicion open that he may return from the un-dead once more, the explosion catapulting his evil into the western skies. My brother Rollo's theory – an excellent one, if I may say so – is that Stoker rejected such a conclusion for *Dracula*, concerned that it would be judged too similar to Poe's *The House of Ushe*r. This find would substantiate that, adding credence to his decision to use the conclusion he had originally wanted, having decided it acceptable to employ in a sequel because of the years dividing the two. Rollo went so far as to speculate that Stoker may have written that chapter first.' He pointed at Florence's letter. 'It is both fitting and ironic that in life Stoker chose to immolate his creation, as he had already done in fiction.'

'Does your brother still have the chapter?'

He nodded. 'We decided not to put it forward for publication. Finding a publisher for a single chapter would be difficult, even one such as this. Instead, we have entered into discreet discussions with a number of private collectors. There has been considerable interest in it as an artefact in and of itself. I have several clients who would adore such a rarity for their personal libraries.' A clever strategy, Ellis thought. Doubtless the Chattertons would make a handsome profit by selling the chapter to a wealthy Gothic enthusiast, while sparing themselves the financial complication of involving Stoker's estate, which would want publication and healthy sales in order to profit.

'And that chapter was found at the Lyceum, you say? With my uncle's long-standing involvement in the theatre world, that makes perfect sense. I have a connection through my mother and Florence Stoker also, who were friends since childhood. I am so pleased I thought to bring it with me today. It's such a curiosity, isn't it?'

'This isn't a curiosity, Ellis, it's a *rarity*. To think we all believed it lost for ever! It's more than a sequel, it's a rightful heir.'

Ellis began to ease the pages from Ralph's hands, smiling politely. It couldn't have been going any better.

'The power of a tether to draw us to another world can't be underestimated,' Chatterton said, and ran on in this fashion for some minutes, expounding on the notion that 'true readers' (by which he seemed to mean Oxford scholars and his own customers) sought out authenticity (meaning anything that substantiated and bolstered their admiration of their own opinions). 'This manuscript,' he concluded, to Ellis's relief because he really did have a train to catch and not mentioning money was becoming exasperating, 'has the power to create a new reckoning for Stoker, proof that he understood his masterful creation so well that he knew the necessity and value of a sequel. Stoker desperately wanted to reanimate the Count, but believed himself to have failed. And yet here he is, un-dead, despite Stoker's casting him into the flames. It couldn't be more delicious!'

Ellis checked his watch. Two twelve: time for the duet of his and Stoker's talent to take a bow and await the applause. 'Gosh, I'll be late! I'm booked on the two-forty. Would you pass me the letters, please?'

'What?' Chatterton looked horrified. He put one hand on the folder, pinning it to the desk. 'How much do you want?'

'Do I *want*? I do apologise, Ralph, have I given you the wrong impression? I wasn't thinking of selling. I wasn't sure what it was and, with your expertise in antiquarian literature, I thought of you as the perfect person to show it to.'

'Under the laws of copyright, the rights to publication of both this and the chapter in Rollo's possession lie with Stoker's estate. His next-of-kin, presumably.'

'Publication?' He paused, as if needing to consider such a foreign concept. 'Why, yes . . . I suppose so. That would be Noel, his son. Nice fellow.' Ellis continued to gather the sheets, secretly thrilled by the stricken look on Chatterton's face as, page by page, *The Un-Dead Count* disappeared from view. The man was taking far too long to – as he had phrased it during Ellis's previous visit – 'talk terms'.

'But this manuscript, on the other hand, is yours to sell, Ellis.' At last!

Chatterton reached into a drawer and took out a large leather folder. 'I'll give you six hundred and fifty pounds. An excellent price. And, as my brother and I already own the final chapter, it would be fitting for the book to be reunited with the finale Stoker gave it, don't you agree? I don't keep such sums on the premises obviously, so I'll give you a deposit if you leave the manuscript with me. Once Rollo and I establish provenance to our complete satisfaction, I'll have a banker's order drawn up for the balance.'

'I beg your pardon? Ralph, I couldn't possibly part with it.'

'Seven hundred.'

'Oh,' said Ellis. 'Oh, my.'

On the train home Ellis sat back, content to watch the greens and treacle browns of the countryside give way to London's red-brick sooty outreaches. Usually such bland constancy – the repeated terraces with their repeated washing lines, the stained intimacies of ordinary lives on vulgar display – hollowed him out. Not today! How pleasant it was, each new sight a glorious note in a wonderful choral composition. A traditional bucolic English pastoral that only he could hear. Fields were full of newborn, unsteady lambs, and clean clothes billowed in each tiny yard, caught up by a breeze that was airy and fresh. The sun winked at him from a thousand polished windowpanes, just as he knew it would sparkle on the waves of the warm and unfamiliar seas that would soon be rolling towards him.

The only other occupant of the carriage, a woman of Virginia's vintage, with large feet and a catarrhal cough, who joined the train at Didcot, was entirely preoccupied with her Booth Tarkington novel. When she wasn't snorting with laughter at the tosh she was reading, she rolled barley sugar around her mouth, each roving bulge a crude shove against her cheek. But even the sound of it crashing repeatedly against her teeth couldn't irritate him for long.

He could hardly control his thoughts, each disparate idea a bubble popping on the surface of his brain. The world was bright and pure and broken wide open, offering from deep within itself the glittering promise of adventure.

He had money, finally. No, more than money, more than the promise of any single thing money could buy. He had success. Freedom. What an achievement! Another fifty in his pocket and the promise of the six hundred and fifty pounds' balance to follow in due course. Plus, he had the forty Rollo Chatterton had given Janey, and he hadn't yet spent his own share from Rollo's original deposit. He'd lost only fifteen to Janey's greed – and to think he'd been planning to give her half of the total proceeds from chapter twenty-two, plus some consideration from the fee he received for the rest! It still hurt that she had believed him capable of double-crossing her like that. He would have given her a cut, of course he would. Why hadn't she trusted him?

Relaxed and happy, he gazed out at the soot-stained brick of London. The glory of picturing his future while knowing he now had the power to send the lifeblood of money coursing through its veins! Finally, an end to all the years of feeling as though he was living his life with one ear pressed against a locked door in a constant, desperate attempt to decipher incomprehensible sounds.

The platform was busy. A woman reached the ticket collector just ahead of him. Sleek blonde bob. Modish hat pressed to the side of her head and an ebony fur coat. His stomach lurched. You fool, he chided himself. Thousands of women in London dressed like that.

CHAPTER 13

'*Janet Gouldstein*?' Virginia echoed Constable Smyth's words. He nodded. Whatever she might have been to her former landlady, she was now Janet Gouldstein as far as the Metropolitan Police were concerned. Smyth sat back, refolding his legs, his boots up on their heels. He had appeared alone on the doorstep ten minutes earlier. His superior, Inspector Morris, would be along in a couple of minutes, he explained, and would like a word. 'Janet Gouldstein . . .' Virginia said again, as if she didn't believe him, and repetition would flush out his lie.

'It's just as you was told yourself, ma'am. Miss Gouldstein was employed in the Lyceum on a casual basis, doing errands and the like. George Atkinson confirmed it. It suited him that Miss Gouldstein upped and left, he said, for he was planning to let her go once the cinema opened. Her primary place of employment was a nightclub.'

'A *what*?' Virginia said.

'Called . . .' Smyth slipped his little notebook out from his jacket '. . . the Bat, in Mayfair. She was a hostess. Paid to dance with the customers for tips. *Gifts*, the girls call them, though a tip is a tip is a tip, if you ask me.'

'I know what a hostess is,' Virginia said tersely. She looked horrified, and Ellis knew she was thinking, *Harlot.*

Sweat bloomed down his back. The Bat was the name of the nightclub she had refused to go to with him! He recalled the evening they had spent in the Nest at Winsome's expense, and the hostess Janey had chatted to for ages. It had struck him at the time that they seemed awfully familiar with each other, yet he remembered her saying they'd only just met.

Smyth had paid a visit to the Bat, he told them. 'I can't say what it's like of an evening, but it's a rum sort of place in God's own daylight, let me tell you.'

'I can't possibly imagine,' Virginia said, which meant she was imagining wildly.

They fell silent. Disquiet wrapped itself around Ellis, a sparky jumpiness worse than the most horrible hangover, making it hard to think clearly. He couldn't get it straight in his head: how did the nightclub and her real name tie together? As with his previous visit, Smyth didn't appear to harbour any suspicions about Ellis, so just how might the conversation involve him? Virginia, trained since childhood to ramrod posture, no matter how uncomfortable the physical or emotional circumstances, remained perched on the edge of her chair. The only indication she was uncomfortable with the situation was a tiny movement of the tip of her index finger against her thumbnail, her habit if she was uneasy, as though her finger was composing a miniature message in an invisible code. Smyth twirled his feet and flicked through his notebook, pausing here and there to mutter to himself. His right eye roved madly.

'She's a wraith,' Virginia murmured, and Ellis recalled one of her stories from his childhood in which a beautiful churchyard demon waylaid bereaved men to poison them, using their lips and hands as weapons. Fairies in Virginia's old Irish tales were always halfway creatures, outcasts caught between Heaven and Hell, roaming restlessly between the two. But Janey wasn't a siren who had lured him into a trap that was now beginning to close. She alone was responsible for her fate. He had done no more than react as circumstances demanded.

A minute passed. The grandfather clock ticked, logs crackled and hissed. Outside, a car backfired. Ellis started from his seat and rushed to the window. Through the gaps in the front hedge he watched a navy Austin turn around and drive slowly away, the sound of its tyres dull and heavy on the road. Blue smoke spluttered from the exhaust. A vast dent creased the bonnet, as though a large object had dropped from the sky onto it. A well-dressed man walking up the street was also watching the car's halting progress.

Virginia looked at Ellis, puzzled. Smyth, too. 'Everything all right, sir?' Ellis nodded. Smyth checked his watch. 'The inspector will be with us any moment, I'm sure.'

'But I still don't understand why he needs to see us,' Virginia said. 'Doesn't the fact that Janey – Janet, I suppose I ought to call her now – lied make it even *more* likely that we will never hear from her again? What date is today, Ellis?'

He didn't move from the window. 'The sixteenth.' Hearing Janey's name was like being stung repeatedly. Was this repetition a spell to conjure her up? The car turned towards Hampstead Lane and disappeared. If only he was inside it, cocooned. Going somewhere, anywhere. The destination wouldn't matter, as long as he didn't have to bother with fools like Smyth once he got there.

'Which makes it, what, six weeks since she left? As I've told you, she hasn't telephoned or sent someone for her case.'

'Yes, well,' Smyth said, but stopped.

'Well *what*?' Ellis asked, but Smyth nodded.

'All in good time, sir.' The clock struck exactly as the doorbell rang. 'Would you hark at that?' Smyth said. 'Good time, indeed!'

Virginia went to answer it, returning with the man Ellis had noticed on the pavement. He was older than Smyth. Clean-shaven, with prominent cheekbones, a set, thin-lipped mouth and thick greying hair brilliantined back from his forehead. A narrow white-edged scar ran from just below his right ear down the line of his jaw, disappearing under a resolute, square chin. It made his head look like an outline, his face a child's paper mask waiting to be cut out and coloured in.

'. . . so you are that Morris!' Virginia was saying. 'How thrilling! I've seen your name in the newspaper. Shall I ring for tea?' She pressed the button, though Ellis knew as well as she did that Virginia would have to go ('Oh, these wretched bells! Nothing is working for me today!') and make it herself. She looked relieved when the inspector declined, forcing Smyth reluctantly to follow suit. 'I heard on the wireless that the search for the torso murderer is expected to bear results any day.'

'The chaps in Devon got him late last night, Lady Spender,' Morris replied. 'Scotland Yard have the pleasure of Alastair Harper's company now. He was dossing down in a disused hide on Dartmoor, and in a very poor state indeed, so I'm told. Admitted everything.'

Smyth nodded approvingly. 'A red-letter day for police work. Harper will get the rope, mark my words!'

'You must be a fan of *Alice in Wonderland*, Constable,' Virginia remarked tartly. 'It appears you are familiar with the words *sentence first, verdict afterwards*.'

Inspector Morris sat down. 'Smyth has filled you in on Miss Gouldstein's real name and employment, I take it.'

Virginia nodded unhappily. 'I don't see why she bothered with the Lyceum at all, if she wasn't much more than a char there.'

Here was an opportunity, Ellis decided. 'She wanted to be an actress.' You fool, he thought immediately. Did anyone notice his past tense? No. He'd got away with it.

'All the girls these days think that working in a theatre or picture house will get them into the movies,' Smyth agreed. 'Crazy for the movies, they are. My missus was saying as much the other week. It was in her magazine.'

His eyes resting briefly on Ellis, Morris removed a small dark-grey object from his satchel and placed it on the table. The small lump appeared to shift, the shape resolving itself into a shrunken glove. White streaks patterned the calfskin, and the decorative stitching around the cuff was filthy. A narrow tear along one seam made it look as though the tiny creature had been eviscerated, its entrails sucked out through a single fingertip. 'Do you recognise this?' Morris asked.

'Should we?' Virginia replied.

'With the heavy rain over the last while, and a build-up of uncleared leaves, a drain at Victoria Embankment near Middle Temple Gardens flooded last week.' He lifted the pathetic glove and turned it inside out, exposing its grubby, stained interior. 'Do you see this laundry mark? Walton

Lodge Laundry. One of the Walton girls recognised it, and the name in their book is that of Janet Gouldstein. She had been using the laundry for some time, and was in the habit of conversing with one girl in particular, who told us Miss Gouldstein worked as a dance hostess at an establishment called the, uh . . .' he paused for a second to recall the name '. . . the Bat. Enquiries at the Bat revealed that she hasn't been seen there since early on Friday morning, April the first. She mentioned to one of the other girls she would be in to collect her wages that evening at six, but would not be working there again because she was going away. She asked this young lady to keep it secret because she hadn't given notice. The guv'nor has a reputation for being difficult with his girls, I'm told.'

Ellis mentally replayed the list of items he'd taken from her bag, re-watching the carousel of her belongings pass through his fumbling, shaking hands as he transferred the money and Rollo Chatterton's receipt to one pocket, and the rest to another, waiting to be emptied, item by item, into bins on the street that evening. Why hadn't he noticed a glove was missing? Yet it was *only* a glove. An innocent man would be irate at a policeman even bothering him about it. He took a breath.

'So she cut out on two employers as well as us? And all in a single day! It's a disgrace. Why, she probably has debts all over town! That laundry you mentioned – I bet she owed them! And it's only a glove – my mother drops hers all the time, don't you, dear? All sorts, not just gloves.' He could hear himself beginning to gabble yet couldn't stop. If anything, he was gathering speed, hurtling into the path of a train on legs that refused to stop running, running, running . . . 'That cashmere scarf Minette sent at Christmas, do you remember? And you're forever losing handkerchiefs and—'

'Mr Spender!' Morris's voice was as forceful as a door slamming in his face. 'Walton Lodge Laundry isn't owed a farthing. And surely you don't believe a lost glove is a matter for the Metropolitan Police?' He reached into his satchel again.

'Oh!' Virginia's hand went to her mouth.

The handbag's black outer surface, which tapered out like the folds of a hard panelled skirt from a decorative metal clasp, was scratched and, like the glove, badly water-stained. The silver handle had worked loose on one side and was scraped, each thin score revealing its true dull lead colour underneath. Ellis cursed his choice of drain: he'd decided on it because it was obscured from the road by trees, which meant nobody could see him as he crouched over it. He had noticed at the time that the water level there and in the gutters was high, but he was so desperate to be rid of the bag and the coat he'd decided to take a chance. Oh, Lord, the coat! He'd clambered down the bank half a mile further downstream to throw it into the river. Surely it was safely lost. It had to be . . . He'd watched it sink with his own eyes, after all. Its pockets filled with stones, Janey's precious coat became a sleek skin disappearing into the brown, churned-up filth of the Thames. A selkie returning to its water home.

Would his fingerprints be still on the bag or would the water have washed them away? His hand was the only one to have touched it since Janey herself had carried it, or to have matched where her own fingers had once snapped open the clasp. It must have. The world rises and falls on the power of the infinitely little, and he shouldn't have allowed panic to make him careless with her bag. But, he reasoned, thinking quickly, hadn't he held the bag plenty of times for her when she was putting on her coat? Yes, of course he had! Stay calm, he reminded himself. There was nothing to tie these drowned objects to him.

'This bag came up in the flood and a street sweeper handed it in to the local station. There was a long tear in the fabric of the lining at the base, the glove must have slipped through and got stuck, as did this.' He retrieved Janey's tiny mirror from his briefcase and clicked its clasp. It glinted in the firelight as he angled it towards them, splayed open. When Ellis leant forward his reflection barely registered in its discoloured and tarnished surface. He moved closer still, yet his face was no more than a shadow, a discoloured smudge across the glass. He wanted to pick it up and hurl it across the room, unable to bear this cheap conjuring trick of objects any longer.

'Perhaps now,' Morris continued, 'you understand my concern. The position of the drain is approximately half a mile from the Lyceum theatre, which is where Miss Gouldstein was last seen on April the first by the doorman. She was in the building when he left to run an errand late in the afternoon. When he returned an hour later, she had signed out on the board. He himself left for the day shortly afterwards and didn't return until Monday morning. Lady Spender, are you sure these items belonged to Miss Gouldstein?'

'The bag and mirror are definitely hers. In fact, she noticed a tear in the lining that Friday . . . Her language was quite choice, as I recall. I can't say about the glove for definite, but as it was in the bag . . . What on earth do you suppose has happened?'

'Clearly, she's run off,' Ellis interjected, every inch of his body aching with the effort of feigning mild irritation rather than the terror he was really experiencing. 'But where to?'

'*Clearly?* From what I've just explained you think it's obvious she has gone somewhere of her own accord? That's interesting, Mr Spender, because I don't believe running off is the only possibility. Lady Spender, you told Constable Smyth that Miss Gouldstein seemed to have more money than usual in the weeks before you last saw her?'

'She had bought a lot of new clothes, yes.'

'Yet she received no increase in wages from either the Lyceum or the nightclub – though it seems to operate on more of a tips basis.'

'Gifts,' Smyth supplied, but Morris ignored him. 'To recap: Miss Gouldstein hasn't been seen since April the first. She failed to collect her wages or give notice at either of her places of employment. She took nothing from her bedroom here. There was no money or latch key in the bag, only this mirror and glove, both of which were trapped in the lining. It's possible that the bag was emptied and deliberately hidden in the drain rather than accidentally dropped. In consideration of these circumstances, foul play is a possibility.'

Ellis felt as though his brain might split in two with the effort of assimilating this information. Smyth sucked his teeth loudly and made a note (What? What on earth could the horrible man possibly be scribbling down?) in his little book.

Virginia gasped. 'How awful, Inspector. Truly. But I don't understand what it has to do with us.'

'I needed you to identify the bag and its contents as belonging to Miss Gouldstein during her time living here, Lady Spender. Which, thank you, you have done.'

Virginia nodded. 'It's the only one I've ever seen Janey – I mean Janet – use.'

Ellis twitched at the constant airing of her name, even in

this new, strange form. He'd have put his hands over their mouths if he could. Janey, his Janey, was dissolving entirely. Not only had she proved herself a liar and a fraud, but now she didn't even own the name he'd known her by.

'She had it with her the last time you saw her?' Morris asked.

'I didn't see her leave the house, but she must have, yes.' Virginia's nods were becoming smaller and more tired, the resigned acquiescence of a child who finally realises they are of no interest to the room.

'I'd like to speak to your other lodger now too, if I may.'

'He's not here. He's rarely home before eight. He tends to go for supper before returning.' She looked embarrassed, a seaside landlady caught being cheap with her guests, adding, 'His mother only requested breakfast.'

'Will you ask him to telephone Constable Smyth at the station to make an appointment to speak with us? In the meantime, I'd like to see Miss Gouldstein's things, if you please.'

'They're in the cellar,' Ellis said. 'A suitcase and a couple of small boxes.' He spoke more slowly now, careful to sound just right. 'We didn't want to dispose of anything in case she came back for them.' He had packed away what remained of Janey's existence in a matter of minutes, heaping her clothes into her suitcase, no longer thrilling to the secret touch of her belongings or desiring the connection he used to feel by simply standing in her room surveying the trappings of her life. After all, who would ever benefit from her belongings? What a strange waste death was, that it caused one's individuality and accomplishments to vanish instantly, while the tarnished glory of possessions faded slowly. The bed had been stripped weeks before, so whatever flakes of skin or strands of hair that were once trapped within Janey's sheets were long gone, sluiced away by the woman who came in to do the washing every Monday. As a king might approach his throne only to realise it was nothing more than an ordinary chair upholstered in cheap, gaudy velvet, the meaning and mystery of her had disappeared and could never be revived.

'Do you know Miss Gouldstein's age, Lady Spender?'

'Twenty-five I should think, or thereabouts.'

'Eighteen, according to the Waltons' laundress.'

The telephone pealed from the hallway and Virginia rushed out, returning moments later. 'For you, Inspector. No, he's rung off. Someone called Davis – at least, I think that was the name – has just arrived at the station and asked for you urgently.'

Morris gestured at Smyth to remove himself from the armchair. 'Thank you, Lady Spender. Perhaps you might have Miss Gouldstein's belongings ready for me to look at when I return in a day or so.'

'Ellis could fetch them up from the cellar now, if you'd prefer to take them away?'

'The station is a place of Metropolitan Police business, not a left-luggage office.' Morris's curt reply caused Virginia to blush again. She assumed deference – if not outright subservience – from men like Morris and Smyth as her due, and anything other than respect at a bare minimum left her at a loss.

Just as Ellis began to close the front door behind them, Morris turned to face him. Ellis swallowed hard, willing himself not to trip up. After a long pause, Morris said, 'Oh, and Mr Spender? Should anything strike you as pertinent to Miss Gouldstein's whereabouts, you will contact the station, won't you?'

'Of course, Inspector. Immediately.' He shut the door, unable to shake the horrible feeling that Morris was still on the doorstep, immobile and listening, waiting for him to let something slip. He took a deep breath and turned to his mother. 'What awful men. If you have a nervous attack it will be that inspector's fault for sure. I do hope you're not blaming yourself for any of this.'

'Blame myself?' Her eyes grew wide at this new prospect: until that second Virginia would have considered herself as playing no more part in Janey's disappearance than an audience member in the front row is responsible for the plot unfolding on the stage before them. 'Ellis, is this *my* fault? Should I have suspected something wasn't right? And she is so terribly young . . .' He watched his poisonous flower bloom, its ugly stalk creeping around her, holding her tight as its petals spread themselves wide.

'No! That's exactly what I said. It's *not* your fault.'

'But it's true, it is! I am to blame. It's my house, after all. Agreeing she could live here was a mistake. Patrick too.' Virginia's eyes filled. 'Why can't everything be as it was before Freddie left? Nothing has been right since he went away.' She began to cry softly. 'The poor girl, whatever can have happened to her?'

'It's not for you to worry about.' Ellis touched a hand to his mother's hair. How easily she could be made to crumble. An odd reversal had occurred, he thought. She was fading before his eyes just as the colours of his life were becoming rich and vibrant. The sketch of his desires he'd always carried around was finally being completed, every complex detail perfect. Whereas his father's portraits depicted the sitter as Sidney wanted them to be, and ignored tedious or ugly realities, Ellis had mastered the opposite technique: he would make his existence match a perfection he had so far only ever created on paper. He had privately begun to make plans to leave and was suddenly so sure of his future happiness that he despised his former self for ever having lacked such confidence: for being a man who moved along a narrow, high-walled track without ever comprehending the glorious landscape that unfolded in the sunshine just beyond the fences on either side of his path.

He tucked a loose strand of hair into place behind Virginia's ear, his hand grazing her earring. The pearl drop swayed to his touch, a single tear falling. Why couldn't everyone just forget about Janey? *Damnatio memoriae*, he thought. Her memory must also be condemned to death if she was truly to leave their house and lives. Only eighteen! It was impossible.

'Whatever happened to her, she brought it upon herself. No matter what those dullard policemen say, my bet is that she took off with some chap from the nightclub who promised her the moon and stars.' A very cheerful little idea was taking shape, one that would help distance him further from the problem of Janey (it was impossible to think of such a beautiful creature as a homely, humdrum *Janet*) and, into the bargain, deflate the irritating balloon that was Patrick. Morris deserved to be tricked too, for his rudeness to Virginia.

Safely alone in his study, it took a while to locate the single sheet Ellis was looking for because his desk was so cluttered, but he eventually found her – phantom Janey, newly pliant, reliable Janey – towards the bottom of a stack of waste paper he kept for kindling. He gently wiped the sheet with a handkerchief, being careful not to touch it with his bare hands afterwards, then slipped downstairs. Just as well he hadn't sent Virginia a letter of apology from Janey with a forwarding address. She'd have been sure to show it to the police.

The kitchen was in silence apart from the drip-drip of a tap. Cold and damp, the cellar stank of a perennial winter decay because no other season ever managed to penetrate its stone walls. The single bulb beside the steep steps that led to the scullery didn't even attempt to illuminate the entire space, abandoning its edges and corners to murky shadows. To step out of the thin spill of light was to vanish into a low-ceilinged, suffocating dark. He crouched uncomfortably and groped his way forward, relieved when his hands touched the case. As he fumbled with the lock, the gloom making it difficult to work the key in, a panicked rustle started up nearby. The case split open with a thud. He fell back on his heels and rushed to right himself.

She was everywhere around him at once, suddenly turned to a heady scent, a flash of amber gold rising through an inky, alien sky. His heart pounded. He inhaled an earthy, intoxicating smell. He sank one hand into the case, cheap lace pressing against his fingertips. It was damp. Perfume! The stopper in her Vol de Nuit must have worked loose. Oh, the irony of her choice of scent. A clue to her true intentions had been in front of him all along, he thought. Vol de Nuit: *night flying*. A phantom of the shadows, she was a vampire who roamed once day was done, but sucking fools' money rather than their blood.

He searched blindly through the case, every movement releasing further waves of perfume. His fingers touched the lock of the diary he'd given her, its tiny brass fastenings cold to the touch. He would take it back, he decided. She'd never deserved it anyway. He picked through her orphaned possessions until he found Patrick's chocolate box. Using his handkerchief, he lifted the sheet of paper he'd brought with him, folded it over and gently tucked it into the box. He repacked the case, leaving the chocolate box at the top, its lid slightly ajar.

In the pitch-dark, a page inside a box inside a case inside a room waited. Despite hating the very sight of the police – they reminded him of vampires, who also required an invitation to enter the house – Ellis wished he could be there when they confronted Patrick. He mentally reviewed the situation: Morris thought foul play was a possibility. That was bad. Smyth was a fool, Ellis had nothing to fear from him, but the inspector was cannier. Yes, he'd have to watch himself should he encounter Morris again. He was relieved that he had thought to change her slider in the Lyceum: the police sounded sure that whatever had happened to her had taken place once she left the theatre on Friday afternoon. Clearly no one was thinking to look for her *inside* the building, which had opened as a cinema three weeks earlier. He hadn't been himself – how could he revisit a place of such terror and pity? – but had seen an article about it in the newspaper. She could never be found now, he reassured himself. He must keep his nerve until Chatterton's money arrived and he could leave London. He had, he was beginning to realise, no intention of ever returning.

Later that day Ellis sat at his desk and began to compile a list of potential subjects for more Stoker stories. Creating the second narrative, the story of the discovery of *more* lost works, would be a greater challenge than writing the pieces. That was going to need a lot of thought. Oh, for another Janey, but an honest one! Why did life refuse to resemble its models? Ellis recalled Nanny's plodding emphasis on the importance of growing up to be responsible, of the rewards that accrued to the just. But existence followed no such rules; kindness was too fragile. On balance, a collection of shorter pieces was by far the best next step, he decided. A cache of lost short stories would be believable to discover, and hard to undermine as authentic. And, with *The Un-Dead Count* as primogenitor, other 'new' works would be more difficult to disprove because the book would become the essential reference for comparison. It was the same with paintings, he knew. Curators defended each new piece by reference to the last, so the simplest way to forge an artist would be to create a body of work and attribute it to one person, rather than eke out single pieces and watch them be examined individually and in isolation.

If anything, *The Un-Dead Count* made Stoker's own fiction more authentic, for without such a momentous find what true measure existed against which *Dracula* could be honestly measured? What better comparison than a sequel? To have created such a sublime book and be unable to assert himself as its creator was his only disappointment. But, he persuaded himself, originality was a pointless delusion, its insistence on purity tiresome and dishonest.

The doorbell rang. A woman, her back turned to him, her figure distorted in the stained glass. The collar on her coat was turned up so it touched her hat. He opened the door slowly. She didn't turn around for what felt like ages, though was probably only seconds. Blonde hair and pale, waxy skin, her lips a slick red bow. Christ, it was – '*Janey*,' he whispered, unable to stop himself. Idiot, he thought almost immediately. How could it be?

'That's who I'm here about.' Her accent was harsh. She was older than Janey, faint lines already etched around mouth and forehead. She was familiar, but he wasn't sure why. 'How d'you know that?'

'Who are you?' he asked.

'Stella Lloyd.'

'Janey's friend? She often mentioned a Stella. But she doesn't live here any more. Didn't you know? Did a bunk, you might say.'

'*You* might say it,' she said, adding, 'I didn't.' She removed her hat and smoothed her hair by holding her hand still and rubbing her head against her palm.

Of course! 'You're from the nightclub!' He paused, remembering the night in the Nest. 'But that doesn't make sense . . . I asked Janey who she'd been talking to, and she said she didn't know your name. She'd never met you before.'

'Sounds 'bout right.' Stella shrugged. 'She's the type who likes to keep things separate. Or maybe she didn't want a fancy chap like you knowing she consorted . . .' she pulled a face, teasing him with the word '. . . with nightclub hostesses? Hey, ain't you going to invite me in?'

What an appalling idea. 'My mother is due home any minute. Janey's awful behaviour upset her terribly, so I don't think she'd be happy to find a friend of hers here.' This is who Janey would have become in time, he thought, her looks settling into a pinched, brassy meanness. No, he corrected himself. This is who she already was. Her trajectory was set.

He recalled Janey mentioning Stella's breach-of-promise action. Some chump she'd tricked into it, no doubt.

'I ain't seen her since the end of March. Now, normally that'd be fine, everyone has their own life to live, as I say. But I'd taken myself to Brighton for a few days and she was s'posed to be joining me, only she never did. I thought maybe she'd gone off with a chap. She'd her eye on one in particular, handsome like yourself he is too, and I could hardly mind that, now could I? Only I still ain't heard from her, and neither have any of the other girls. I stopped by the Lyceum yesterday, and that old drunk on the door says the peelers was in asking about her. Found her handbag, he says.'

'The police called here too, but we couldn't help.'

'Couldn't or wouldn't?' Her eyes met his, her stare hard and even.

'What do you mean?' he asked.

'Janey told me as how you two had a racket going.'

'I don't know what you mean.'

'You know more than you're sayin'.'

'*Ellis?*'

Hell. The hedge was so overgrown it blocked the view of the path. He hadn't noticed Virginia open the gate.

'Who on earth is this?'

'I'm a pal of Janey's,' Stella answered, before he could speak.

'I see. And has Miss Gouldstein sent you for her case?'

'No, I ain't heard from her.'

'Neither have we. Now, please, go, or you will leave me with no option but to telephone for the police.'

CHAPTER 14

Since Patrick had announced his intention to go home for a holiday, Virginia had nagged Ellis about going to Ireland with him. He had continued to refuse, even when she offered to cancel her own trip to Carlsbad to fund it. But the second visit from the police, followed by the unexpected arrival of Stella like a spectre of Janey come to haunt him, changed his mind. Stella had left without another word when Virginia had told her to, but it was possible he hadn't heard the last of her. If only he could be sure how much she actually knew. Perhaps last year's breach of promise had given Stella a taste for blackmail and she was bluffing: considering the extent of Janey's lies and omissions, she was unlikely to have told her much. Either way, while he was still waiting for the balance of the money from Ralph Chatterton, he would be better off away from Fitzroy Gardens, and being limited in what he could yet finance for himself, why not take the ticket and spending money on offer? Virginia had been right all along, he finally conceded. He did need a break after months of work, adding, 'I'm annoyed with myself for not realising it earlier. Patrick is leaving in two days.'

'I'm sure it's not too late, Ellis. I can wire Minette now, and you can collect a ticket at the station.'

'Do you really think so? It seems awfully short notice.'

'No, not at all. Minette wrote twice to say she would be only too delighted to have you, and she was so disappointed when you refused.'

'I know,' Ellis said. 'I did feel horrid about that.'

'All the more reason to go, darling. You'll be leaving for Europe soon and I shall miss you desperately – I've been swanking about you terribly to all my friends, you know. A travel book about the Mediterranean is such a coup. It's bound to be a wild success, too – but that's a working visit, not a holiday. A short break first would set you up wonderfully.'

'You're quite right. What would I do without you? I have been tired recently and, as you say, Minette was so kind with her invitations.'

Delighted with his decision, Virginia hurried off, booking him to travel with Patrick and return alone five days later.

As Ellis was getting ready to leave for the train Ralph telephoned to say *The Un-Dead Count* had been definitively validated. Just as Ellis had assumed it would be, the authenticity of the first twenty-one chapters had been determined by the same two experts who had certified chapter twenty-two. Needless to say, it was declared to be a perfect match. Also, Ralph told him excitedly, they were entirely overwhelmed by its skill as a novel. Jaffe marvelled at what he called its 'contemporary relevance', while the curator from the British Museum was terrified by the book's depiction of intense dread and unease and 'the threat of obliteration that hangs like a dark cloud over this second generation', declaring himself shaken to the core by the characters' fears of invasion, the threat of sullied bloodlines, and its clamorous unease.

Ellis's heart filled with pride. When Rollo rang off he remained in the hallway, unwilling to replace the receiver and disconnect himself from such a rapturous conversation. Never once had he experienced such pure, untainted joy. He held the moment in his hand, the way a fortune-teller does a crystal ball, seeing in it only true, happy things.

Implying that impecunious family members would make life difficult for him should they discover his good fortune, Ellis made it a condition of the sale that he remained anonymous. Ralph agreed readily: the firm of Chatterton & Chatterton was only too happy to be considered solely responsible for this remarkable treasure trove. Ralph had begun to use the word 'unearthing', Ellis noticed, delighting in its subtle suggestion that the Chatterton brothers were vampire-slaying sleuths, dogged hunters of Stoker's lost work. Constable, *Dracula*'s original publisher, had expressed interest in buying *The Un-Dead Count*, as had Victor Gollancz, the fool who had rejected *Varnishing Day* just months before. Ellis didn't begrudge the Chattertons their profit: they deserved to make money, just as he had. Ralph had established contact with Noel Stoker, recently arrived home from the Continent, to discuss copyright and terms. Noel had given his seal of approval too, professing himself delighted that the sequel to his dear father's masterpiece had been discovered, and unwittingly adding to the book's provenance by commenting, 'my mother never truly believed that my father could willingly destroy his own work; she would have been so gratified by this exciting discovery'. The *Times Literary Supplement* had interviewed both Chattertons for an exclusive article, due for publication in a fortnight. Ellis listened enthralled as with each new opinion *The Un-Dead Count* became even more incontrovertibly genuine: the more experts who believed it real, the more real it became. While the whisper of one man would be easy to doubt, the heartfelt conviction of so many was irrefutable.

And in all of this there was nothing, absolutely nothing, to tie the book to Ellis.

'Which means,' Ralph had concluded the telephone call, 'that the balance of payment can now be issued.' Those words, so crisp and business-like, compounded Ellis's joy. The cheque would be waiting for him when he returned from Ireland. And, he reminded himself, there was valuable research to be done in Dublin, which would be necessary for the Stoker short stories. He and Stoker were united now, a conjoined force, but with *The Un-Dead Count* complete, Stoker's voice had fallen silent. As soon as he began the short stories, Stoker's imagination would return, he was sure of it.

His entire life had been building up to this. He was prepared. He thought suddenly of that day in the Royal Academy and the stinging barb of shame he'd felt while watching Sidney make minuscule corrections to the terrier's tongue. Ellis was his father's pentimento: scrubbed out and painted over. *Repentance!* Sidney Spender didn't know the meaning of the word.

Patrick's distress about the interrogation the police subjected him to proved more than enough compensation for Ellis having to put up with him as a travelling companion. What a shame he had spent the entire afternoon and evening of April first at the hospital so couldn't have been the last person to see Janey! Still, for an innocent man with nothing to fear, he made delightfully heavy weather of his conversation with Inspector Morris. Over and over during the train journey from Euston, and then again on the boat, Patrick returned to the subject of a note the police had found in Janey's case, which implied they might have been more than two strangers with a landlady and a bedroom wall in common. Delighted as Ellis was, even he found himself tiring of the subject of the surprising contents of the chocolate box after the first hour. It didn't help matters that Patrick alternated this conversational theme with a treatise about Ireland's status in what he insisted was the forthcoming war. Democracy was dying, he insisted. Only fools believed in everlasting peace. He talked on and on as the train rattled forward, pushing through the looming shadows of the countryside. The issue was not whether Ireland should remain neutral – for what attacking enemy would hesitate to give her a choice in the matter? – but the decision that had to be made.

'What decision?' Ellis asked.

'Whether she should throw in her lot with the democratic states or risk the alternative: being overrun by the combined forces of the dictators. Neutrality is impossible for a country such as Ireland. If we were to enter a war on the British side, our independence could be completely lost to the hands of the Nazis. And it would be our own fault for being so damn stupid as to join the losing side!'

'Both options sound unpleasant to me,' Ellis said, recalling the newspaper story about the heartbroken old woman's offer to pay for the screening of an anti-war film whose title he'd forgotten. 'And I'm not even sure the latter should be considered an option, anyway.' Even though he disliked most of Patrick's opinions, privately Ellis found himself agreeing with his assertion that a war was becoming more and more likely. It would be nothing on the scale of the previous one, obviously. How could it? The very idea was ridiculous. Ellis was determined that any such conflict wouldn't affect him: now that he was finally the master of his own destiny, he was determined he would find a way to evade its net entirely.

Patrick excused himself to go to the WC. Bored, Ellis leant across the table and opened Patrick's satchel in search of a newspaper. The latest edition of *Action* was folded inside the *Daily Telegraph*. An article headlined *Oxford Falls Upon Evil Times*, which described its graduates as 'the products of perversion', caught his eye: *British Union undergraduates*, it intoned, *yours is the task of driving from our Universities the filth and decay which a declining Social-Democracy brings in its wake. Yours is the task to rid our Oxfords and our Cambridges of their Left-Book Clubs, their Daily Workers, and the remaining impedimenta of the Pink and the Pansy.* Its rhythmic rhetoric irritated him. Vicious lullabies, preying on primitive emotions, seducing people into block-headed stupidity.

'What are you doing?' Patrick slid back into his seat.

'I was looking for something to read.' Ellis held up the newspaper. '*Britain for the British.*' He quoted the masthead. 'What's a British Union rag got to do with an Irishman?'

'Can't a man be interested in the affairs of the country he's living in? You would benefit from looking beyond your own walls, Ellis. You might see that politics doesn't respect borders or citizenship.'

With a shrug, Ellis pushed the newspaper across the table. The last thing he wanted was another pompous lecture. They sat in silence as the train rattled through the Welsh countryside. 'So, you think,' Patrick asked after a while (and not for the first time), 'that Janet really *did* have intentions towards me?'

'Yes. Definitely.' Ellis nodded. He pictured the note the police had found in the suitcase, a single sheet of paper with nothing other than the handwritten words *Miss Janey Gould*, and underneath, *Mrs Patrick Arcourt.* He could see it as clearly as if it rested on his lap in place of the newspaper. As clearly, in fact, as the day he had written it, in pitch-perfect imitation of her handwriting. *Cheeky sod.* She'd laughed, red lips peeling back over her white teeth. Ellis was looking out the window, glancing at everything, at nothing. As the train passed a large stone farmhouse, the first building for miles, a light came on in an upstairs room. A woman was suddenly illuminated in a window, staring out at the tracks, her silhouette as clear as if shot through by lightning. He saw her for only the briefest second yet was sure he would have known her anywhere from then on, as long as he lived, as if some current had passed between them, a secret exchanged.

The seat under him wobbled slightly as the train wound a wide arc around the base of a hill. 'Janey had a particular way of watching you from across the table. I often observed it, though of course it was none of my business what the two of you did together, so I would never have said anything that might have drawn attention to it.'

'But we *did*, as you put it, nothing together!' Patrick protested. He was torn, Ellis could tell, between his desire to indulge the newly legitimised erotic thrill that the beautiful woman in the bedroom next door genuinely had been attracted to him, and the necessity to distance himself from the lying lodger who danced with strange men – and who knew what else? – for money. Patrick was desperate to reminisce about the ways in which she must have fallen for him, while equally desperate not to be implicated in any way in either her manner of living or her disappearance. To be fair, Ellis thought, that would be a tricky balance for any man, and Patrick was not the chap to pull it off with aplomb.

'Anyway,' Patrick had reached an end to the subject many times only to resuscitate it once more, 'as I told the police, I was in surgery so obviously my movements are accounted for.' He paused, petulant as a child who has been told to pass a beloved toy to another to play with.

'But didn't that patient die?' Ellis enquired.

'The patient was not the alibi I was referring to,' Patrick snapped. 'As you well know!'

Once settled on the boat Patrick went in search of a meal, and Ellis walked the deck alone, his footsteps in harmony with the ship one minute, willing it to Ireland, then the next a narrow current running contrary to it. The vessel pushed along with a regular, bullying rhythm. The sea was choppy, and though Ellis was aware of the force of the water rising high against the prow, the ship continued to attack the waves, its passage as imperious and impartial as that of a tank. While he waited for the milky flank of the Irish coast to emerge over the horizon, he pictured himself on a sleek liner steaming towards New York rather than the night mail-boat to Dublin with only Sawbones for company. How wonderful it would be to sit in a stylish suite, tantalisingly fresh beads of condensation forming on a cocktail shaker, happily readying himself for a visit from new, boat-made friends. Some day, he promised himself. Soon.

Many tedious hours later, on the pavement outside Cousin Minette's home on Lower Baggot Street, Ellis and Patrick parted company. The Arcourts' house was across the road, three doors up. Patrick pointed it out but, to Ellis's relief, didn't issue any invitations to visit. Doubtless Ellis would be dragged over there by Minette soon enough, so he wasn't particularly inclined to make his own arrangements.

Cousin Minette, the youngest of a spindly branch of Broughton cousins, had spent her life in the home she was born in. Its inhabitants had slowly died or left until, as the last surviving member, she was alone. A tall and narrow Georgian mid-terrace, her house was less down-at-heel than Ellis's, yet the exterior had a similar quality of a slow, peeling descent from grace. It had a decidedly more subdued presence than some of its neighbours – including the Arcourts, whose neat-as-a-uniform navy-blue door stood to attention across the road, the polished door brasses sparkling like fool's gold in the May sunshine. Minette's house and the three on either side of it were covered with some sort of dense creeper, its small leaves too bright a green to be ivy. The rain that had greeted them from the boat had stopped and a wind had got up instead, turning and twisting the leaves so they twinkled like sequins in the sun.

It was almost twenty-five years since Ellis had last been in Ireland, and the scant memories he retained of his previous visit were distorted, barely animated flickers, a confusion of sights and unfamiliar smells and voices. He'd been sent away almost immediately after Lucy's death: Nanny told him she was taking him to cousins in Dublin the following day, and when they returned, two months later, it was as though his sister had never existed. For the first year or so he was liable to get confused, wondering if he had conjured up the pretty baby who was there but then gone, never to be mentioned again. Perhaps she was a friendly ghost who had come to keep him company only to be called away to look after some other lonely boy. But in time even imaginary-Lucy began to fade, becoming ever more dreamlike, until by the time he went away to school he had more or less forgotten her.

Standing outside Minette's house, he recalled the feeling of Nanny's large chapped hand wrapped around his own, of being queasy and tired from the journey but also aware of a cold confusion, a horrible clenching feeling that had taken residence deep in his stomach. Neither Sidney nor Virginia had said goodbye. After the first week he began to wonder if *he* was somehow responsible for his sister being alive one day and not the next. Had he been rough and hurt her? Somehow wished death upon her? As the days passed, he became increasingly certain that he would never see his mother again either. Though he had very little memory of where he went or what he did during those weeks in exile, he knew he had spent most of the holiday worried and alone in an unfamiliar nursery. Nanny came from a village just outside Dublin, and was so happy and distracted to be as good as at home that she was completely oblivious to his wordless distress. To make matters worse, she was ensconced on the floor above instead of being, as he was used to, with him or in the room next door.

Standing alone in an unfamiliar place outside a house he

hadn't visited for more than two decades, he felt horribly aware of his sister – not of Lucy herself exactly, but more of the fact of a sibling's existence. Her long death was a sudden intrusion into his life, as though the two had been diligently, secretly, playing out in parallel all these years and could easily become intertwined. It troubled him to wonder what part the past was playing in his present.

As Patrick crossed the road, a young girl with a dog clutched tight under one arm rattled open a high window and shouted something unintelligible before slamming it shut again. The front door opened almost immediately, shrieks of delight clearly audible from across the street. Patrick and his suitcase disappeared, swallowed by arms and barking and excited shouts. Finally alone, Ellis glanced up and down the pavement. Baggot Street was wide and pleasant, two straight-backed terraces of narrow houses, Lower and Upper separated from each other by a stone bridge. It was quite different from the oppressive stillness of Fitzroy Gardens, where tall, densely planted hedges and trees created barriers between its row of houses and the pavement that wound to Hampstead Lane. Here, each house opened straight onto the street, with only a short set of steps and a small railed basement area creating a void between the front façade and passing pedestrians. St Stephen's Green, its duckpond one of the few places Ellis vaguely remembered from his previous visit, was about a mile further on.

He glanced at Minette's windows, each identically swagged and draped in a complicated arrangement of lace and trimmed with ribbon. As with its neighbours, the house was constructed of a soot-stained yellowish brick, with two sets of paned windows on each floor. The steps led to a heavy-looking panelled door with a fanlight above it. Despite the fussy dressings, the overall effect was of a forlorn quality conferred by years of never-quite-enough attention. Not neglect exactly, more a genteel acceptance that its best days were over. A figure with one arm half raised was staring down at him from a small attic window. Through the lace he could just make out a round face, framed with pale hair, but not the woman's features. Flashes of sunlight bounced red and orange from the glass, obscuring his view. Two floors below, a first-floor curtain twitched, telling him someone else had observed him. He sighed and picked up his suitcase.

The door was opened by a young woman who introduced herself as the housekeeper, Mary. She wore a shawl over a cardigan over an apron over a jumper over a dress: did these many layers mean the house was freezing? Minette's small, stooping frame looked lost behind Mary's sturdy, padded body. A girl, her thin mousy hair tied so tightly back it must have hurt her scalp, hovered in the hallway, apparently nonplussed at being summoned up to be presented to 'the gentleman Mr Ellis Spender, our very special guest'. She wobbled into a quick, awkward bob, then stared at the floor until Mary grasped her upper arm and marched her downstairs. Two servants! And ones who could be relied upon to present themselves, clean and deferential, for inspection by guests! Virginia would bristle with jealousy when she heard.

Minette received him as a man lost in the desert greets an unexpected and lush oasis. In person she was true to her letter-writing style: busy and emphatic, every pronouncement and statement underlined with a supplementary opinion or undermined by a challenge or question. Her conversational style was remarkably self-reliant. Was it the lack of companionship in later life that had made her so, he wondered, or a surfeit of older, opinionated people around her as a child?

In her first-floor sitting room, while Minette busied herself with the spirit lamp and a complicated arrangement of plates and doilies and tray cloths, Ellis glanced over the newspaper on her reading table. How entirely parochial a neighbouring country's news was, even when the reports had protagonists in common. What with its quaint advertisements for second-hand furniture, agricultural demonstrations and advance booking notices for films that had already been and gone in London, the *Irish Times* could have been any regional newspaper. Laughing, he read aloud a short piece about a man posing as a priest in a wealthy parish in Ballsbridge ('Sure that's only up the road,' Minette said). This imposter had been hearing confessions and instructing sinners to donate to the poor box in the church porch as they left. He'd made seven pounds in two days. What admirable opportunism, Ellis thought, and with the added pleasure of duping the fools into believing themselves absolved. 'It did seem a bit off,' an unnamed penitent commented, 'when he told me to say twenty-seven Hail Marys. The usual chap only ever gives the one Our Father.'

An advertisement for a new Blue Star Line cruising liner caught his eye: an eighteen-day tour from thirty-two guineas, calling at Algiers, Naples and Malta. One to consider, he thought, as was the weekly P&O mail steamer calling at Southampton on its way to Bombay or Japan. The address listed was Cockspur Street, and he decided to write away for a brochure, so it would be waiting for him when he got home.

The room was as busy as Minette's letters, an incoherent

babble of ornaments, furniture, dowdy oil paintings and great towers of newspapers and magazines. He craned his head towards the Arcourts' house, uncomfortably aware of feeling like a friendless child spying on a more popular boy at school. The lace curtains filtered the daylight, turning the air around them opaque, creating a place of shadow and smoke. Minette was like a once-loved toy, now forgotten and abandoned to rot in an outgrown nursery. As with the rest of the house, the room was high-ceilinged and divided into pockets of extreme heat or extreme cold, depending on how close to the fire he sat. The wallpaper below the dado rail was a nondescript milky colour, its design faded and indecipherable, but above it was an interlocking pattern of leaves, long and thin as reeds, a chaotic explosion of blacks and thick, rotting greens. On the ceiling six feet above him, ornate plaster figures growing from floral borders gurned down, their cherubic faces smeared with dust and cobwebs. The two servants aside, Minette was a model of the type of old-fashioned gentility that was scared of penury without ever really suffering it, yet suffered it anyway because living in the fear of it for years had eventually rendered it true. Would his mother's situation have been similar had she not had a beautiful face and gone to London in search of a suitable husband? Society viewed Virginia's life the more successful, yet Minette was considerably better off.

Despite describing herself as 'only desperate for news of London and our dearest Virginia', her monologues gave him little opportunity to update her on the city or his mother. She had a lot to say on the subject of Patrick Arcourt, his myriad talents and achievements, most of which was already tediously familiar from her correspondence and Patrick himself. Not being required to contribute to the conversation suited him, though, as he was tired and hungry after the journey. She would fix on specific personal details (the local fishmonger's missing finger; a neighbour's outrageous hemlines) and, without offering any proof why, treat them as codes, suggestive of deeply held convictions or attitudes (the fishmonger was as careless with his customers' change as he was with his own knife; the neighbour wasn't to be trusted near any woman's husband). Minette, he decided, was someone for whom the passing of each uneventful day reinforced the lie that everything would for ever remain entirely knowable, unchanged and unchangeable. She had no idea that the world could change at speed, turning inside out on a sixpence or a lie.

Quite quickly, she lodged herself firmly within the subject of death, a topic with which she was extremely familiar and which appeared to give her enormous satisfaction. She described the final illnesses and unexpected demises of many people he'd never heard of with such detail that he began to imagine these recent dead filling the room, as though Minette shared her house, lit and unlit corners alike, with muted friends and relatives. Another Arcourt, an ailing elderly great-uncle of Patrick's now nearing the end of his life, received top billing. 'He never married,' Minette concluded, having already reviewed his early years, long career as a judge, and those whom she expected to be at his funeral service when the time came. 'He once had the most enormous pash on Florence Lemon Balcombe, but she was engaged to marry . . .' she blushed, and mouthed the next words, as if too scandalised, or too nervous of being overheard by the invisible phantoms that surrounded her, to permit them breath '. . . that awful

Oscar Wilde. Those Wildes! Aptly named, believe you me. A desperate family.' Reinstating her earlier volume of speech, she added, 'But Florence was no fool. Didn't she catch hold of Bram Stoker instead and move to London, and that, as they say, was that.'

It was strange to hear such familiar words fall from her mouth, her soft accent a butter knife across Bram's name. 'You knew the Stokers?'

'I never did meet Bram as it happens, though his brother Thornley – he's dead years, the poor man – and my brother Jonathan used to be very tight. Your mother and I knew the younger Balcombes well as children. Florence could be quite a one, forever batting those eyelashes of hers.'

'I remember her as very amusing. Kind, too.'

'Not to everyone, she wasn't.' Minette's thin lips folded inwards, her voice acidic. This was an old spite clearly, one cured to perfection by time. 'It must be a year since she passed. Your mother wrote.'

'Yes.' He nodded. 'She was very upset. Uncle Freddie was also.'

'Was he? Hmm. Frederick is still away on his travels or whatever, I take it.' Her voice – *was he? . . . or whatever* – had shifted again and Ellis regarded her carefully, trying to decode her tone. Was it possible that Minette, too, saw through Freddie's fakery and lies?

'The last we heard, he had left New York for Hollywood.'

'America is a big place, so I'm told.' Big enough for Freddie to get lost in permanently, he thought, suspecting she would agree were he to voice the thought.

'Bram Stoker's book *Dracula* – you know it, of course?'

He nodded, becoming accustomed to her jumps back to

pick up on a previous topic. He had originally assumed it was because she wasn't sure of the conclusion and wanted to rewrite the conversation, then began to wonder if in fact, because she was so unused to regular company, she knew there would be no opportunity to correct a misapprehension later. Minette was a woman, he decided, who probably believed herself a devout keeper of confidences, yet could be relied upon to tell anything and everything to anyone who asked.

'There was a woman, Thornley told Jonathan, so I have this on the very best authority, who claimed *she* was after writing *Dracula*, and hadn't Bram only gone and stolen it from her! It's a woman's book, she said.'

As if Stoker would steal from anyone! 'A woman's book?' Ridiculous idea.

She pursed her lips. 'Whatever that means. I never liked Florence,' she added, doubling back on herself once more.

'Why?'

'I overheard her once telling your mother that I wasn't pretty. *Minette has nice, quiet manners, which is something, I suppose,* she said.' She flushed, her jaw set and tense.

He wanted to ask her how long it was since she had last had a visitor. A pause grew between them instead, a silence that seeped out from the walls, draping itself heavily around his shoulders and breathing in his ear. Desperate to push it away, he said, 'I didn't know you had a companion, Minette,' recalling the pale-haired face he'd seen at the window.

'Whatever do you mean?'

'When I arrived this morning, I saw a woman looking out from the top floor.'

She placed her saucer on the tray, the cup rattling slightly. Tea splashed, a brown stain discolouring the white cloth. 'The attics are empty. Haven't I been living alone these last thirteen years?'

After a day and a night in Minette's house, Ellis discarded any thoughts of treating himself to a hotel on the pretext of an unexpected invitation from a friend. His bedroom was old-fashioned but comfortable, which appealed to him, and Mary's food, though plain, was excellent. He felt agreeably alone: safe, not enclosed. Minette was eager to help him plan a daily itinerary, then discuss its implementation and execution in detail afterwards. She had some sort of internal complaint, referred to with an awkward expression and the words 'a spot of bother', and needed plenty of rest, so he was spared the trouble of having to fend off her company. He was already in a hotel, he realised, so why waste his money going to another? All the talk of the possibility of war meant he should plan for the longer term, so the more he could save now, the better off he'd be.

On the basis that a day that didn't go anywhere ended much the same as every other, he asked nothing of himself. By comparison with home, the streets had a hollowed-out quietness. A couple of days passed, calm, pleasant days in which he strolled around Dublin, stopping here or there to sit with a newspaper or book. It was as though the city centre had been constructed using only a limited colour palette, which he preferred to the garish lights of home. He enjoyed the fact that the streets lacked, as Stoker had written of London, *the muffled roar that suggests the life of a great city*. Dublin was made of sky, its grey domed roof scattered with clouds that loomed over the buildings or scudded blithely over good and bad alike, ignorant of the gladness and sorrow that flowed beneath.

On Sunday morning he walked down Baggot Street towards St Stephen's Green without seeing a single open shop, tea-room or restaurant. He was surprised to come across a crowd, until he noticed the church behind them. A service had just ended and people were streaming out, some fervently blessing themselves, eyes downcast, hands incessantly touching foreheads, breasts, mouths. He found Catholic devotion excessive and distasteful. He couldn't understand such fervent idolatry, though some of the churches were beautiful, with stained-glass windows that glowed like treasure chests. Who had designed them? he wondered. Who cared about the detail of their construction? They were monuments without signatures, each alone in its anonymous glory.

That afternoon, he strolled around the grounds of Trinity College, paying particular attention to the buildings he thought Bram Stoker would have frequented during his student days. The quadrangle was quiet, and the endless tide of young men he would have expected to encounter during a weekday, that restless, rustling stir and movement caused only by undergraduates in a hurry either to a lecture or escaping one, was absent. He patrolled the campus for an hour, noting his observations in a small journal. While these lines had no particular purpose – aside from possibly proving useful for provenance and authenticity in the Stoker short stories – they felt vital to the future somehow. Each page he filled became a promise to himself, a tether to as-yet-unimaginable experiences. No matter that the line lay slack: that it existed was enough. He held it in his hand and would pull it taut soon enough. The entire visit was an interlude, he decided, a necessary division between the tedium of his past and the glittering excitement of the life to come.

He visited the National Gallery and amused himself by imagining what his father would have made of its collections. A newish Yeats painting of a huge gathering watching the last moments of a swimming race in the river Liffey would have given Sidney a bilious attack, which made Ellis admire its fluid lines and loose, generous style all the more. Sidney would never have located himself, the superior artist with his superior vision, among the thick of the flat-capped, cheering crowd, pressed tight against the river wall. The figures in the water were blurred, the artist's charged palette creating an impression of the swimmers' strong, pale shoulders and lean, unseen limbs, of gasping mouths desperate for breath.

Minette mentioned that the Stoker brothers had once lived nearby, so he walked to their former home too, and stood outside on the path for a few minutes, until a woman polishing the railings shook her cloth at him.

Though the weather had been mild and bright, the parks full of flowers and birdsong, the morning of his last full day began cold and dreary, a high wind whistling through the gaps in the window frames. He had woken from a nightmare, sweating and uncomfortable, his legs trapped in a tangle of blankets. In his dream he was standing behind a woman with long hair, which was pale but not the fixed platinum blonde of Janey's. The woman's skin was the colour of fresh snow, as though she – whoever she was – had grown to adulthood without ever knowing sunlight. He'd grabbed her hair from behind so as to turn her around to face him, but it continued to pour down from her head, silky and snakelike, slipping through his hands as he tugged and tugged, unable to get any closer to her. Hair began to wrap like a rope around his shins then his knees, moving higher and higher up his body until he could feel it tight around his groin and up, compressing his chest. He made a final lunge and grasped her. She had a baby's face. Lucy's face, her eyes shut tight.

He lay in bed watching a thin blue sky break while he waited for the nightmare to drain from him. He needed fresh air so after breakfast, on the advice of his guidebook, he decided to visit a scholars' library a half-hour walk away.

He went through the graveyard of St Patrick's Cathedral, following a winding path past the gravestones to a flight of narrow stone steps and the sign for Marsh's Library. An acrid smell of animal glues rose from an open window in the basement bindery. Ellis walked through the first of two long galleries, in which ornate oak bookcases, each finished with a carved gable, sliced the main passageway through the room in half and drew him on towards a gloomy interior that ended abruptly at a narrow window. It was curtained, the lace reminding him of Minette's attic. How foolish he was, he thought, recalling the face at the window in Minette's house. On his first evening there he had quietly slipped upstairs alone, and discovered that the woman he'd seen was nothing more than an oval white-framed mirror propped up on an unused dressing-table in front of the window, half hidden by the drop of the lace curtain. He had stopped in the doorway and looked into the room. No wonder it was strangely familiar: it was where Nanny had slept, all those years before.

Three tall narrow cages, in which readers of rare books

were once customarily locked, sat empty and lightless, their wire frames cold to the touch. With no one to tell him not to, he stretched out one hand, running his fingertips down a row of gilt-inset brown leather spines, pausing at a thick volume entitled *Touching Witches*. He slipped it down from the shelf and opened it at the title page. Marsh's Library was more than three hundred years old; Stoker must have visited it. Perhaps he had once stood in the same spot, touched the same spine, read the very same words silently to himself, just as Ellis was doing now: *An Advertisement to the Jury-Men of England, Touching Witches, Together with A difference between English and Hebrew witches.*

'Handling material without permission is expressly forbidden.' Ellis jumped. A librarian had appeared soundlessly beside him. 'A treatise on astrology and magic in the prediction of political events,' he continued, with the weary air of a man surprised to wake up every morning and find himself not dead. 'Which must have been a perilous occupation for those involved in its practice.' He took the book from Ellis's hand. 'We request that all scholars discuss their requirements with us in advance, as books must be signed in and out by myself.' A slight rustling from above caused Ellis to glance up. The ceiling was shadowy and still, yet the noise continued. 'Bats,' the man said, and sighed. 'We'll never be free of them.'

Ellis apologised and left. He paused to glance through the Visitors' Book on the desk near the door. An entry on April the first caught his eye: *What a world it is, that a library is full of things which we cannot understand, yet which are.* The signature was indecipherable, and he wondered briefly whose invisible steps he was treading in; which man's pen was marking this page on the same day he had followed Janey to the Lyceum.

He set off for Baggot Street, walking quickly through a misty drizzle. He would begin to pack when he returned to Minette's, he decided, for he was leaving the following day and they were invited to the Arcourts' for supper that evening, with Patrick's parents and sisters. At least Patrick wouldn't be at home, now that he and his brothers were plodding up and down hills somewhere in the north. He had neither seen nor heard from him before he left, which was irritating: Ellis had been expecting Patrick to pester him with invitations, and had anticipated the precise level of ire such neediness would create. But nothing! Not a word. The annoyance he had prepared himself for had never occurred, which was, of course, even more annoying. Minette had insisted on taking him across the road to meet Patrick's parents within hours of his arrival, but he hadn't seen them since either.

Alice Arcourt, a stout woman with a soft voice, was pleasant, unchallenging company. Customarily deferential to men, she was doubly so with him, as an Englishman. Ellis disliked her husband, whose many and varied opinions danced through a bewildering range of topics, each pronouncement delivered with the same thin-lipped smile. Older people had always been easy for Ellis: at prep school his combination of politeness and deference could disarm the most hardened visiting grandee father or cheerless snob of a mother. It was his contemporaries he constantly struggled with, as though they could somehow see through him, to where his heart was missing, its place taken by a glass substitute. He had tried often to reshape himself, modelling his reactions on other people's, yet he knew he was never quite able to carry it off. In the past he had noticed new acquaintances looking at him curiously, apparently puzzling over his purpose in their company, as if they couldn't be sure what he wanted, or was for. Patrick's youngest sister Eileen had dropped into a blushing curtsy when she was introduced to him, prompting him to wonder had Minette made the Spenders sound like minor royalty. When she went to help with the tea things, Alice Arcourt smiled and touched his arm gently. 'I think you've taken Eileen's fancy, Ellis! And sure, who could blame her?' His expression must have betrayed some horror, because she frowned and, looking uncomfortable, said, 'My apologies, I'm after embarrassing you,' and turned away, fussing about Minette being too far from the warmth of the fire.

Minette was standing at a ground-floor window, one hand holding the lace curtain aside. She was staring at the street like a cat stalking a small bird. As soon as she spotted him she began to wave something, he couldn't make out what. A handkerchief? No: a piece of paper. Flushed and excited, she appeared on the top step hopping from foot to foot, the page flapping in her hand.

'A telegram! Almost an hour since. Ellis, I've been going mad waiting on you!'

With the thin sheet waving like a white flag, he could make out only the word *STOP*. And suddenly he was made of lead, his blood thick and pounding, his legs weighted, their joints rusted. He grabbed the iron railing that ran alongside the steps. The very movement of his arm as he reached out felt like an unravelling.

Janey, her sealskin coat rising through a great press of water, bulging and distorted, its swollen arms splayed wide as an eagle as it floated down the river in search of her.

'London?'

Minette nodded, her eyes wide, cheeks suffused pink. She was overwhelmed by the fleeting sense of importance that possessing information generates, and desperate to tell him, even though the very act of doing so would leave her powerless once more.

'From your mother!'

Janey undead, her body pushing up through the masonry and rubble, bloodied and vengeful. Her strength building now, possessed.

His lungs were empty. He was choking.

'It's your uncle.'

Janey, falling backwards once more, her bloodied head striking the floor hard. Her attempt at rising from the grave thwarted, stones pelting down on her.

'Freddie?' He gulped. 'What about him?'

CHAPTER 15

'He's back!' Minette's words lodged in his mind, immobile as a stone. All evening at the Arcourts, while he ate and drank and answered questions about London, as though he was an explorer just returned from the jungle, he was two creatures: polite, charming Ellis, thoughtful guest and kindly companion to his elderly relative; and a panicked animal, backed into a corner, prepared to snarl and bite its way out. He found himself thinking of the torso murderer hiding on the Devon moors: had the man ever realised that hiding was simply another form of *waiting*?

As the long and tedious supper wore on, Patrick Arcourt senior refused to abandon the subject of politics, no matter how unforthcoming Ellis was in his responses. Like father, like son, he thought. The newly signed treaty, which returned several ports to Ireland, was, according to Arcourt, a British ploy, a dowry of sorts to buy the nation's goodwill when war broke out and the British would need to shelter under Ireland's flank. Ellis sighed inwardly but nodded along, keeping his responses to vague murmurs. They slowly bade goodnight to the Arcourts at ten, accompanied across the road by Alice Arcourt's repeated exhortations to send her very best regards and sincere thanks to his mother. Minette, who rarely ventured out in the evening, went straight to bed, exhausted from three hours of ceaseless gossip and speculation about her entire acquaintance.

Ellis would have set off for home immediately if he could, but he had to wait. With the curtains open and the lamp switched off, he sat on the edge of his bed for hours, smoking, staring at the Arcourts' house across the road. He watched its windows go dark one by one until only a small yellow flicker from the attic told him anyone was awake. The servant, he supposed, though Patrick's curtsying sister Eileen, a soft-spoken, shy girl, whose intelligent but tired eyes spoke of late nights reading in poor light, seemed more likely to be up when the house had finally fallen still. The street lamps were of poor quality, nothing like at home, and Baggot Street lay swaddled in a soupy blackness. Perhaps it wasn't there at all.

'Well, how about that!' Minette said, more than once, the following morning, after she had wrung dry her memories of the previous evening, and was ready to move on to other topics. 'Frederick back from his sprees! Your dear mother is only thrilled. Beside herself.' He nodded curtly, resisting the impulse to question just how Minette had deduced quite so much from a telegram that read only FB HOME STOP ALL LOVE STOP V STOP. But he knew she was right: Virginia was giddy with pleasure. *All love* told him so.

He began to feel physically uncomfortable in Minette's company during those last few hours. Her house became oppressive, its long-dead phantoms wrapping themselves around his ankles, like mist, murmuring and muttering, bemoaning their unending, unwanted existence. He could think of no errand that would take him outside, no last thing to see or do or buy. Everything Minette said, every speculation about Freddie, about where he had been and what he had been up to, made him uncomfortable.

On the boat he stayed on deck. Later, while the train pushed through the countryside, the horrible thought returned over and over, its motion matching the clack-clack of the carriage on the tracks beneath: *He's back.* On the train he began to collect himself once more, and calmly consider the possible scenarios that might await him. Assuming that his mother had sent the telegram within a day of Freddie's sudden appearance in Fitzroy Gardens, it was unlikely he had looked through the Marsham Court boxes, not to mention audited their contents. Even if Freddie did notice that things were missing, Ellis could blame the incompetent removal men. Virginia would be sure to back him up. No matter how many times he reminded himself that Freddie had abdicated all rights to his possessions, he knew his uncle would never honour his note if it suited him to do otherwise.

Freddie was an ugly mirror, which made Ellis uncomfortable and self-conscious. When he was a child, guests often commented on the strong resemblance between them, adding something horrible, such as 'You shall grow up just like him, I'm sure!' He'd hated it, appalled that he was either the same as Freddie or a younger, diminutive version. What was it people believed they noticed in *him*, Ellis used to wonder, to see a plausible young surrogate for a monster? A man who was always able to insinuate himself into places he shouldn't. Lives he shouldn't, rooms he shouldn't. When Ellis and Nanny finally went home to London from Dublin after Lucy's death, Freddie began to visit the Spenders' house more often. He had few memories of Freddie before then, and far too many after. Freddie was a whisper in the dark, a hand under a sheet, a shudder of damp, woody, tobacco-scented breath.

Ellis hated his uncle. The thought had the power of a fine blade pressed to his skin. He felt powerful then, filled with a purity that a single, perfect realisation brings.

Yes. He hated him.

CHAPTER 16

Ellis was rummaging in his pockets for his latch-key when the front door swung open. Without moving his feet, Freddie leant to one side until his shoulder came to rest against the door jamb. Freddie wasn't a drunk (at parties he was often the only man in the room *not* tipsy, which Sidney had always found deeply suspicious, as though sobriety was nothing more than the perpetuation of a sly trick on one's companions) but he had a sot's confidence, the bone-deep belief that the world would forever turn, and effortlessly, just for him, no matter what. Perhaps, Ellis had wondered more than once, that was why life did flow smoothly for men like Freddie. Perhaps there was no sleight of hand to it, and simply acting as though everything is yours to have makes it so. It was fools like Ellis, people who studied the actions of others and emulated their responses in the hopes of passing for them, who lost time and time again.

'Look who it is. My dearest nephew, returned.' Freddie twisted a silver-tipped black cigarette into a long ivory holder. New affectations both, Ellis noted sourly. 'How was Dublin? Dreary as ever, I expect.'

In a fashionable pale linen suit, he was plumper than Ellis remembered, his face fuller and tanned, years of sooty late nights smoothed away by the Hollywood sun. America suited him, Ellis thought angrily, wishing that country had kept him. 'Who else would it be? I live here, after all.' He heard the petulance in his tone and silently berated himself for it. 'I'm not the one who treats this house as a –' he faltered, disconcerted by the child's emotion that was rising, threatening to flood his throat and mouth '– a left-luggage office!' He could have kicked himself for quoting Inspector Morris's uppity comment.

Freddie's smirk broadened. He always did find another person's discomfort massively heartening. 'Aw, I missed you too.' His accent had a new drawl, and Ellis hated him for that as well. How easy for Freddie to go wherever he wanted, to become whoever he wanted. To abandon an old life as a snake sheds its skin.

'Darling! Was the crossing terribly bad? It used to simply destroy me, every time.' Virginia appeared from behind her brother, slipping past him and onto the doorstep to embrace Ellis. 'You got my wire? I was too excited to keep it a surprise. I knew Minette wouldn't reply. Every farthing is a prisoner to that woman – isn't that what you said, Freddie? Oh, Ellis, it was the most amazing thrill! I simply couldn't believe it. I was here by myself on Friday morning – the girl took off the day after you left, the horror – and being alone becomes desperately tedious, I must say – and I heard the door . . . and . . . well! There he was.'

'There I was!' he echoed, draping his left arm around

Virginia's shoulders and kissing the top of her head. 'And, lo, here I am. You look well, nephew. Or as well as any man who has spent time in Min Broughton's ghastly company possibly can. It has always been my belief that every cultured Irishman's first and foremost duty is to get the merry hell out of Ireland.'

'Oh, Freddie,' Virginia remonstrated, but gently, leaning into him.

'How long are you staying?' Ellis pushed past them and on into the hall.

'Ellis, please!' Virginia said, surprised. 'I don't ask that of any guest, and particularly not this one!'

He slipped his suitcase under the table in the hall and picked up the post in search of Chatterton's letter. Just as well he had planted the story of a publisher's advance with Virginia before he went to Dublin because, with Freddie back in their lives, Ellis was determined not to stay a day longer than necessary in Fitzroy Gardens. It was so unpleasant to see how Virginia turned against other people once Freddie was there, as though his approval lay beyond a heavily guarded gate, with access dependent on her dismissing all other claims to her affections. To have to stand in his uncle's overpowering presence, breathing in his expensive cologne, and be wrong-footed by him so smoothly, so swiftly, was unbearable. Ellis's hate for Freddie had flourished like an untreated tumour in the months he'd been away. If only his mother could feel the same! She had worn her brother's absence as chainmail, every movement and utterance constricted, defined by it. His return liberated her, and Ellis wasn't much enamoured of this newly freed Virginia.

'Who knows, old thing, who knows?' Freddie waved his

cigarette-holder like a wand over Ellis's hand. 'Looking for something? I moved your letters to your desk. For safe-keeping.' The tiny red tip glowed fiercely as it moved. 'How rotten it would be, should one's things go missing while one was abroad.' He raised his eyebrows.

Freddie knew! Or knew *something* . . . but what? Ellis's stomach lurched, but he kept his face neutral. Virginia's interest in his week away was half-hearted, her questions faltering after the most basic enquiries about the journey and Minette's household arrangements. His replies – or attempts at them: he did the best he could, given the distraction of his uncle standing close by, smoking, staring – served only to remind her of something Freddie had said or done since he returned. She showed slightly more curiosity about the Arcourts, and delighted in Ellis's description of Patrick senior ('Of course he *would* be Patrick too,' Freddie cut in. 'I can imagine how completely dull they are. I'm surprised all their sons aren't called Patrick') and Patrick's mother. Pleased to have hooked her attention, Ellis continued, fashioning Alice Arcourt into a matronly Widow Twanky, bemused and outsmarted by her family in equal measure, rather than the welcoming, content woman he had found her to be. Patrick's youngest sister became a shy and charmless spinster-in-waiting, her existence a source of embarrassment to her family. It was cruel to squander a family's generosity and kindness on such a fleeting purchase as his mother's smile, but what else was he to do?

Only when he had exhausted the Arcourts did he allow himself nonchalantly to enquire whether there had been any further contact from the police. 'No,' Virginia replied, 'not since the inspector spoke to Patrick.'

'A rum business, isn't it?' Freddie said. 'She never struck me as the type to take off.' That she was Janet Gouldstein not Janey Gould was new to him too, he claimed, as was the job in the nightclub. He barely knew her. How typically Freddie. He didn't care a jot for any of them: had it suited him to move Dr Crippen as a lodger into his sister's house he would have done so.

Ellis didn't want to linger on the subject of Janey. Curiously, hearing her name spoken aloud didn't affect him as it had a week earlier. Her death no longer besieged his dreams. Going to Ireland had put more than distance between their lives – more accurately, his life and her death – and despite his return, she had remained in the past, a creature of a different, long-ago time. She was a character in a play, and the company had moved on to a new script and production, discarding their old selves as easily as last week's costumes.

'I must swing by the Lyceum, see what George is up to.' Freddie checked his watch. 'Perhaps I'll catch him later, before the evening performance.'

'It's a cinema now, don't you remember?' Virginia said. 'You shan't find me going there, for one.'

'Oh, Ginnie, not even with little ol' me?' He pretended to tickle her under the chin. 'Not for a box of Black Magic?'

She smiled. 'Save your cheap chocolates for chorus girls, Freddie!'

Ellis couldn't bear it. He excused himself and went to his study, itching to open his post. There it was! A Chatterton's *With Compliments* slip and a cheque for six hundred and fifty pounds. His hands trembled. He had kept the deposit, holding on to it like a talisman, and so had the full seven hundred, finally.

One evening, a couple of years earlier, he'd walked through Sydenham, passing the Crystal Palace. It couldn't have been long before the fire that would destroy it – a couple of months at most. It was September, the night air already heavy with autumn's earthy, sunken tang. A brilliant moon sat heavy and full, almost over its very centre point. The roof had glistened as though sprinkled with fine splinters of light. It had struck him at the time as the most unimaginable cliché – the twinkling glass, the suspended moon, a steel-grey sky as background to the entire scene. But now he recalled it and realised how wrong he'd been. It was beauty, pure and simple. It was a castle constructed of hopes and dreams, perfection and might realised, a crystalline glory rising towards the sky. Testament to what man could create when his heart, his strength, was kept right.

He could not turn away from his own truth, not now. He held the envelope tight, aware of a soaring feeling in his chest, as though his heart had physically grown larger, lighter, and was fluttering against his ribcage, like a bird at a door that has unexpectedly swung open. Life had become immediately simple: he had money, and the police were no longer interested in his household's relationship with Janey. So what if Freddie knew Ellis had gone through his possessions and taken a few paltry things? Freddie had given Ellis the lot: what happened to his books and papers was no longer Freddie's concern. Ellis was the one with the upper hand now. Money was power and he had a vast rushing torrent of it, enough to crush whatever obstacles Freddie would try to place in his way – which, given Freddie's selfish and cruel complexity, could be of vast or minute proportions, it was as yet impossible to tell. How foolish he'd been, to have spent the entire journey from Dublin in a fret.

It was vital to be business-like, he decided. It would be careless to allow any possibility of his plans to be derailed by some trifle, so he would settle up with every single one of his creditors immediately. He found himself quite looking forward to the prospect of sitting down with his cheque book and ledger, dispensing money and good wishes in every envelope. As soon as he could get out of the house, he would deposit Chatterton's money safely in his account and book the first decent sailing he could get.

Virginia went to rest and Ellis to unpack. When he returned downstairs, the door to the Music Room was open. Freddie was standing in the large bay window, staring out over the Heath, smoking one of his foul cigarettes. Several boxes were upended, their contents – a familiar mix of handwritten pages, typescripts, old playbills and shop accounts – scattered around his feet and fanning out into the room. Dust motes stirred by a recent commotion filled the air near him, their dancing flurry a choreography of impatience and anger.

'So, how *is* your writing coming along?' Freddie asked, as if taking up the threads of an earlier conversation. He began to wander around the room, randomly lifting pictures from the canvases stacked against the walls only to discard each one with the barest glance. 'Your mother tells me you have a commission to gad around the Continent and write about it, though what editor would be idiot enough to send *you* away alone, I can't imagine. Your career will go the same way as your father's, no doubt – though at least he experienced success. Decades of it, in fact, but what use was that? Sycophancy, then bankruptcy. The ignominy of being forgotten while he was still alive to watch it happen.'

'My work has nothing to do with my father.'

'It should. Learn from his legacy, Ellis. Success isn't about artistry, or even endeavour. Your father and his art were one and the same, so when society no longer valued his work, by his own monstrously vain logic he was worthless. I believe in taking what I want, when I want it, and I always assume every other intelligent person is doing exactly the same. The world is fake, Ellis.'

Ellis looked at him carefully. Why had he used that word? Freddie began to hum, a tune Ellis recognised from *Iolanthe.* He broke off abruptly, and said, 'You've been unlucky, old thing,' his voice so stonily calm and unmoving that the words seemed almost to come from somewhere else entirely.

Ellis glanced around the four walls, sure a third person was hiding in a shadowy corner. 'What are you talking about?'

Freddie ignored the question, and instead began to sing. *'When darkly looms the day, and all is dull and grey, to chase the gloom away, on thee I'll call . . .'* He added, 'I adore Gilbert and Sullivan, don't you?'

Ellis tensed. 'Not particularly.'

Freddie stood in front of the mirror over the mantelpiece. Ellis could see a faint reflection of himself, as though his and Freddie's heads were side by side. It was true how physically similar they were, his own face and wide mouth a younger, slimmer version of his uncle's. He tried to smile confidently, yet watched himself produce only a narrow, ugly grimace.

'Henry Warner took me to a party,' Freddie said. 'At Yip Harburg's. As soon as Yip heard my accent, he insisted on showing me the autographed Gilbert and Sullivan librettos he'd just acquired from a rare book dealer in London. Imagine my surprise when I recognised my belongings . . . The Harburgs thought the name was a marvellous coincidence, and I didn't disabuse them. *Well, what ya think of that?* Yip says to his wife. *We got ourselves two Limey Freds in one day!* How we laughed.' Freddie stared at Ellis. 'While you and Min were fussing about like two old spinsters – oh, and don't get any ideas about inheritance there by the way, her money returns to a Broughton trust – I was busy auditing my possessions.' He gestured to the boxes. 'In addition to my darling librettos, some fine books are missing. Ah, I said to myself, I know what's happened here! Little Ellis has been up to his tricks once more.'

'I don't know what you mean.' He kept his tone offhand, but felt his breath thinning.

'But, old thing, I think you do. You've been helping yourself to things that don't belong to you.'

'If you're referring to that business with the Prudential, I—'

'You might have convinced your mother otherwise, but I know you tried to cash in that policy by forging her name.'

'That was a misunderstanding. And have you forgotten that you dumped your belongings on me? Even you know this is all rubbish, worthless rubbish. Your actual words were: *Keep the lot and consider what you insist on referring to as my "debt" duly discharged.'*

'As if that would stand up in court! The lot of *what*, exactly? Harburg's delightful acquisitions are troubling me. You stole them, and either forged Gilbert's handwriting, or paid someone else to do so in order to elicit a better price. Which was it? Actually, don't answer: you're too tight to pay someone. And you always were good with your pen, despite not being able to fool the man from the Pru.' Freddie giggled. Ellis hated his laugh. 'Your mother is an idiot. Always was. But I'm not, so don't think you can get away with conning me, like you do my sister.'

How Virginia would wither to hear him! 'I'd have let the bailiffs take every last scrap of yours and be damned,' Ellis snapped. 'Have you any intention of repaying her?'

'Me repay *her*? All she had to do was take over the lease at Marsham, so I would have had my own flat to return to, but she was too stupid to think of it.'

He couldn't bear to hear Freddie say such things. That he was right, and Virginia was a blind fool, was irrelevant. 'How dare you! She could barely afford to clear your debts, not to mention take on an expensive lease as well. Do you have any idea how much money she has? *None*.'

'She's been had, then.'

'Yes! By *you*! It's always you, Freddie. I can't understand why but she adores you. And you know that, and you take advantage of it, time and time again.'

'You have no right to lecture me about owing my sister money while you, a grown man, live off her. What a pathetic child you are.' Freddie picked his way through the mess on the floor. He crossed to where Ellis was standing and paused, staring straight into his face. He lifted one hand and put it to Ellis's cheek, gently, his thumb moving to and fro. Ellis froze. 'And a child is all you'll ever be.' The first time Freddie had touched him like that he had been four, his neck craning as he looked up at his uncle's reddened, intense face, lips whispering of secrets, of silence.

'I've pitched a new show to Harburg, so it doesn't suit me

for him to discover he's been the victim of a fraud involving my name. But if you want me to continue to lie on your behalf, you're going to have to make it worth my while.' He moved a step back and checked his watch. 'Just something for you to think about. Time for me to be off, if I'm to catch George.'

He left without another word. Ellis leant forward, his hands on his knees. His head was full of needles; a buzz in his ears told him he might faint. He forced himself to breathe slowly, counting to ten before standing upright. Smoke from Freddie's cigarette thinned and disappeared, yet his uncle's malign presence – worse – hung over him. *The money*, he reminded himself. *It changes everything. He can't touch you, not now you have money.* The thought was a spotlight suddenly illuminating a murky corner. Right there, in the dazzling glare, happiness waited.

It was desperately bad luck about the librettos. Ellis recalled Chatterton mentioning the name Yip Harburg as the buyer. Tipping the scales in his favour was that Freddie hadn't noticed Winsome's letters were missing. Ellis thought it through quickly. Freddie knew nothing about *The Un-Dead Count* and Ellis's newly made fortune. Fine, he decided. He'd admit to the Gilbert and Sullivans, and maybe a dozen or so first-edition books, and make a show of reluctantly compensating Freddie for his pilfering. He'd begin by offering ten pounds, knowing Freddie would push him to fifteen, or even twenty. The prospect of having to give that beast money made him feel ill, but it was the safest way, and he could – the thought cheered him immensely – afford it. He would have to act swiftly, he decided. He wasn't going to let Freddie threaten his plans, or take his future from him as he had taken so much else.

CHAPTER 17

The following morning Ellis left the house early, went to the bank, then booked his passage as far as the Côte d'Azur. The Calais-Méditerranée Express wasn't what it had once been since the addition of second- and third-class cars, according to a punctilious agent with overly tinted hair whose manner reminded him of Ralph Chatterton, but because Ellis wasn't intending to mix with his fellow passengers during the journey, he wasn't deterred. The night ferry to Calais, *le train bleu* and the Côte d'Azur Pullman Express – he booked the most expensive sleeping car – to the French Riviera. He would spend at least four weeks there, followed by another month travelling Italy from top to toe.

He was leaving in three days' time. There was so much to do. He put aside twenty pounds to pay off Freddie, and allowed himself another twenty for shopping. The first lightweight linen travelling suit he tried on was perfect, right off the peg. Simply touching it filled him with such unexpected pleasure. He bought cream summer shoes, a gold tie-pin, and a leather suitcase with his initials tooled on its lock. He also permitted himself the private pleasures of a monogrammed leather washbag, a silver-plated shaving kit and, in a final, irresistible splurge in Selfridges' stationery department, two leather-bound notebooks, one navy, the other oxblood, with his initials debossed on their covers. To have the monogramming done immediately incurred an extra charge, and he was happy to pay it.

The joy of running his fingers over these – his! – possessions! How perfect it was going to be, in city after city, to pack and repack such beautiful new companions, their unity that of cordial strangers who find themselves travelling together in one strange land after another. The world had filled with promises and thrills, every city a romantic, radiant entanglement. He would go further east after Italy, to Greece and Turkey, possibly even Bulgaria. He would settle somewhere warm and cheap, he decided, where he could live easily and with dignity. His was not to be a self-serving wandering odyssey. Nor would it be the relentless and unfeeling journey of an insolent, friendless Englishman, determined to scour the world and find it wanting by comparison to the bland perfection of home.

That afternoon he showed Virginia the case and suit, but kept the rest hidden lest she queried his extravagance. He had given her a highly redacted version of his schedule. His trip would take two months or so, he explained, having decided that eight weeks sounded a believable duration, and in line with his modest budget. She was to write *poste restante* for the first fortnight, he told her, because the best-value digs were always to be found on arrival. He would be staying in a succession of expensive hotels, but she did not need to know that. And Freddie certainly didn't.

Assuming that his uncle would be trying to get him alone again to ask for money, Ellis had deliberately stayed out until four o'clock. He needn't have bothered, because Freddie wasn't there, arriving back just as he and Virginia were having tea.

'Even though I can't bear that you're leaving, I'm so proud of you,' she was saying, as the door opened. 'Will your publisher – what was his name? – want the book out this year? Freddie, darling! How lovely. Shall I pour for you?'

'Martin Secker,' Ellis replied. 'And, no, next summer at the earliest, I should think. I have to write it first!'

'Indeed,' Freddie cut in, nodding at the teapot in Virginia's hand. 'Indeed, he does,' he said, a brittle edge to his voice as he grabbed the saucer she offered him.

'Careful, darling, you'll chip it,' Virginia said. 'Isn't it thrilling, Freddie? Our Ellis, a man of letters!'

'To the papers maybe!' Freddie snapped.

'Oh, Freddie, you're terrible!' she scolded playfully, as she rose from the table. 'I'd better change. I'm dining with the Grades before bridge. Can you both forage for supper? I wrote to the agency again yesterday. I can't understand why it's taking them so long to send me a new girl.'

Ellis went to his study, noticing for the first time how chaotic it had become over the previous few months, with pamphlets and magazines piled in unruly stacks, and draft pages from *The Un-Dead Count* in little heaps under the desk. When he had begun working on it, he had got into the habit of locking the door when he was out, telling Virginia it was because he kept money in the desk and didn't trust the ever-changing parade of servants. He spread his collection of maps and travel brochures across the desk one last time. He would burn them first, he decided, then work through all the rough pages from *The Un-Dead Count.* How he had enjoyed planning his itinerary! The entire world at his disposal . . . big-game shoots in Africa, bear shoots in Russia, mahseer fishing and the Taj Mahal in India! Spain was off, of course, yet with so much of the world open to him, having to exclude some countries hardly mattered. Yugoslavia, Scandinavia, Turkestan, the Brazilian jungle . . . The very names were the stuff of poetry. First into the fire was the Thomas Cook *Pilgrimages to Lourdes* catalogue he'd received in error. The papal seal on the cover fizzed yellow, orange and blue in the flames. The Poly Tours *Rhine Cruise* with its swastika emblem and coy promise of *The Land of Dreams Come True* went next, along with the agent's covering note and gloomy suggestion that such an itinerary was less likely to find favour with 'this season's traveller'. A long voyage taking in Lisbon, Gibraltar and Istanbul waxed too lyrically about pink sunsets and lapping azure waters, so it, too, deserved its place in the flames, as did the Wayfarers' activity cruise programme, crammed full of awful-sounding lectures, madrigals and music.

A photograph of a harbour reminded him of a trip to the seaside with his parents and Freddie, years before. He was only, what, nine? Ten? That first touch of the sand . . . the warm soft grit flowing between his fingers as though he was powerful enough to grind it! The water, glittering with white light, rippling and curling, constantly folding over on itself, the sea forever made and remade. Almost as soon as they arrived his parents had announced they were going to a hotel for lunch. Freddie suggested he take Ellis for a walk through the sand-dunes, which, hidden behind high grasses, wrapped around the curve of the beach.

'I don't want to,' Ellis said, his heart thudding. He had been taught never to disagree. Sidney frowned but – surprisingly – raised his hands in acquiescence. 'Oh, leave the boy to his sandcastles,' he said, holding out his arm for Virginia. Freddie strode off by himself, and Virginia and Sidney went to luncheon, telling Ellis to wait where he was.

As time passed, he grew hot and thirsty, and increasingly envious of the families around him. Ordinary people, playing cricket, chewing macaroons, chatting and squabbling, passing each other fish-paste sandwiches and comparing the merits of summer landladies and the cost of room-and-board versus room-only. He had his bathing suit on, but was afraid to go into the sea alone, or even the water's edge. What if they came back and didn't see him? What if a wave swallowed him and he drowned? Or a shark? On the way there, Freddie had whispered in his ear – his mouth so close that Ellis had felt the warm rain of his uncle's spittle hit his cheek – a story about a bloodthirsty, child-eating shark. Little kiddies were grabbed from the water and gobbled up – he swore it, swore on his oath – on the self-same beach their train was thundering towards, without so much as a finger or tiny toe spat back out. Ellis sat on the sand and shuddered, nervous for the other children larking about in the water. If the shark attacked, would it be his fault for not having warned anyone? Desperate for a drink of water, his shoulders and arms pinking horribly, becoming taut and sore in the sun, he distracted himself by building a fort. Hours later, as the tide was coming in, his parents returned with an ice for him. He watched in horror as water flowed into his moat, swallowing the neat perimeter picked out with shells, before breaching the low walls and retreating again, taking half the fort with it. Only ridges and a square-shaped hollow remained in the sand, his entire day reduced to soft, blurred edges. His attempt to make something, to hold his day tight, safe, was ruined.

Freddie strolled down the beach towards them, Malacca cane twirling in one hand, cigar in the other, the very picture of a man enjoying an afternoon of leisure. The ice made Ellis's head hurt but his thirst was so great he crammed it into his mouth nevertheless. Freddie leant forward and prodded the flesh of Ellis's reddened thigh with the tip of his cane, and the burning sensation in his leg combined with the ferocious cold made him feel sick.

The harbour lights disappeared as he closed the brochure. Then it, too, at last, went on the fire.

Virginia left at ten to six, calling her goodbyes from the hall. Ellis popped his head around the study door and waved. 'Enjoy your evening. Good luck!'

'Bridge is at the Astons, so supper is bound to run terrifically late – you know what they're like. I shall see you in the morning, darling.'

'Wait!' From upstairs, Freddie threw an envelope over the banister. 'Be a dear and pop that in the post-box?'

She picked it up from the floor, glancing at the name. 'A woman? I do hope you're not causing trouble for husbands again!' Despite being raised in the blackout of ignorance, Virginia didn't care what people did, or who they did it with, as long as they did it in private. It was bred into her generation that desire was a weakening influence, an illicit otherness that could prove fatal and so was best denied. She did little to force ignorance on Ellis, but it is a virus that spreads easily.

Sidney's single nod towards educating his son in what he confusingly referred to as 'the ways of a man's world' had come not long after the war ended, when he informed Ellis of the death by wounds of Nancy Grade's son – who, although he was ten years older than Ellis, had always struck him as childish, prone to silly giggling in Freddie's company – with the words, 'It must be a consolation for the Grades that Douglas has been spared further temptation.'

'Me? Trouble?' Freddie laughed, feigning outrage. 'Never! It's boring old theatre business. You have nothing to fear, dearest. You're the only woman in my life.'

Ellis returned to his study. His next task was to ensure every page and tattered scrap that could cast doubt on *The Un-Dead Count*, or trace its origins back to him in the spring of 1938 rather than to Bram Stoker's pen decades before, was taken care of. He ought to have dealt with it weeks earlier, but hadn't wanted to do so while waiting to hear that Chatterton was assured of the book's authenticity. Then he had thought, given the hours he had put into perfecting Stoker's composition style and handwriting, it would be foolish to discard all his work. Now he began to make two piles: one of material to destroy, the second to go into a trunk he had arranged to store with his bank. The fire in his study had gone out so he relit it, fanning the scrappy flames impatiently until they took.

He was leaving his Varityper behind. He'd had to think quickly when Virginia asked why, and whether he was planning to write in longhand. He'd arranged to pick up a cheap portable in Nice, he told her. The typewriter he used on *The Un-Dead Count* went into the trunk for storage. He had no way of discovering what sort of typewriter Bram had owned, but Ellis reasoned that as the Stokers had been prolific correspondents – he recalled Florence once marvelling that her husband produced a minimum of 'fifty good letters' daily during his time at the Lyceum – he would have had a hard-working, well-made machine with a manifold function for carbon copies. In *Dracula* Mina Harker refers to the advantages of her new portable Hall typewriter, so it was reasonable to assume Stoker had used the same model himself to write *Dracula*, and changed it in favour of something newer before writing the sequel. When he had found Virginia's long-forgotten forty-year-old Hammond portable in the attic, needing only oil and a new ribbon to work perfectly, he decided that Stoker had employed the very same make and model.

He checked carefully through his pages of notes and ideas for other Stoker stories. It would be foolhardy to destroy them. He missed Stoker, missed his company. *The Un-Dead Count* had lived suspended inside him as the earth is in space, and he was lonely without it. Day after day as Ellis sat at his desk, he had watched his hands fill with another man's talent. The characters he had created – even those phantoms sired by Stoker's original creations – had remained no more than fictions to him, puppets to be manipulated, but Stoker himself was as real as life. For sport, he took a pen and wrote a few lines. *The man's nib pierced the paper's taut skin,* he thought, with a smile, *ink dripping down the soft, snow-white page.* He delighted at how smoothly his hand could become Stoker's. He no longer saw himself as a sort of phantom trying to animate a long-dead man's mind and talent. Instead, they were connected, a fused creative identity. Ellis had never experienced that before: his own attempts at fiction had, he now understood, each been a small death. *The Only Boy* and *Varnishing Day* were nothing more than a displacing of some part of himself that could never be corrected, an attempt to click a dislocated bone back into place. While they had obsessed him during their creation, they had never haunted him afterwards as *The Un-Dead Count* did. They were not of his soul. Without Stoker, his destiny as an author would have been to pull from his own small, dwindling stack of ideas until he arrived at nothing, the thread of his own being unspooled to a vacant, pointless centre. He understood plagiarism as more relevant to his own attempts to shape his existence into a story, than in relation to Stoker's writing. Falsity depends on the reader being unable to recognise the point of origin, whereas his achievement with *The Un-Dead Count* was far greater.

He sealed the trunk carefully and labelled it, ready to despatch first thing. He composed a letter, explaining he would be on the Continent until further notice, and would send for it by telegram, for delivery to an address he would advise. Finally, he began to stack up all the discarded pages, ready for the fire.

He heard Freddie's footsteps in the hallway outside. He appeared to be pacing up and down. Whatever was he up to? Just as the grandfather clock struck half past, the doorbell rang, immediately followed by Freddie's shout of 'Ellis?' Had he been waiting for someone?

Ellis stared at the man standing on the threshold. 'It's you.'

'Indeed, Mr Spender.'

'To what do we owe the pleasure? If you're looking for Patrick, he's in Ireland.'

'Believe me, there is little pleasure in my occupation. I'd like a word with you, as it happens.'

Freddie hovered nearby, his tanned face and cream suit a curious reversal of the inspector's pallid complexion and dark trench coat. When he turned his head, Morris's scar stood out, pink and ridged, against his cheek. 'And you are, sir?'

'Frederick Broughton, Mr Spender's maternal uncle.'

Morris nodded. 'Mr Spender, do you know a Miss Stella Lloyd?'

'I don't think so . . .' He pretended to think, his heart thumping uncomfortably. 'Wait a moment . . . Does she work in a nightclub?'

'The Nest, yes. She made a statement this afternoon to the effect that she believes you have information about Miss Gouldstein's activities around the time of her disappearance. Perhaps there is something you did not think to mention during my previous visit?'

'But I didn't give you any information—' he protested.

'The point exactly.' Morris lit a cigarette. Freddie remained silent and completely still.

'—because I don't have any! Janey ran off with a man from the club.'

'How do you know that?'

'I don't recall. Possibly your constable – Smyth, isn't it? – mentioned it.'

'I doubt that.' Morris exhaled a curl of blue smoke, his breath a genie spilling from a lamp. 'Miss Lloyd claims that you and Miss Gouldstein were engaged in an illegal activity. Blackmail, in fact.'

'*Blackmail?* What complete rot! Sadly, it doesn't surprise me, Inspector. She's been here, you know, trying to peddle her lies. My mother was most distressed by her rudeness.'

He thought quickly. Yes, it was possible Janey had told Stella about Winsome and the letters, but surely highly unlikely. Damn that Stella! It was all about money, of course. She was the blackmailing type, not him. Let her bloody well whistle for it. She wouldn't get a single farthing.

'Where were you on April the first?'

'I can't possibly remember. It's two months ago.' Recovered from his initial fright, Ellis felt he was carrying it off better than he would have otherwise. Having Freddie for an audience seemed to be helping. He gave a slight shrug of acknowledgement and lifted his hands: a polite young man who would help, if only he could.

'It's the day Miss Gouldstein was last sighted, as you know.'

'Yes, of course.' Ellis kept his face attentive and serious because he was, he reminded himself, on the same side as the inspector: two men concerned for the girl's welfare. 'Working in my study, I suppose.' He shouldn't have mentioned the study while the desk was littered with his practice sheets for *The Un-Dead Count*. But surely there was no reason for the inspector to want to go there, or to look through his papers if he did. 'Inspector, this is completely ridiculous. Janey left here owing us money. If you want to investigate an illegal activity, I suggest you begin there.'

'I see,' the inspector said calmly. He paused, as though he had run out of questions. Ellis relaxed. The three men stood quietly for a few seconds, the clock a metronome keeping time with their silence. But the pause stretched out, gaining strength and sound, a peculiar thudding in his ears. The air grew cold around them.

Morris moved first, holding up one hand and ticking off his fingers as he spoke, his voice colder than before:

'Miss Gouldstein is missing since April the first. Her empty handbag is found in a manner that suggests foul play. Miss Lloyd claims Miss Gouldstein was engaged in an illegal activity with you, which was coming to a head.' He dropped his hand. 'Mr Spender, when I was last here, you referred to Miss Gouldstein with the words, *she wanted to be an actress*.'

'Did I? What of it?'

'It strikes me as interesting that you spoke about her in the past tense.'

Ellis felt hugely aware of his own body and its discordance. Every limb was an encumbrance, unwieldy and useless. He would give himself away, he was sure of it. He swallowed hard, as Morris continued, 'I'm going to ask again: can you or anyone else account for your movements on April the first?'

'Inspector!' Freddie spoke at last. 'This is an outrage! How dare you come here and challenge my nephew, a young man of excellent standing, with no more basis for your filthy accusations than the word of a girl in a nightclub.'

'Questions, sir, not accusations.'

'Miss Gouldstein came to live here on my recommendation, so if there is blame to be attached for her behaviour in this household, it is on my shoulders. Her callous disregard for my sister's kindness was appalling. Lady Spender was like a mother to her.'

A mother to her? What rot. Ellis stole a glance at Freddie's face. Freddie glided through every situation on raffish charm. Ellis had never seen this imperious and authoritative version of him before.

'With all due respect, Mr Broughton, her behaviour while living in this house isn't the subject of my enquiries.'

'I can vouch for my nephew's character, and were his mother here, she would vouch for his whereabouts. Do you have any proof, or merely slanderous lies? So what if he spoke in the past tense? Perfectly reasonable when talking about a woman whom none of us has any expectation of ever seeing here again. Inspector, if you have nothing better to do than waste our time, I bid you farewell. Unless you would prefer me to talk directly to the chief constable, a personal friend?'

Morris's pale face grew paler. 'That will do, for now.' He turned away, and Ellis realised this wasn't merely another interlude between rounds but that the inspector was definitely leaving, defeated. The front door slammed behind him.

Emboldened by Freddie's righteousness, he felt as innocent as his uncle believed him to be. Innocent and free and strong. How dare Morris talk to him like that. Throwing around – what were Freddie's words? *Filthy accusations*, that was it. And not a shred of proof! Freddie was right: it was outrageous. He took a breath, allowing his shoulders to relax. He was out of the woods.

In silence Freddie strode towards the Music Room. Ellis followed him. The room was dim, illuminated by a lamp in the hallway just beyond the door and the fading light spilling through the large picture window. Full-leafed branches outside created soft shadows on the floor, their shapes that of the swish and flick of forgotten ballgowns and long-dead feet dancing to inaudible music. Freddie turned to face him, laughing. 'Didn't the bobby do well? Morris and Spender . . . two leading men of my latest show. All *that* particular production needs is a bag of toffees and a programme!'

'What? I don't understand.'

Freddie's laugh fell away instantly. 'And your stupidity

makes you dangerous. Allow me to explain. Last night I met George Atkinson. Exactly as I could have predicted, he's in a terrible mess. As if the projection-operators' strike wasn't bad enough, he couldn't get distribution rights from those crooks in Film Circuits. He's been told to close the cinema and reopen the theatre.' Freddie lit a cigarette, his eyes dark and glittering. 'Silly me! I forgot to mention *where* George and I were. The Nest, where we met a delightful creature – if a touch mutton for my tastes – called Stella. When the subject of Janey came up, she told me she'd been here to ask about her friend, only to be sent away with a flea in her ear by you and my sister. She has the very strong suspicion that you, dearest nephew, are not to be trusted.'

What of it? Hadn't he just heard as much from Morris? It meant nothing. Typical, this dangling, this slow, torturous drip. He wished Freddie would name his price and leave.

'No one at the Lyceum has the faintest clue what's happened to Janey since she— Actually, old thing, what *are* we calling it? Did a bunk?' Freddie raised one hand and made a *pfft* noise, as a conjuror would, his fist opening to reveal nothing. 'I don't believe a word of this travel-book nonsense. *You?* Why, you barely leave your mother's skirts! So this morning, I made it my business to seek out an antiquarian dealer highly recommended by my new associate, Yip Harburg. Rollo is quite the chatterbox. Aptly named, one might say. Times have been good at Chatterton's recently, he told me, enthusing about the remarkable find of a Bram Stoker novel believed to have been destroyed. He was sworn to secrecy about the circumstances of the discovery, but when he let slip that one chapter was unearthed by a young woman in a former office of Bram's, I smelt your dirty hands all over it.'

Freddie's expression changed, becoming the clouded, harder one Ellis was so familiar with. Slowly, Freddie withdrew a couple of sheets of paper from his jacket pocket and held them up. Early discarded pages from *The Un-Dead Count,* with Stoker's name written – the words jumped up, shouting to him for rescue! – several times, a ragged penstroke up and down the margins.

Ellis reached out a hand to steady himself against a table. He wasn't out of the woods – far from it. He had the dizzying sense that he had wandered in far deeper than he had realised, and was lost, the trees suddenly vast and dense around him, blocking out the sky entirely.

'While you were gallivanting around Selfridges this morning – oh, and you're returning the lot tomorrow, you're not wasting my money – I had a good look in your study. You don't suppose you're the only one with keys in this house, do you? Gosh, you've gone quite a funny colour, Ellis. Are you all right? And what I found was so exciting that I rang up Stella and suggested she contact Inspector Morris immediately. She'll do anything for a quid. She was to express her concerns at her own behest, you understand. My name was never mentioned, not in the bookshop or to the police. Stella's an enterprising tart, I'll give her that much. Pegging you for a blackmailer was her idea.'

Freddie picked up a neat stack of letters and cards, and fanned them out across the table. The postcards' colour illustrations – a fat, cheerfully smutty policeman on a beach leering at a woman in a bathing suit lay directly under his thumb – looked garish beside the neat monochrome sheets. Each one was signed by Bram, or by him and Florence. Beside them, he set out the pages from *The Un-Dead Count*, lining up the sheets so that Bram's signatures, despite having decades separating them, were beside each other, each one identical.

'As if the world needs more of Bram's drivel,' Freddie sneered, and Ellis felt he might weep in frustration and sympathy for a friend under attack. He thought of the poor fool Godalming, attacked by bats and drained of blood until he dies, under the illusion that he alone is being seduced night after night by the un-dead Lucy Westenra. He had written him as a man beguiled not just by a strange woman's touch but by the very idea of what she represented: Godalming yielded to her as the fleshly manifestation of the power of a mighty and commanding force, a will bigger than his own feeble, singular desires. Quincey Harker, too, is being visited by her, but because neither man confides in the other, it is only after Godalming's death that Quincey uncovers the truth of what has happened to his friend. From the outset, Ellis had decided that only the stronger of the two would survive.

He stared coolly at his uncle. In life as in art, he told himself. Nothing had to be real, everything could be false. One rarely knows the actual point when life's reticulations change, when the map is redrawn, yet Ellis knew with a cold certainty this was one such moment. When Janey lay dying at his feet, he had understood for the first time that existence is a series of separate and often entirely random moments, and fixating on it as an ordered, interlinked sequence is the road to damnation. Life was connected, yes, but only in the way Virginia's pearls were: each separated from the next by a small, tight knot.

Anger was swelling, like a blimp, inside Freddie – Ellis could almost see it pulsing against his uncle's skin. 'I know how rotten you are, Ellis. Foul to the core – I've said it since you were a child. A firm hand is what you need. I used to tell your father as much.' He smirked. 'A very firm hand.' Freddie walked to the mantelpiece and put the letters down, echoing Janey's steps months earlier when she had left Winsome's correspondence there for Ellis to find. He lit another cigarette, looking at Ellis's reflection in the mirror. Ellis didn't move. He regarded his uncle as he would a stranger in a dream, one in which nothing is real and everything moves to its own unfathomable, jerking dance. Freddie smoked and stared, reaching out his right hand idly to stroke the small bronze bust of Ellis's head. His fingers cupping the hair, he ran his thumb over and back across the child's sightless eyes, as if trying to press his lids shut. Over and back his thumb went, without ever once dropping his gaze from Ellis himself. Ellis was hot and cold all at once, full of a familiar fizzing dread.

'I warned you yesterday that trying to trick me is a mistake. You know how this works: I assume you've already paid off Janey, but I want every penny you got for that book, or Morris gets these forgeries and Chatterton's address tomorrow. Your mother doesn't believe me and, I'm sure, living in your ridiculous fantasy land, you don't either, but there's another war coming. I'm not staying around to witness the carnage when Hitler leeches Chamberlain down to the last drop. Any chance of an honourable peace is over, which leaves either a dishonourable peace or a fight – and neither suits me. I'm leaving again for Hollywood. I only came back to raise some cash. That place is dripping money, but you have to look rich to get rich. Your mother's a dead loss. If only I'd known she didn't have anything left I wouldn't have bothered . . . But *you*, Ellis, you can fund me. Oh, and in case you think you can fob me off with a clever story and a couple of guineas, this came for you in the second post today.' Freddie took his hand from the sculpture and turned from the mantelpiece, taking an envelope from his pocket. He shook out two pieces of paper and read the first aloud: *'Dear Mr Spender, Deepest apologies; your receipt was omitted in error when settling our account. Please find enclosed. Sincerest wishes.'* He held up a smaller piece of paper. *'Enclosed banker's order for six hundred and fifty pounds for the manuscript as presented of* The Un-Dead Count *chapters one to twenty-one, written by Bram Stoker Esquire deceased, in full and final settlement et cetera.'*

His face flushed with spite and greed. It was clear that consequences meant nothing. 'We both know a forger is nothing more than a monkey swinging from the talent of others, but you're better than I had expected,' he said. 'You'd fool anyone, bar me. The price to keep yourself out of prison is six hundred and fifty pounds. I'm a generous man, so I'll let you keep whatever you made when you stole my librettos. Can't say fairer than that, now can we? Choose your reply carefully, Ellis, because I can cause a lifetime of trouble for you.'

A sound was building inside Ellis's head, clamorous and wild, capable of knocking him off course entirely.

'A lifetime of trouble,' he repeated, barely above a whisper. How ugly the words were in his mouth. He knew what he was going to do. Knew that he could not – would not – have stopped himself, not now. He moved closer to his uncle, as if looking to inspect the receipt. Ellis picked up the sculpture, the bronze curls and face – his! – still warm from the caress of Freddie's fingertips. He shuddered.

He turned quickly, straightening himself.

'What on—' Freddie began, surprise and confusion in his eyes.

Quickly, softly, his feet joining the shadows cast by the trees, Ellis had moved so close as to be beside him. He lifted the sculpture and, drawing his arm back as a boxer might, slammed his fist against the side of Freddie's head. The hard edge of the plinth caught his left temple and blood spurted out. Freddie fell towards his right, all arms and legs, one hand trying to grab the edge of the table but failing to get purchase on it so that he twisted and landed face-down, palms splayed in front of him. He got himself to his hands and knees, limbs loose and uncoordinated. Ellis lifted the statue again and slammed it into the back of his neck. His head tilted backwards so quickly that their eyes met for a single, horrible second. A rasping, coughing noise came from Freddie's chest as he fell forwards, the sound abruptly cut off as his face hit the wooden floor.

Ellis stood over him, the tiny head in his right hand, desperate to turn Freddie onto his back and smash it into his uncle's face over and over, bronze lips hard, vile, against Freddie's own. He used his left hand to hold back his right. *Stop*, he told himself, or maybe he said it aloud, he was immediately unsure. *No.* He was panting, and took a step back in case Freddie, though completely still, might rise like the devil he was and swing one arm around to grab Ellis's ankle. Ellis kicked out, hitting his ribcage hard. Freddie's chest contorted against his foot, but he put up no resistance. Nervous, he bent down and took Freddie's wrist, fumbling for a pulse. The skin was warm and pliable against his own, its touch immediately familiar and sickening. All those times it had been Freddie's hand tight around *his* wrist!

But Freddie was dead. In life as in art, finally. And entirely, he thought coolly, what such a vampire deserved. Ellis rose again, leaning forward over the body. He was still clutching the bust, so loosened his grip and dropped it directly on the mound of Freddie's back. How grotesque to see his own little face bounce from another's body and land on the floor with a dull clang. Ellis dashed across the room and grabbed one of Sidney's old dust sheets to wipe the blood from the floor before it began to stain. He tucked it beside the body, leaving it wedged between Freddie's head and the edge of the hearth. A thin waft of turpentine, its original sharpness long dissipated, rose from the sheet. He wiped the sculpture clean and returned it to its usual home on the mantelpiece.

He checked his watch. Eight thirteen. Assuming the Astons' supper ran as late as usual, he had no more than two and a half hours, three at best, before Virginia would be home.

Ellis stuffed the Stoker pages and Chatterton's receipt into his jacket before going through Freddie's pockets. A half-empty cigarette case, an empty gold calling-card-holder inscribed FB in large, cursive initials, and a latch key. A robbery, he decided, when Freddie was drunk, crossing the Heath in the dark. If he could hold off until after ten it might be dark enough to bring him into the back garden and through the door onto the Heath. He'd find somewhere dense and wooded to dump his body. He'd take a bottle of gin from the pantry and douse Freddie in it until he stank, then plant the empty bottle in his pocket . . . Yes, that might work. Virginia never drank gin, and wouldn't notice a missing bottle. Almost immediately he began to fret. Over-complicated plans rarely worked out, but was this the opposite? Too thin and full of holes to succeed? Possibly, but what else could he do?

Helpless and panicked, his stomach spasmed. He lit a

cigarette and went to the window to check the easiest route through the garden to the wall and door. Heavy clouds were gathering, causing the light in the room to change as suddenly as if he'd drawn a curtain. It hadn't been a warm day, and the forecast was for an unusually chilly night. A gloaming mist was dropping low over the Heath. Good. He was to be lucky, again.

He turned and stared at his uncle's body on the floor, one limp arm flung wide, his palm tilted back. Why did people keep interfering? It was so unfair. Clumsy and dangerous. But while he had felt sad for Janey, even though she had treated him so cruelly, he could never have sympathy for rotten, filthy Freddie, his death determined by his actions in life. Disgusting Freddie, blackmail now added to his list of dark talents. He turned over the empty card-holder in his hand, imagining Freddie as stateless, impoverished and adrift. He hoped his uncle's last conscious thought had been split-second surprise at his defeat at his nephew's hand. Paid Janey off? Once again, Freddie had underestimated what Ellis was capable of: a man who had written an entire book as Stoker as well as constructing the story around its very existence in the world was more than capable of defending his creations. Freddie had thought that by simply feeding the unwitting police a script, Ellis too would reel off his lines and slink away? The fool. Freddie had wandered onstage during the third act: of all men, he should have known anything might happen.

He left the Music Room, locking the door behind him. Freddie's bedroom – which had once been Sidney's, Freddie

sleeping in the bed his former brother-in-law had died in –
was chaotic, a mess of ashtrays, newspapers and magazines,
with clothes spilling from open suitcases onto the carpet. He
grabbed Freddie's smallest suitcase and packed it with his
overcoat and a distinctive pale blue linen suit, and took his
sponge bag from the bathroom. In the furthest attic, he put
the suitcase into a large trunk which he covered with dust
sheets. Covered in sweat and dust, he ran back downstairs,
where the fire in his study had come along nicely. The room
was warm, tongued shadows running up and down the
walls. To distract himself while he waited, he began to burn
his papers. Sheet by sheet he watched them go, but happily,
because he wasn't destroying treasures: he was sealing his
future. It took a full half-hour to rip each page into strips and
burn it, with regular pauses to tamp down the growing pile
of ashes. Finally, he reached into his pocket for the pages,
originally intended for the conclusion of *The Un-Dead Count*,
that Freddie had stolen from his desk:

Veronica Holmwood's diary

. . . I am fearful to continue, but feel I must, as I have no one
to talk to about the latest developments until Ernest returns
from Berlin. 'We stand and fall by our own acts,' Quincey cried,
with such honour and conviction that even had I been of a
different mind from his, I would have found it impossible to
tell him so. 'Your heart has too many rooms, Veronica, that you
believe a man such as he – no, not a man: a phantasmagoria
of evil! – deserves housing there. No, let him cry out for our
mercy. Let him beseech us.' Still, I made no reply, tho remained

fearful nervous, for the silences that followed each scream were more deadly still, holding murder in each breath. Am I foolish to commit such words to paper? What if I am writing the very script that may someday be evidence between myself and a rope?

Ellis spotted immediately where this attempt had erred both in style and handwriting: how his *f*s in the handwritten addition of 'fearful' were too timid; how he hadn't allowed the words ending in *m* or *n* to trail off into a line, the way Stoker did, as if he was so keen to move on to the next word he couldn't bring himself to complete them fully. But even had it been perfect, he could never have included it in the final manuscript of *The Un-Dead Count* because he had accidentally used the wrong type of paper, recognising it as a creamy art stock rather than his customary typewriting paper. It must have come from one of Sidney's old sketchbooks. He turned it over. There was a faint pencil drawing on the other side. He tilted the sheet closer to the fire and watched the small face come into focus on the page, the lines flickering, dancing in the firelight. His father's drawing, suddenly appearing finer and more detailed than he remembered, almost as though she was at that moment returning to life. Wide, serious eyes that understood nothing of the world; a neat, unknowable mouth that was neither smiling nor downturned; dark eyebrows that traced the topmost curve of her eye sockets before ending in a short drop.

Lucy. He touched the curves of her hair, the pencil strokes so wispily perfect as to be barely there. He stared at her face for a long time, willing it to spring up inside him, to rise gladly, gleefully, from the page and fill him. He wanted her for the air inside his blood. He would eat her sins if it would free her tiny winged soul.

He tore the page, carefully, into four jagged strips and threw them onto the fire. She flared for a second before crumbling, blackened. Smoke disappeared up the flue, as what remained of his sister slipped out of the chimney and joined the clouds hanging low over London. Another child forgotten, lost to the night city.

CHAPTER 18

At five past ten he heaved Freddie's body up from the floor, only to stagger backwards under its weight, losing his grip. He tried again, this time managing only a couple of tottering steps. Moving this flaccid mountain was impossible by comparison with Janey – and he'd struggled with her at first. He couldn't do it! Ellis's energy fell from him, swiftly and cleanly as a bloodletting. He slumped against the wall, his head in his hands. It was over. Freddie had won. He'd been right: stupidity had made Ellis dangerous. He began to cry almost without realising it, until tears spilt uncontrolled down his cheeks, tickling his neck as they dripped under his shirt collar. His entire life had been shrouded in a thick grey fear, a constant state of dread, in which he was always waiting for Freddie either to leave or to return. Freddie would never care whom he manipulated, whom he hurt. Ellis had been part of Freddie's wreckage all these years, he realised, just another chump, there to be had. He looked at the bronze sculpture on the mantelpiece, feeling desperately sorry for that child, and the adult he became, and the legacy forced upon him. His own small face stared back.

No, he decided. Freddie would not win. He could not. Hate was a better servant than tears, anger a better fuel than sadness. He rose unsteadily to his feet. He'd dragged rather than carried Janey, hadn't he? He began by removing Freddie's shoes, slinging them around his own neck, the laces tied loosely together. That helped a little. By leaning forward, bending low at the waist, holding Freddie's body close to the floor and tugging, Ellis was able to move him. Freddie's feet began to bump quietly along, but he remained a dead weight. Ellis's back was aching almost immediately. Progress was slow and exhausting, and when he tried to pick up the pace on his way down the kitchen stairs, banged Freddie's head against a wall.

'Hell,' Ellis muttered, leaning forward to check whether the skin had broken. It hadn't. Good. The muscles in his shoulders and arms stung as he manoeuvred Freddie through the scullery to the small door that opened onto the grubby yard. From it, a narrow and overgrown path tracked the garden wall as far as the kitchen garden. While he was grateful for the cover of the wilful hedges and overgrown currant bushes, he repeatedly snagged their clothes on loose twigs and broken canes. He crouched as low as he could without breaking his step. Should anyone be looking down from a neighbouring house, he hoped they might just assume any faint blur of movement against the hedges was foxes on the prowl.

When he reached the door in the back wall he was reluctant to put Freddie down in case he couldn't lift him again, so he propped him against the wall, steadying him with one hand while he shoved at the door. The wooden frame was so rotten that the catch gave easily. He was on the Heath! What should have been at most a three- or four-minute walk had taken almost half an hour. His thighs screamed in pain from the constant squatting. His hands shook as he straightened up, the heels on Freddie's shoes clicking under his chin like castanets.

Using all that was left of his strength to hold Freddie a little higher, as one might support a desperately drunk friend, he picked his way carefully through the grass. He breathed deeply, relieved that the rain-misted night was sure to have kept late walkers at home. He glanced constantly from side to side, shuffling his feet to feel for any sudden dips. Poorly filled-in trenches from the war still littered parts of the Heath, often surprising walkers unfamiliar with their surroundings. He reached the edge of North Wood, the dense gloom of its oak trees darker than the sky behind it. He listened intently for the rustle of an animal or, worse, a voice or bark, but there was nothing. He struggled along, the burden in his arms getting heavier and heavier, until the path narrowed and the branches on either side began to crash together overhead. It was colder there, which meant it would remain badly lit and secluded during the day too. When he'd struggled along for almost ten minutes, he moved from the path and through a ditch to a thick clump of bushes. It was a good thing he was wearing gloves: fingerprints aside, he'd have been terribly scratched without them, which would have been hard to explain to Virginia. Awkwardly, he shoved the bushes apart with one foot and an arm, creating a little clearing. He laid Freddie on the ground and raised his head, then carefully poured half the bottle of gin into his mouth and the rest over his shirt and jacket. Liquid dribbled from his uncle's lips and onto his shirt. Damn. He'd just have to hope enough had gone in so that he'd stink of it. He unbuttoned Freddie's trousers, tugging them down a couple of inches. The touch of the man's flesh was unbearable, even with gloves. Finally, he pushed Freddie into the gap, taking care that he landed on the side where the gash in his head was.

Ellis took the shoes from his neck. Damned laces were tied too tight. He attempted to tug them apart, but that caused the laces to knot further. His fingers were shaking violently by now, so he teased them open with his teeth. Sweat dripped into his eyes. He leant in to put the shoes on Freddie, but couldn't reach his feet without disturbing the branches. The best he could do was to throw them as close to Freddie's feet as he could manage. Finally, he tossed the bottle onto the body. It landed in the crook of an arm, as though he had been clutching it when he fell. A nice touch.

He hurried home as quickly as his exhaustion allowed, using a broken branch to obliterate his footprints as he walked. Every muscle hurt, and a saw's blade pressed against the full width of his shoulders and neck. There were two things wrong, he decided. Why would a drunk who stops to urinate in a deserted part of the Heath remove his shoes? The police would be sure to consider it odd that Freddie's shoes were beside rather than on him. Even though Ellis had retied the laces, only an imbecile could believe that a man could trip in such a way as to cause both shoes to fall off simultaneously. But had Ellis climbed into the bush himself to return them to his feet, he'd surely have left some disturbance to suggest a second person, or even a trail out of the wood. Second – and this was probably a bigger problem – there was no murder weapon with the body. There were plenty of large stones, so it was conceivable that he had fallen, drunk, and hit his head, or – and this was the explanation Ellis hoped the police would arrive at, should he ever be found – Freddie was indulging his filthy perversions with a bit of rough he'd picked up on the Heath, only to be robbed and killed, accidentally or otherwise.

Would they be able to tell that he had already been dead for a couple of hours and his body had been dumped? He wasn't sure. Oh, what was the use? It was done now. He'd just have to hope that if Freddie was ever found, his body would have decomposed to such an extent as to make the cause and scene of death at best undeterminable and at worst unprovable. He buried Freddie's latch-key under a tree a good fifty yards away from the body, and shoved his card-holder far down into the earth under a bush. He took the rest of the cigarettes from the case, then buried it under a hedge.

It began to rain heavily. More luck! That would wash away any footprints he might have missed in the dark. Less than ten minutes later, he was at home, locking the kitchen door behind him. It seemed unbelievable. The house was exactly as it always was, as though he had come home from a walk, or merely popped out for an evening drink or newspaper. The same cold sense of being on the other side from life, of putting up a new barrier between him and the world, came over him, just as it had when he'd walked through the London streets after Janey's death.

Forcing his exhausted limbs to move fast, he cleaned the Music Room floor. In the study he used the poker to spread out the embers and scorched papers, checking until every scrap was burnt. He was tired, so tired he could have lain down by the fire like a dog and slept till morning. What had happened to his life? He had never considered himself either good or bad, but assuming he was a good person, circumstances had forced that goodness to turn a full half-circle, converted to vice. What did that say about the world, about humankind? Evil was no mystery: it was goodness, turned by pressure into something else. A pearl in reverse . . . Humanity was slowly peeling away layer by layer, reverting to its original state of grit. Janey was right: people were weeds.

He needed to be in bed when Virginia returned. He locked the study door behind him, tugging off his filthy jacket. He'd hide his clothes and dispose of them in the morning. Sweat had cooled on his body and he shivered, even though his head was burning. At the bottom of the stairs he paused by George Thompson's portrait. His face was cold and unforgiving. Sarah Bernhardt, Ellen Terry . . . one after another, they shut their eyes to him. He put out a hand to cover Freddie's portrait as he passed it. At the top of the stairs Henry Irving pointedly turned away his head in disgust, the very frame glowering with displeasure, his long chin tilted in the air.

A voice whispered, '*I am beginning to feel this nocturnal existence tell on me.*' It took him a few seconds to realise he himself had spoken. It was one of his favourite passages in *Dracula*, the words of Jonathan Harker while trapped in Dracula's castle as his supposed guest. '*It is destroying my nerve,*' he continued, turning back to look at Bram Stoker's face. '*I start at my own shadow, and am full of all sorts of horrible imaginings.*'

All ten *Greatest Theatrical Figures* were dead now. 'I will protect you,' he told Stoker's portrait. 'I promise.'

He closed his bedroom door and fell into bed, naked and feverish. All he would have to do was weather the next two days and he'd be gone for good. He slowly stretched his arms and legs, burning muscles unable to find comfort. He lay awake, watching faint strips of cloud drift about the night sky, thinking of that long-ago day on the beach and his sandcastle, smooth and solid, and how the whorled ridges on the shells, grainy with sand, formed perfect patterns against his fingertips.

On a night such as this, the difference between moments and years could feel like nothing at all.

The Un-Dead Count
Chapter XVII

Papers Found in the Possession of Lord Godalming

London, 18 October. The world is over for me, tonight. The end! Oh, my God! And in this dark place, forsaken by God and man alike. I can see my page but barely, yet I must do something or go mad as I wait, so I write. True, too, that my duty as an Englishman is to commit to paper such facts as I have for the poor soul who will find my lifeless body – *you*, I suppose. While I have the strength and can stand true unto God as my creator I shall tell you the truth. Oh, what a spiritless fool I have been! To believe that our combined forces – that is, Quincey's and my own – our united powers of reason and logic, supported by God Himself, would overcome the evil march that is the Count and his leeching army. The resources of science – of daylight, even! – have proved no match for the evil that has unfolded across London these last days. Quincey is also recording our travails, though I have seen but few of his writings (nor he many of mine). Veronica recently began to transcribe his shorthand, and is doing her best to compile a timely account, commencing with the papers Quincey's father inherited from Professor Van Helsing. A number of his books were in Dutch and German, which are being translated, also at V's instigation. When I conclude this short account I will secret the Note-Book about my person for you to find and then, what? Wait. Yes, what else is there? I am locked in the Westenra crypt in Highgate Cemetery, completely alone, waiting. I have but these pages and pencil and a single flame . . . Please, reader, I implore you, pray for me. I am the scourge of my own mortal flesh, destroyed by my sins. I cast myself into this perilous state – but, please, I beg you, forgive my sins and help my soul find safe passage.

Van Helsing's journals foretold that, should the Count revive from his hellish resting place, he would marshal deadly creatures to his side in his attempt to subjugate the forces of goodness. A fortnight since, a pack of wild wolves, over a thousand deep, traversed the breadth of Russia, killing and scavenging their way across Austria-Hungary as far as the Netherlands without a single cessation. They abruptly turned north at Bremen and moved as a pack, their speed that of devils, until they reached the coast. As one they flung themselves from sheer cliffs and disappeared into the German Ocean. Not a sound was heard, reports had it, not a single wave crashed or howl unleashed. And yet our newspapers cried to us not to be afraid, that such a plague emanated from a far-off place, subject to commands of nature that do not apply to England's green fields! What rot! What hubris! Three nights ago, a plague of bats – each larger than the handspan of a grown man – descended on London from the skies with the speed of lightning in the dusk of a single evening, their raid that of a thick, fast-moving mist one might see on a deserted moor in winter. The colour of soot, they arrived first in their hundreds, then hundreds of thousands, until the sky was thick with wings and the air suddenly warm and oppressive. It was as though the very spirits of the earth and air remade their shapes, warning the city about the mighty, grim forces waiting to attack. Within an hour, the clock face of Big Ben was unrecognisable, its spire turned to a shifting blur, and Tower Bridge had become a blackened, seething mass, seeming to shake under the weight. Come morning, all was normal. The bats had disappeared but reports from the night before began to accrue from far and wide. Chalky cliffs made grey and shifting. Ships sunk, dragged down by extra hundredweights of filthy, disease-ridden cargo. And every one of the foul creatures biting – men, women, tots in their cribs, animals . . . it made no difference! With each vicious bite the bats swelled further, engorged, until the smallest had the wingspan of a seagull and the largest, so I am told, were the size of eagles.

My flame gutters. I must hasten. You, who next see these words, I beg you please read no further but ensure these pages go to Harker & Partners of Sackville Street and are given directly & only into Quincey Harker's hands:

Oh, Quincey! Dearest, oldest friend, a thousand apologies . . . You will find all my journals and the maps I made in Budapest in my nightstand. The appalling danger that has fallen on us from the east is more volatile and horrifying than you or I ever predicted, even in our most tortured imaginings. Oh, that we had never boarded that ship, for that was when the vicious evil chose us for his own! The nosferatu seeks revenge for his fate at our fathers' hands, and determines to employ us to his evil ends. Dracula has no death, as Van Helsing's papers taught us: he is not a bee that stings and dies. He becomes but more powerful, his brutal strength and cunning that of twenty fellows, but with necromancy as an ally. That you survived the first attack is a miracle for which I thank God daily.

Last night, during the bats' plague, you and I were in your lodgings, exhausted from the day's futile efforts. From fireplace to window-seals, we checked and closed every possible means of ingress, and the bats were, albeit temporarily, unable to reach us. I confess I had been ready to throw our mission over entirely, but your words gave me strength: 'He is attacking the Empire,' you said. 'The heart of our religion, our trade, our very government. We have taken enough, man. Enough. We must continue our fight, and we must defeat him and his filthy allies.' When you were away from the room I watched a man collapse from an old barouche onto the street, so entirely hidden by attacking bats as to be rendered into the most basic arrangement of arms, legs, head and torso. A moment later he rose, his shirt and trousers a tatter of rags, as though he had slept on a bed of nails, and stumbled but two paces before falling direct to the ground, on his face, and moving no more. These vicious creatures do not suck the blood, but instead lap it, as a cat does a saucer of cream. The sound as they assaulted their victim, that licking and scraping, it was a hornets' nest magnified by a thousand. It assaults the ears, a vicious drone that warns that terror is about! Horrendous through closed window-glass; in reality must be terrifying! We spent the night closeted in that room, talking incessantly over every aspect of our battle to date. Exhausted from the weeks of struggle, and despite our avowals not to, we fell asleep shortly before dawn – and I have to own that I was grateful for it: I craved rest. When we woke, I told you I was convinced these predators returned to Highgate Cemetery en masse, to sleep in the many tombs and crypts there during the day, and would be back to terrorise the country once dusk fell again tonight, descending from the skies on our great country's citizens with no care for who, or where. I told you I could bear it no longer and would go in search of their master.

'You must not, John,' you said repeatedly. 'It is too dangerous alone or for us both. We must find an army to march with us.' But I took no heed, claiming that no true Godalming would permit duty wait upon fear. And I hate that I lied to the man who has been a brother to me all these years, a man I love – but lie I did, for these last ten days. Because it was not the bats' master I was seeking: it was their mistress.

Forgive me, Quincey, for keeping this from you: for nine nights of the last ten a poisonous creature came to me while I rested. Whether I was awake or asleep I do not know, nor did I care, for she could not be resisted. Something would jolt me awake in the darkest hour and she was there, at my bedside! Beside me, leaning over my breast. On the first occasion I called out, but discovered that no matter how I tried, I was unable to form any sound, nor move. I strained every muscle as one does in a nightmare, but I was hypnotised by her, and felt the wicked burn of desire as her pearl-white teeth and red lips bent over me, a longing I could not resist, yet despised. It was the strangest dream, I decided afterwards, yet for reasons I could not quite fathom, I remained silent. She returned, time after time, and I . . . I ached for her. I would, could, not refuse her lips on me, though I understood their purpose and felt the sweet drain as she lapped life from me.

She never spoke, not once, but somehow it came in a dream, it must have, because that morning, when I woke, truly awoke, I knew that her name was Lucy Westenra, a name both strangely familiar and unknown to me. For nine nights I went on so in this glorious, demented horror.

But last night, because I was with you, she did not come to me, awake or asleep. I could not bear it! I have to see her, to feel her touch. As I woke, I felt more than heard a whisper in my ear, telling me that I must wait in this crypt, her crypt, this evening.

Wait! A sound! Is she come? The dank chamber all about me has begun to quiver – the very walls are trembling. No, not the walls! But not my beloved! Bats! Come to life as though the very patina of the stone has lifted and quivered and is breathing. The very room was full of them all this time but so silent and still! And now! Eyes, glassy and glinting everywhere, a rustling getting up. The stench! The evil stench! No! I cannot—

Telegram, Lady Godalming to her son
17 October: WHY HAVE YOU NOT REPLIED STOP AM GRAVELY UPSET STOP INSIST YOU LEAVE LONDON TODAY BY ANY MEANS STOP TAKE YOUR SISTER AND GO IMMEDIATELY TO MAUD I IMPLORE STOP MOTHER STOP

Note from Quincey Harker, affixed to Lord Godalming's pages:
How heavy my heart is . . . My fallen comrade's note breaks off abruptly at this point. As he predicted, it was found on his lifeless person. And now I, too, must live in a hell of my own making.

Westminster Gazette, 20 October
Extra Special
Lord Godalming Fatally Injured
Menace of 'Bat Plague' strikes at the heart of society

We have just received intelligence that Lord Godalming, a young man of great character who had but recently acceded to the title on the death of his father in February, has fallen victim to the plague of bats that descended on our great city for three successive nights this week. He was discovered, in an entirely unconscious state, in a desolate corner of Highgate Cemetery by a grave-digger late in the morning, half hidden under a furze bush. He had been punctured by hundreds of tiny wounds and his body was entirely emaciated.

CHAPTER 19

Knowing Virginia wouldn't be up early after a late night, he despatched the trunk first thing the following day, his back and shoulders stiff and protesting as he helped the two delivery boys manoeuvre it over the threshold. Not a shred of *The Un-Dead Count* remained in the house. The book was gone, divided between the fire and the future.

He listened carefully until he heard Virginia go into the bathroom, then counted to ten and opened the front door. 'Goodbye, Freddie,' he called, as if shouting to someone already halfway down the path, 'Yes, I'll tell her! Yes, lots of postcards, I promise. Best of luck, Uncle Freddie!' Was that last *Uncle Freddie* hamming it up too much? He slammed the door and waited in the hallway, counting softly again. He had got as far as seven when Virginia appeared at the top of the stairs, one hand clutching the neck of her dressing-gown, the other holding a bottle of Kemdex. Her face was slicked with cold cream.

'Was that Freddie? Where was he going?' Her lips moved awkwardly, as her tongue manoeuvred her teeth into place.

This version of his mother always made him uncomfortable. Not because she was dishevelled, her hair unbrushed (she didn't make up her face or follow fashions in clothes anyway, and he imagined that the contrast in an equivalent scene with someone like Janey would have been far more pronounced) but because she was unravelled: an old woman with a slack, toothless mouth, standing vulnerable and alone at the top of the stairs.

'You've just missed him! He's been called to Manchester on business. They sent a motor and he didn't want to wake you up, so I told him I'd pass on the message . . . A new revue apparently. He's very excited.'

'*Manchester*? He never said anything to me!'

'The director telephoned late yesterday, while you were out. Very urgent and hush-hush, apparently. Big names and all that.'

'One of his new American contacts, do you mean?'

'He was sworn to secrecy, he said, but, yes, you've hit the nail on the head as always. Remember what he told us the big studios are like about their stars? It would be more than his life's worth to breathe a word in case a newspaper got hold of it!'

She frowned. 'When will he be back?' Snowdrifts of cold cream began to gather on her forehead.

'Next week, he hopes' – well done, Ellis, he thought, recalling Inspector Morris's needling questions: he must ensure Freddie continued to thrive in the present tense – 'though he said it could run into the following week if it goes well. He'll be in touch.' He would book a telegram from Freddie, putting off his return for ten days or thereabouts, he decided, for delivery when Ellis would already be in France.

And a second deferral, to come a week or so after that. He might even send him back to America – who knew? Freddie was his puppet now, and other than to a funeral march, Ellis would make him dance along with any tune he chose.

'You won't see him before you leave!'

'That's all right, dearest. Freddie and I have said our goodbyes.' The bell rang and Ellis jumped.

'Freddie!' Virginia was back at the top of the stairs, smiling, bending low and craning her head to watch while he opened the door. 'He must have forgotten something, you know how he is!'

'Probably!' It couldn't be, could it? No! Even if he had been found – itself highly unlikely given that it was barely twelve hours – it was incredible that a man in an American-made suit with nothing on him to reveal his name would have been identified so quickly, or tied back to this house. Ellis had been careful about his tracks. At dawn he had double-checked all the floors and the garden path to be sure there was no trace of his and Freddie's laborious exit.

'Well?' The impatience in her voice irritated even while it saddened him. For she had always been so about Freddie: nothing less than his presence was good enough.

'Telegram from Alice Arcourt.' He ripped open the envelope. 'Oh dear! Patrick has broken both legs mountain climbing. He isn't coming back. Will write re belongings, she says.' He stood at the bottom of the stairs, looking up. 'Did you hear me?' But there was silence, the landing was empty.

Certain situations in life demand an audacious response, he thought, recalling a newspaper article about the theft of a priceless medieval Italian artwork. Dressed as a museum guard, the unidentified thief's plan was no more complex than to place a cloth over the painting and leave the building with it tucked under his arm.

When one's opponents expect subterfuge and secrets, then surely the trick is to stand, arms spread wide as Christ's, in open ground.

The street door led into a distempered hallway, which ended abruptly in a dreary room, no bigger than a large alcove. The public counter was a shelf under a hatch recessed into the wall. Never having been in a police station before, he was surprised at how bland it was. He'd been assuming he'd enter a scene from a Dashiell Hammett novel: a room full of noise and smoke and movement, typewriters cracking like gunfire, policemen shoving hard-boiled criminals along in front of them. Instead, three empty chairs the colour of Windsor soup waited against one wall in front of a lacklustre corkboard dotted with notices. The posters divided into two types: threats in the form of fines for various misdeeds, and entreaties for help disguised as rewards. A Metropolitan Police recruitment poster made a lone plea for more men. Smaller, newer notices about trench-digging and gas masks were pinned to the frame.

He knocked on the hatch door and stood back, waiting. A mask without a box dangled on a peg beside it; Ellis had only ever seen them in pictures. Those nightmarish, sightless eyeholes! Gingerly, he lifted its oversized, drooping snout, the rubber cold and tough to his touch. He couldn't bear the idea of putting such a thing on, shuddering at the memory of the horse's head in the Lyceum.

The hatch rattled open, a policeman's head and shoulders appearing like a sideways jack-in-the-box. 'Rum old things, aren't they?' The man gestured at the mask. 'Mark my words, we'll all be carrying one before the year is out.'

Not me, Ellis thought, but said only, 'Ellis Spender for Inspector Morris, if he's available?'

'Got an appointment?'

'No.'

The policeman closed the hatch without responding. Ellis stood immobile, unsure what to do. Could they see him without his realising? He glanced surreptitiously around, looking for a peephole in the wall. A concern that he was being watched kept him on his mettle, the way a tightrope walker in a circus must feel at the beginning of his act, savouring the gasps and fears of the audience while focusing with an almost unnatural clarity on the rope ahead. The first policeman reappeared through the hatch, leaning forward, his elbows propped up on the ledge, watching him. He said nothing as a door behind Ellis opened.

Morris looked at him, clearly taken aback. 'Well, this is a surprise, Mr Spender. I didn't have you pegged as a willing visitor to the Metropolitan Police.'

Willing? The rudeness of the man! Ellis smiled. 'I'm so sorry for the intrusion, Inspector. I've come to apologise for my uncle's behaviour last evening. He was horribly rude to you. It's completely out of character.'

'I'll have to take your word for that.'

'It puzzled me I must admit . . . And then something happened today, which—' He broke off, his worried sigh that of a nervous sinner in the confessional, then continued:

'You may recall my uncle mentioning he had insisted Miss Gouldstein rent a room in my mother's house.'

Morris nodded.

'I found her diary earlier today.' He became deliberately hesitant, just as he had when first showing Ralph Chatterton *The Un-Dead Count*. 'And I wondered if perhaps it might, oh, I don't know, shed some light on Freddie's odd reaction?' Shivers of pink and white glinted in the narrow mother-of-pearl surround that framed the words *Engagements Diary 1938* as Ellis passed it to him, with a small key. 'I know it's private and I shouldn't have . . .'

Ten brief entries, between January and March. Five tiddlers swimming alongside five red herrings. Morris read through them in silence. The inspector would be sure to bite. Ellis watched him turn the pages quickly, mentally reciting the significant lines to himself as though preparing for an examination.

29 January. 5 months to the day here. Glad I didn't move when FB started carrying on cos then he upped and went. Hope he never comes back, bastard.

14 February. Valentine from P – my sweetheart!!

16 February. Postcard from FB. Hollywood! V. awful cut up but she put on a brave face. Good news for me – I'm safe.

30 March. Letter from FB. Money of course . . . Someone will be in touch, he says, & I'm to do what I'm told or he'll tell Atkinson everything. He'll bleed me for ever.

Morris paused and examined the covers of the book, then leafed through the pages to check if any loose sheets were tucked inside. He found nothing. The final entry read:

1 April. Embankment, 6 p.m. How am I to break free of the devil?

'And the FB referred to here is definitely your uncle, Frederick Broughton?'

'Yes.'

'Where is he now?'

'In Manchester, on urgent business. He plans to leave for Hollywood as soon as he can.'

'You're sure this is Miss Gouldstein's diary?'

He nodded. 'It was a Christmas gift. I was rearranging the furniture in her bedroom – my mother might re-let it – and found it hidden between the bed and the wall. In fact, it appeared to me as though it might have been deliberately tucked behind the headboard.'

'This is her handwriting?'

'Yes. I believe you have something of hers to compare it against?' Did that sound as though he knew too much, or was unnaturally interested? Ellis added hurriedly, 'Patrick Arcourt mentioned something about a note of Janey's. I can't quite recall . . . something to do with chocolates, I think he said.'

'Mr Spender, potentially this is evidence that may implicate your uncle in a crime. Why are you bringing it to my attention?'

'My mother is the most important person in the world to me, Inspector. I lost my sister at a young age, and as my uncle told you, my mother treated Janey as though she were her own daughter. It simply wouldn't be right to . . .' His face fell, a young man wrestling with his finer feelings, desperate to do the right thing. 'My uncle is an honourable man, Inspector.

I'm sure there's a simple explanation. But for my mother's sake, it would be wrong to hold on to anything that could be of some small help.'

If Morris sent someone to make enquiries about Freddie, Virginia wouldn't be able to shine any light on his whereabouts. They would be forced to assume that following Morris's visit to the house he had returned to Hollywood in a hurry, keen to put the ocean between him and whatever unprovable ill he had orchestrated for Janey. Let the police try to figure that one out! A nice little knot tied between his pearls, Freddie and Janey. Two interconnected alibis, both unable to confirm or deny anything, dependent on each other in death as they never were in life. He had to stop himself grinning in delight at his own performance. Freddie hadn't produced the show, Ellis had. He buttoned up his coat, ready to leave the station.

'Mr Spender?' Morris was regarding him curiously, as one might a wild creature in a zoo, newly aware that its cage may not offer enough protection.

He was immediately taken aback by the inspector's tone. 'Yes, Inspector?' he replied, careful to be as cheerfully agreeable as before. Suddenly he imagined Morris calmly laying down fact after fact in front of him in a neat sequence from the moment Ellis had sold Winsome his own letters until this second, and challenging him to disprove that every movement between those two points was a lie. At speed, he imagined a number of different beginnings. *She threatened to expose your forgery scam, so you killed her,* or *Why have you never mentioned you were at the Lyceum on April the first?* or even, in the sort of quiet tone that carries its own icy menace, *Mr Spender, don't you think it suspicious that Mr Broughton too has vanished?* No, he reminded himself: he was being paranoid. Whatever he might suspect, the inspector didn't know anything, and could offer no more than silly speculation disguised as reason. Most importantly of all, *The Un-Dead Count* wasn't a lie. It existed, a shining gem.

'I have been with the Metropolitan Police for twenty years and—' He was interrupted by the sound of the hatch rattling open at speed once more. Smyth this time, clutching a telephone receiver. In his agitation, he didn't notice Ellis. 'Inspector, quick!' He as good as shouted it. 'Brixton – an emergency. It's Alastair Harper!' Morris waved a hand and Smyth fell silent.

Morris turned away, moving towards the door. 'Men, Mister Spender, harm their fellow citizens for a thousand different reasons, each one believing their actions to be, if not justified then certainly exculpable. My job is to catch them all.' The door closed, and he was gone. Still clutching the telephone receiver, Smyth slammed the hatch shut.

What a foolish, narrow-sighted man, Ellis decided as he walked home. The real question isn't why some people kill: it's why more people don't.

Virginia was in the Music Room, standing in the bay window and staring out towards the Heath, her face pressed close to the glass.

'Hello – what are you doing in here?'

'Nothing.' Her voice was low.

He crossed the room to her side. He hated this room now. It was full of shadows and stale lives. His father was an exhalation, Freddie an inhalation still, but his breath was held, as if he had plunged into cold, deep water. Together they looked out over the back garden at the Heath and the gloomy sky hanging low over it, its sullen greyness broken by patches of charcoal clouds that made even the grey look brighter. Two men, so close to each other as to be almost touching from shoulder to hip, walked across the grass in the distance, pushing forward into the rain. The taller of the two was holding an umbrella over the other's head, and a barrel-bodied dog with spindly legs danced around them, its ears pinned back by the wind. Ellis envied them terribly in that moment, those ordinary people out for an ordinary walk. Such simplicity was denied to him now, he knew it. That they were walking towards death step by step in the same way he was made no difference; not now that he had been dropped onto an alternate path. He would have to be forever on his guard, waiting and watchful. There was more space around him now: the gulf between him and everyone else had been forced wider. What had happened with Janey, with Freddie, had been no sudden and brutal jolt into another world, no desperate swerve from a workaday, knowable situation into an unseen, untested one. Nor had it been an overwhelming, unstoppable propulsion of evil. It was simply the way it had had to be: Janey and Freddie had tried to block the road he was fixed on.

'I wonder where they are going,' Virginia said, her voice still flat and unreadable.

'Those chaps? You know them?'

'No. But everyone seems to be going somewhere, doing something while I . . .' Her voice trailed off and she shrugged, her eyes still focused on the scene outside. Her fingertips skittered over and back across her necklace as though the pearls were komboloi. 'I merely exist. And there are days, Ellis, when I no longer know *why*.' Finally, she turned and looked up at him. Her face was tired and lined. She had lost more weight too, he realised. 'Perhaps I never had a purpose, and have lived as a fool might, dancing to a tune that no one else cared to hear.'

'Nonsense! Why, I for one would be lost without you. I adore you. Freddie too. Surely you know that.'

'But you're going away, and so will he . . .' she said. 'And if there is another war, as people keep telling me there will be, who knows what will happen?'

'I'll be back. So will Freddie. And don't forget Lord Halifax's announcement last week: even if there is a fight over Czechoslovakia, it shan't involve us . . . You know how blue you feel when you're tired, but there's nothing to fret about.'

He expected her to reply, but she didn't. She put her hand to his shoulder briefly, the lightest of touches, then went to leave, one hand still worrying her necklace. At the door she turned back. Was it his imagination or was she staring at the spot where Freddie's body had fallen?

'We used to be so gay here, once,' she said. 'This room, full of people and music and laughter. Time could have stopped for ever and I would have been happy.'

Ellis peered at the garden, searching once more for any trace of his agonising journey with Freddie's body down the path to the door in the wall, then his stumbling track across the Heath to the woods. But the grass kept his secret, hugging it tight into the earth. Who was to say what each of us was capable of doing, what secret poison was capable of spilling out, when we are pushed beyond our customary limits by desperate circumstances? And even then, he wondered, why should one action alone become the very definition of a person's life? There was no single moment that could possibly capture the complexity of a human mind or predict one's most innate responses. It was no different from having suffered the most appalling pain, an agony that was entirely consuming and debilitating. But once the pain was anaesthetised, the memory of it was gone too, every feeling now inaccessible.

If the two men were to look at him, what would they see? A single figure at a grubby window in a neglected house. The emptiness of his bedroom one floor up, and Janey's room one up again. But they didn't look in his direction. Instead, they moved out of sight and into the twilit world of the for-ever unknown.

The Un-Dead Count
Chapter XXII

Quincey Harker's Journal

How I wished I had heeded the warnings of my father when he would call me to his side and, after extracting a faithful promise that I would relay none of it to Mama, recount the tale of his journey that long-ago time, and how unbearably altered a landscape he discovered there. It was almost impossible to believe, he recalled, bar that he had to, with the evidence provided by his own eyes. Oh! that I had listened to him! What I might have spared myself! For I shake still at the memory of watching that castle begin to quake. How it suddenly began to crack and split as the very ground it was built on began to part, opening up like a secret dark fissure in the very depths of the earth, and drawing the castle to itself, inside itself, to draw it inside its red, fiery heart! That place of evil was once alien to me – and, oh, that I had stayed away from those eastern lands, and remained desolation in ignorance of the devastation wrought by the hands of that creature and his desperate plague of cruelty and damnation. But no! I rush ahead of myself. I must begin my tale, unfurl it as an Indian fakir does his rope, watching it stretch straight and high and true, unravelling into the blue sky above his head . . .

CHAPTER 20

Virginia is tearful and trying not to show it. 'Freddie was sure you wouldn't go,' she says to Ellis, and then, as if to herself, 'He told me you wouldn't, not when it came down to it.' She gives him a present of a small, leather-bound book, not nearly so fine or expensive as those he bought himself. It was his father's, she explains, sketches of the Italian lakes Sidney made while on their honeymoon; perhaps the drawings will inspire his essays. He will treasure it, he tells his mother, and her eyes fill once more. 'You will write, won't you? Postcards will do, if you haven't time for letters.'

'I've promised, haven't I? As often as I can.'

He glances up at Bram Stoker, trapped in his gilt-edged prison on the stairs. How cruel of Sidney to cram a magnificent giant of a man into such a mean, hard seat and leave him to rot for decades. Ellis imagines Stoker hauling himself up, no longer able to tolerate the restrictions of the canvas. Shoulders swelling and chest heaving, feeling the prickle and pinch of every painted vein, he lumbers to his feet, the chair overturned. The frame shatters into a hundred golden pieces as he bounds down the stairs, shards of umber and red paint flying through the air. Not alive, but free. And free is good enough for this Lazarus: by rising, he will silence every critic who sniggered, every editor who disregarded.

Ellis's new suitcase is heavy, and bangs against his knee in a sudden whip of breeze. He swears softly but is too joyful to be irritated by the pain for long. For it is almost half a year since that night when, worried he was being followed, he ducked into the Golden Lamb. How trapped, how futile, he had felt then, when even unlocking his own front door seemed an act of surrender. And look at him now! He smiles. That very encounter was, in its own small way, the first rattle of the key in the lock. *Gain and loss*, he thinks. And what gains! He has wealth and the Count flourishes once more: the previous evening Chatterton had telephoned with the news that *The Un-Dead Count* will be published the following January, forty-two years after *Dracula*.

Ellis arrives at Victoria in plenty of time. How bland and ordinary it is, he thinks. Everyone with the same dull-eyed automaton expression, their thoughts a stodgy routine of work and meals and that evening's wireless programmes. An *Evening Standard* poster tied to a pillar by the ticket office carries the headline: *Alastair Harper Shocking Jail Suicide! Torso Murderer Dead!* A newspaper seller stands to attention alongside it, one arm held high, at once proffering and saluting the news. Ellis strides past and onto the platform, sloughing off the city with every step. Let London continue in his absence: he and it will not miss each other. He imagines himself in Paris, relaxing in the golden glow of sunlight, inhaling the unfamiliar, intoxicating smells of a summer's day in a large, pleasantly empty city square where dust rises from the dry streets and the sky is clean and limpid. Sitting with a notebook and some pastis, carefully carving out writing time before the day ends, and night, with its parade of intimate dinners with new friends, and literary parties with the gayest society imaginable, lays its claims to his attention. When he tires of that image, he pictures himself on a sailboat excursion in Nice, listening to soft lullaby clinks from moored yachts and watching the blue water give way to the warm dusty browns, whites and reds of the buildings that circle the harbour, green hills rising behind them.

He cannot see that across the sea a plague has come to life and is spreading. A phantom gaining power, materialising as the shape of an eagle, its vast wings stretching to life. Yes, it is coming. A night-shadow flying high above millions of people whose eyes are shut, lost to the gleaming world of sleep, unaware that a great wind is gathering up its armies overhead, its sound that of the march of thousands upon thousands of boots striking hard against concrete.

Four miles away, Stella Lloyd perches on a stool at the bar of a nightclub. The Nest is a miserable place in daylight. Two elderly cleaners sweat like shire horses as they scrub the previous night away, but the entire place is a vast, ugly stain. Stella paints her nails, one slow red stroke after another. The boss tosses an envelope onto the counter beside her and throws her a reprimand too, for getting a personal letter at work. What can this be? Stella wonders, for no one ever writes to her. Taking care not to ruin the fresh lacquer, she rips it open. Three typed sheets, the margins dotted with handwritten comments in an old-fashioned script. She notices the words *vampire* and *blood* almost immediately, and shivers. A note pinned to the topmost page reads, *Keep these safe for me. I'll make it worth your while. FB.*

Cocooned in the quiet luxury of a first-class carriage, Ellis arranges his things, delighting in the new suitcase and the elegance of the letters *ES* on the lock. In France he will buy a second case to match, he decides. Everything from now on will be like this, he is sure of it. Everything will be the best. He knows he is leaving unfinished accounts behind him in Fitzroy Gardens, picturing Virginia with her hands folded loosely in her lap as she listens to the wireless, slowly fading into the walls of her creaking house. Waiting, forever waiting. What will his reckoning be? He will not be back this decade. He will move forward, only forward, following each new daybreak, each horizon. There will be an audit later: she is his mother, it has to be so. But that will be another day, in another time. Equations will be made to come out at last, the dead and un-dead alike accounted for. Everything comes down to one thing, he decides: one day each of us will die and, in that moment, every heartbeat and desire, every fear or flare of self-deceit, will no longer have any value. All that will matter is what was done to whom, and how, and why. Every human utterance is constructed of truths and falsehoods. Honest in its own moment, but doubtless a plagiarism, a forgery of a million others. In that, if in nothing else, he is no different from any other man. The will to exploit runs deep in every human soul, he is sure. He has done terrible things: he knows this, though cannot make himself feel it. But his life before those things was lies too.

Ellis rings for a drink, to steady him for the journey. He stares at his palms for a few moments, thinking of all they have done, of what has been destroyed and what has been created. He has given himself life and need no longer fear the stuttering hunger of his heart's desires. And though the price for becoming Stoker's pen is the sacrifice of his own, the thought causes him no anguish: Stoker thrives inside him; their talents will continue on together, a joint future forged in two solitary pasts. Faking did not lay waste his creativity, for the state of being himself did not die when it was set to one side. He doesn't care that he passes blithely through the anniversary of his own death every year without knowing it, unable to comprehend the significance of the date.

The train begins to rumble, forcing the porters to raise their voices as they hurry the last of the passengers on and begin the business of shouting and slamming doors. Ellis reaches up to shut the window against the noise of the platform. But when he catches sight of himself in the glass, he sees only a handsome, brown-suited man in late middle age with a short reddish beard and neatly combed hair whose small, dark eyes shine with love and pride. 'Bram?' Ellis whispers. He blinks and the man is gone, replaced by Ellis's own face once more.

The newspaper seller rips the poster from the pillar and replaces it with one advertising the final edition. It is so fresh the ink smudges against his hand. '*Evening Standard*,' he shouts, with relish, for who doesn't like a good murder? Death is good for trade. 'Gruesome scene at West End theatre! Woman's body discovered!'

A whistle blows. The train pulls slowly out of the station.